Praise for
Quickstep to Murder

"Perfect for all your dance-show fa— Barrick brings a
light step and an upbeat tempo to b[   ]Who
wouldn't want to spice up their live[   ]ll-
room?"

[   ]*nal*

"A new series that looks like fun." [   ]ws

"Barrick keeps them hopping with a[   ]ery
set in the world of professional danc[   ]

[   ]*nes*

"[A]n engaging debonair amateur [   ]ve
readers dancing the Lindy."

—Genre [   ]ews

"[A] great mystery." —Fresh Fiction

"Absolutely delicious . . . The mystery is substantial, the
murder is piquant, and the characters are fun-loving,
quirky, and provocative . . . 10s across the board."

—seattlepi.com

Other Ballroom Dance Mysteries
by Ella Barrick

Quickstep to Murder

Dead Man Waltzing

A Ballroom Dance Mystery

Ella Barrick

AN OBSIDIAN MYSTERY

OBSIDIAN
Published by New American Library, a division of
Penguin Group (USA) Inc., 375 Hudson Street,
New York, New York 10014, USA
Penguin Group (Canada), 90 Eglinton Avenue East, Suite 700, Toronto,
Ontario M4P 2Y3, Canada (a division of Pearson Penguin Canada Inc.)
Penguin Books Ltd., 80 Strand, London WC2R 0RL, England
Penguin Ireland, 25 St. Stephen's Green, Dublin 2,
Ireland (a division of Penguin Books Ltd.)
Penguin Group (Australia), 250 Camberwell Road, Camberwell, Victoria 3124,
Australia (a division of Pearson Australia Group Pty. Ltd.)
Penguin Books India Pvt. Ltd., 11 Community Centre, Panchsheel Park,
New Delhi - 110 017, India
Penguin Group (NZ), 67 Apollo Drive, Rosedale, Auckland 0632,
New Zealand (a division of Pearson New Zealand Ltd.)
Penguin Books (South Africa) (Pty.) Ltd., 24 Sturdee Avenue,
Rosebank, Johannesburg 2196, South Africa

Penguin Books Ltd., Registered Offices:
80 Strand, London WC2R 0RL, England

First published by Obsidian, an imprint of New American Library,
a division of Penguin Group (USA) Inc.

First Printing, June 2012
10   9   8   7   6   5   4   3   2   1

PUBLISHER'S NOTE
This is a work of fiction. Names, characters, places, and incidents either are the
product of the author's imagination or are used fictitiously, and any resemblance
to actual persons, living or dead, business establishments, events, or locales is
entirely coincidental.
   The publisher does not have any control over and does not assume any responsibility for author or third-party Web sites or their content.

For my brothers, James and John:
good brothers and better friends.
I love you guys.

ACKNOWLEDGMENTS

I'm grateful to Dr. Terry McGee and William J. Loskota, PhD, MD, who provided me with the expertise necessary to knock off Corinne Blakely. They gave me enough information on pharmacology and the effects of readily available prescription medicines to kill off another eight or ten books' worth of characters. Who needs a gun?

Thanks also to my agent, the fabulous Paige Wheeler, and my editor, the insightful Sandy Harding. (They are both much more than fabulous and insightful, but I didn't want to use my day's adjective quota all at once.) I continue to be grateful to my writing buddies, friends, and others who don't think I'm insane for wanting to be a novelist, and who indulge me by kicking around plot ideas, coming up with titles and character names, and listening to me babble about writing esoterica.

Finally, thanks and much love to my husband, Thomas, my mother, and my girls for being part of my life. I am constantly astonished and uplifted by their love, generosity, imagination, and general wonderfulness.

Chapter 1

"*One*, two, three, *one*, two, three," I counted, landing heavily on the downbeat for the six elderly couples waltzing around me in my ballroom as rush-hour traffic honked outside in the Old Town Alexandria streets. "Waltzing" was a bit of an exaggeration, since collisions and missteps marred what should have been the graceful flow of the dance. Four of the six couples, though, were beginners, friends from a retirement community who had recently signed up for lessons, and I had hopes they would improve.

"Keep your frame up," I suggested, nudging one large man between the shoulder blades. He drew his shoulders back stiffly; all he needed was a blindfold to look like a prisoner facing a firing squad.

"Better." I sighed, thinking we could work on relaxing and getting into the feel of the waltz in another couple of weeks. This was only their second lesson.

A short, plump woman in her seventies stopped moving, causing her even older partner to stumble. Mildred Kensington had been taking lessons at Graysin Motion for months, but hadn't shown much improvement. Still, she arrived each week with a sunny, pink-lipsticked smile and lots of energy, frequently with a new friend or two in tow. I had a soft spot for the spunky old lady. "Can you show us how to turn again, Stacy?" she asked.

"Of course." I glanced toward the door, wondering for the third time where Maurice was. He was supposed to be coteaching this class with me, and it was totally unlike him to forget a class. Closing in on seventy, I suspected, although he looked ten years younger, Maurice Goldberg had worked as a cruise ship dance host before I hired him away to teach at Graysin Motion, my ballroom dance studio in Old Town Alexandria, Virginia, just outside the nation's capital.

Selecting the least rhythm-challenged of the men, I led him through the steps several times before encouraging the group to try it again. "Weight on your *right* foot when you offer your partner your *left* hand," I reminded the men as I cued up the Strauss CD.

"Hoover would pick this up faster than I am," Mildred complained after another circuit of the room.

Hearing his name, the Great Dane lifted his head and pricked his ears forward. White with black splotches, he usually lay quietly in a pool of sunlight under a window when Mildred came to the studio. No one had ever complained about him and I liked having him around, so he'd become almost a studio mascot. I gave him a surreptitious pat as I passed him, and he thumped his black tail on the floor, not, unfortunately, in tempo.

"Stop that, Hoover," Mildred complained. "You're throwing me off the beat."

The class ended fifteen minutes later and the group lingered, poking fun at one another's dancing as good friends do. The words "elephant," "rhino," and "diplodocus" occurred frequently. The early June sun still rode high at six o'clock and laid a yellow sunbeam road where it streamed through the street-facing windows onto the wood floor. Some of the boards showed blackened strips where a fire had charred them a couple months back. I'd asked my refinisher to save the boards, if at all possible, because they were original to the Federal-era town home my great-aunt Laurinda had left me. He'd had to replace some of the more heavily damaged planks, but many of them were the very boards James Madison might have trodden when the house belonged to his cousin.

Urging the group to practice at home during the week, I shooed them out the door by my office. It led to an exterior staircase that allowed ballroom students to come up to my second-floor dance studio without going through my living quarters on the first floor. A darn fine arrangement. Before Great-aunt Laurinda had left me the house and I'd opened my own studio, I'd lived in an apartment nearly an hour from where I taught and danced, and the hideous commute had left me alternately drained and homicidal.

I had barely closed the door behind the seniors when a brief knock sounded. Unusual . . . most students and the instructors walked right in. I opened the door and stood dumbstruck at the sight of the man standing on the small square landing.

"Detective Lissy," I finally said. "To what do I owe the"—*imposition, intrusion, nuisance*—"honor?"

The man pursed his stretchy, too-red lips and crossed the threshold. Comb furrows tracked through his thinning, dishwater-colored hair, and his head seemed slightly too big for his thin neck. He wore an immaculate suit and a bland tie. He straightened the knot and the gesture slammed me back two months to when he had wanted to arrest me for shooting Rafe Acosta, my dance partner, coowner of Graysin Motion, and former fiancé. I shivered.

"Ms. Graysin." Lissy acknowledged me with a sour smile.

"I'm guessing you're not here for the Latin class?" I said.

"Astute of you." He stepped farther into the narrow hallway and I backed toward my office. "Actually, I'm looking for Mr. Maurice Goldberg and thought I might find him here."

"Maurice?" What in the world could the police want with Maurice? "I haven't seen him this evening. Have you tried his house?"

"Now, why didn't I think of that?" Lissy said with mock dismay. He passed me and poked his head into the ballroom.

I followed, becoming a little annoyed. "I told you he wasn't here," I said. "Why do you need to find him?"

"It looks much better than the last time I saw it," Lissy said, ignoring my question. "I like the new drapes." He gestured to the ivory velvet drapes I'd hung to replace the curtains incinerated by the fire. "Elegant."

His critique of my decorating efforts didn't distract me. "Why do you want Maurice?"

"You don't mind if I look around?" Lissy started for the smaller room at the back of the house that we called the "studio" to distinguish it from the "ballroom."

"Actually, I do," I said, stepping in front of him. "Unless you have a search warrant." Being a murder suspect had taught me a few things.

Lissy stopped, looking down his sharp nose at me. He was only a few inches taller than my five-foot-six, but he still managed to look down on me. It was an attitude thing more than a physical thing. The way the light from the hallway sconces hit him, I could see every little freckle across his cheeks and earlobes. "You don't have anything to hide, do you, Ms. Graysin?"

I balled my hands on my hips. "Tell me why you want Maurice, or say good night."

"Perhaps you know Corinne Blakely?" he asked, watching me closely.

I nodded. Who in the ballroom world *didn't* know Corinne Blakely, the grande dame of American ballroom dancing, a former champion, teacher, judge, and competition organizer who was leading the push for ballroom dancing to be admitted as an Olympic sport?

"I thought so." He made it sound like I'd admitted something criminal.

"Good night, Detective," I said, leading him back toward the door.

His voice came from just behind me. "Perhaps you haven't heard that she's dead?"

I whirled to face him. "No!"

"Yes."

"How?" Corinne must have been in her seventies; maybe she'd had a heart attack. But that wouldn't explain Lissy's presence. I cringed inwardly, awaiting his answer.

"Murdered."

Chapter 2

Detective Lissy and I stared at each other for a moment, my green eyes meeting his gray ones. Apparently, neither of us wanted to be the first to speak, so the M-word dangled in the silence between us. I cracked first. I frequently wish I had more self-control, but my impulses rule me more often than not.

"What happened?"

"That's what we'd like to talk to Mr. Goldberg about," Lissy said. Putting an index finger to the framed dance photo on the wall, he straightened it with a little push.

"Why Maurice?"

"He was lunching with her when she collapsed. He brought her to the emergency room."

Relief flitted through me. "Well, there! If he took her to the ER, he couldn't have wanted her dead. And if she keeled over while they were eating, maybe it was a heart attack or a stroke. Maybe"—I tried to think of medical conditions that resulted in sudden death—"an aneurysm."

"You've acquired a medical degree since we last spoke?" Lissy asked, gently sarcastic.

I glared at him.

He moved toward the door. "If you see or speak to Mr. Goldberg, please let him know that I'd like to talk to him at his earliest convenience." He put a dig in the last word. "It's in his best interest to explain his ... disappearance from the hospital as soon as possible."

"Of course," I said, holding the door wide. "Good-bye." I couldn't make myself go with a polite, *Nice to see you again.*

"I'm sure we'll chat soon." He stepped onto the landing and turned to give me a look. He was the kind of man who should've had a fedora; he had a 1950s kind of air about him, despite the modern clothes. "Don't go sticking your nose into this case," he said. "And you don't need to bother with that 'Who, me?' look. Remember what happened last time." He started down the stairs with a heavy tread.

"I caught a murderer and cleared my name," I called after him.

He didn't reply, just lifted a hand in farewell or dismissal, and strode toward his car parked at the curb. It was up to me to add in a whisper, "And got shot and got my studio set on fire."

Locking the shiny new dead bolt after him and turning out the lights in my office and the ballroom, I walked to the end of the hall where a door marked, PRIVATE, led downstairs to my living quarters. Going downstairs was a bit like leaving the twenty-first century to enter the 1930s; I didn't have money for new furniture or redecorating, so everything was as it had been when Aunt Laurinda lived here. A fusty lavender velvet settee was near the marble fireplace in the "parlor," as my great-aunt called it. Scattered about the room were a tarnished silver bowl and porcelain knickknacks, and old-fashioned paintings in heavy frames, including one of Aunt Laurinda as a 1923 debutante. The kitchen was no better, with its mismatched appliances, cracking linoleum floor, and turquoise-tiled countertops, the result of a misguided redecorating experiment in the 1960s. As soon as I had money to spare—in another decade or so—I was redoing the kitchen.

Finding some leftover salmon from last night's dinner in the rounded front fridge that Aunt Laurinda probably bought when the Beatles first stormed the States, I worried about Maurice. He was not a murderer. No way. Detective Lissy, as usual, had the wrong end of the stick. I thought how pathetic it was that I could attach the phrase "as usual" to a murder investigation. Considering I lived in an upscale area that I couldn't hope to have afforded without my aunt's bequest, I'd come into contact with a lot of homicide cases recently. Okay, two might not count as "a lot" to a police officer, but it seemed like two too many to me.

Washing my plate in the sink—no dishwasher—I put it in the dish drainer to dry, trying to think where Maurice might be. If he'd been lunching with Corinne Blakely when she fell ill, and had taken her to the hospital, where would he be now? He didn't have a wife, or any kids that I knew about, so he hadn't taken refuge with family. I trusted that Detective Lissy had checked at his house, so he apparently wasn't there. I tried to put myself in Maurice's place. If I'd seen my lunch partner pitch facedown into the bouillabaisse and had to hang around an ER that smelled of various body fluids, desperation, and nose-singeing cleaners, I'd need a drink.

I'd met Maurice once, shortly before I hired him, at a little pub around the corner from his house. I thought I could find it again, although I couldn't quite remember the name. The Fox and Hen? Fox and Hound? I was pretty sure it was something to do with foxes. Pulling the ponytail elastic from my blond hair, I shook it free, ran a brush through it, and changed out of my dance gear into capris, a tank top, and gold sandals. A shower might've been a good idea, too, after three hours of back-to-back classes, but I didn't want to take the time. Within seven minutes, I was out the back door and getting into my yellow Volkswagen Beetle parked under the carport that abutted my tiny courtyard.

Maurice lived west of Old Town proper, in an area dominated by streets named for trees: Linden, Maple, Cedar. Starting from his house on Walnut Street, which had a patrol car parked in front of it—very subtle—I circled the area, searching for the pub. I finally located the Fox and Muskrat on a corner four blocks from Maurice's place. The parking looked to be on the street, so I found a spot and slid into it, then walked back. The pub anchored a block of stores dropped into the middle of a residential area. Mature trees overhung cracked sidewalks, and the stores, like the pub, all looked like they'd been open since the Woodstock era. I passed a wine store, an antique books and maps shop, and a place selling fabric and sewing supplies that had a lovely quilt patterned with stylized mountains in the window.

A wooden sign with a top hat–wearing fox poking his cane at a weaselly-looking muskrat swung from a wooden arm over the pub's door. Why a muskrat? I craned my neck to study the sign, but had to move aside when a patron exited the bar, letting a burp of air-conditioning escape. I caught the door before it could close and went in.

The place smelled like cigarettes, even though Virginia had a no-smoking law on the books. It took me two seconds to realize the odor wasn't new; it seeped from the walls, the beamed ceiling, and the wooden floors. In the fifties and sixties, probably every drinker in the place had a cigarette going, and the smoke had, over time, sunk into every fiber of wood in the place. My fascinated mind wondered whether smoke from one of the founding fathers' pipes still lingered here.

A small place, the Fox and Muskrat was picturesque veering toward shoddy. It could have been transported in its entirety from an English roadside, complete with pint glasses, snug booths, and scarred oak tables. The dim glow from electric candles centered on each table provided insufficient illumination, and two big-screen TVs over the bar didn't help much. Two men tossed darts in a desultory way on the far side of the bar. Once my eyes adjusted to the gloom, I spotted Maurice on a stool at the end of the bar, a half-empty yard of ale in front of him, his gaze lifted to the nearest television, where an obscure channel broadcast a cricket match.

I made my way past a group of thirtyish men arguing about whether Bud or Miller Lite commercials were funnier. They paused, midargument, to eye me as I passed. I ignored them, used to the attention. When you're blond, stacked, and move like a dancer, men tend to notice you. I slid onto the stool beside Maurice and said, "Hey."

After a too-long moment, he lowered his gaze from the television to note my presence. It took another moment before he said, "Anastasia."

No matter how hard I try, I can't convince him to leave off calling me by my real name and use Stacy like everyone else does. He blinked twice, looking perplexed by my presence, and I began to wonder how many yards of ale he'd already drunk.

"Fascinating game," I said, nodding toward the TV.

"I don't understand a single thing about it," he said, eyes cutting back toward the screen.

Ordering a glass of chardonnay from the middle-aged, aproned bartender, I studied Maurice. Although garbed in a double-breasted blazer and tailored slacks, he looked less dapper than usual. A lock of Brylcreemed white hair drooped onto his forehead, his shirt looked tired, and even his perpetual George Hamilton tan looked washed-out. Stripped of his usual élan, he seemed a stranger.

"Sooo," I said when my wine appeared. "I heard Corinne Blakely died today."

He turned his head to look at me and swayed on the stool. I reached out an arm to steady him. "I'm not drunk," he said with the careful diction of someone who was drunk.

"You have a right to be," I assured him.

"Rinny Blakely died," he said, as if I hadn't just mentioned it.

"I know."

"We were having lunch and then—" His head flopped toward his chest, and for a moment I thought he had passed out. Then I realized he was demonstrating what had happened with Corinne. He snapped his head upright. "Then she slumped over and fell out of her chair. I didn't know what to do." Taking a swallow of his beer, he wiped at a smudge on the bar with his elbow.

I took advantage of his distraction to order a couple of coffees from the bartender, who nodded her graying head approvingly. "What did you do?" I asked Maurice.

He rubbed a finger against his prominent nose. "They

have very effishun—efficient—waiters at the Swallow," he said. "They called for an ambulansh—ambu*lance*—but I lifted Rinny and carried her to the hospital. She weighs less now than when we danced together forty years ago."

"You carried her to the hospital?" No wonder the man looked gray and weary. "How far was it?"

"Couple blocksh."

Setting our coffees in front of us, the bartender told me, "You'd be doing your grandfather a favor to take him home. He doesn't usually put it away like this, if you know what I mean. Bad day?" She waited for me to fork over some good gossip.

"You could say that."

Disappointed by my discretion, she drifted to the other end of the bar to wait on new customers. Everyone in here looked like regulars, I thought as she greeted them by name. I sipped my coffee and Maurice followed suit, not even seeming to notice that his beer had disappeared. Maybe he'd pickled his taste buds. We sat in silence, finishing our coffees. Maurice set his mug on the counter with a snap, and looked at me, his eyes less bleary than earlier.

"Anastasia, what are you doing here?"

"Looking for you."

His brow crinkled. "What on earth for?"

"I heard you were with Corinne Blakely when she died," I hedged, "and I thought you might need a friend." I didn't think he was in any condition to hear the police were after him.

He gave me a sad smile. "I don't have a lot of friends. It's hard to keep in touch when you're cruising to the Bahamas one week, Mexico the next. New passengers every week or ten days. You start getting to know some-one, to like someone, and they're disembarking with a

'We'll have to keep in touch' you know they don't mean. It's not that they don't like you; it's that the cruise was a fantashy world, and once they're back in their real world, going to library board meetings and working with Meals on Wheels and keeping the grandkids for the weekend ... well, it's hard to shtay—stay—in touch."

I hadn't thought much about what life as a cruise dance host would be like, but his words painted a picture more lonely than glamorous. "You didn't always work on a cruise ship."

"No." He seemed disinclined to discuss his earlier life.

I helped him down from the bar stool, relieved that he could stand on his own. "Let's get you home." I remembered the cop waiting outside his place. "On second thought, why don't you come home with me for the night? You can sleep in the guest room." I thought I'd changed the sheets on the guest bed after my brother, Nick, visited three months ago.

"That's very kind of you, Anastasia."

Several patrons called good-nights to Maurice as we left. The fresh air outside perked him up a bit and we walked the couple blocks to my car without incident. He dozed off on the way back to my place, but woke easily when I tapped his shoulder. "We're here."

Inside, I heated a bowl of soup for him, pretty sure he hadn't eaten since his lunch with Corinne, and re-made the bed while he ate. By the time I returned to the kitchen, he was sitting straighter and finishing a big glass of water.

"My head is going to ache abominably in the morning," he said with a rueful smile.

"I expect so."

He looked around the kitchen and said, "I shouldn't impose. I can go home, Anastasia."

"You might not want to do that." When he looked a question at me, I explained about the police looking for him.

His brows climbed toward his hairline in astonishment. "For me? The police think I had something to do with Corinne's death?"

"Apparently."

"That's preposterous!"

"Detective Lissy thinks it's suspicious that you 'disappeared'—his word—from the hospital."

"Disappeared? I sat in the waiting room for over an hour, until I gathered that the doctors had been unable to resuscitate Corinne, that she had passed. In truth, I think she was gone from the moment she hit the floor at the restaurant. I went straight to the Fox and Muskrat and I've been sitting there ever since, drowning my sorrows, you might say." He stopped abruptly. "Why do the police care about a heart attack, anyway?"

"They think she was murdered."

"Ridiculous," he said forcefully. "How?"

I realized Detective Lissy hadn't given me any details. "I don't know." They'd been lunching, she'd keeled over.... "Poison?"

The idea seemed to stun him.

"What, exactly, happened? Did you pick her up or did you arrive separately at the restaurant? Did anyone join you? What did you eat?"

Maurice rose and refilled his water glass from the tap. Leaning back against the sink, he took a long swallow. "We arrived separately," he said finally. "I was running errands and drove to the Swallow from the library. Corinne was there, seated at a table, when I arrived. She looked fabulous."

Corinne always looked fabulous. She had a slender

Audrey Hepburn–ish figure that looked marvelous in clothes, and thick, angel-wing white hair she always wore in a chignon. Photos revealed she'd had the prematurely white hair from her early thirties. She favored suits in clear pinks and reds and blues that flattered her complexion, and had a collection of shoes I envied. I won't even mention her extraordinary wardrobe of competition dresses. "Had she eaten or drunk anything before you arrived?"

"I don't think so, although she'd ordered a bottle of champagne."

"Quite the ritzy lunch," I observed.

"She wanted to celebrate. She'd signed a contract for her book on very favorable terms, and she wanted to celebrate."

"What book?"

"A memoir. I believe she was calling it *Step by Step*."

"So what happened then?"

"I kissed her and sat and we had some champagne."

"Both of you?"

He nodded.

Scratch the champagne as the poison source, I thought.

Without further cue from me, Maurice continued. "We talked for a while before ordering—and then I ordered the ginger-squash soup and the portabella-spinach ravioli. Corinne had a salad and an asparagus–goat cheese quiche, if I recall correctly. We shared a slice of a flourless chocolate torte for dessert."

Sharing a dessert . . . It sounded like Maurice had been considerably more intimate with Corinne Blakely than I realized. How interesting. I left that thought for the moment. "And she ate some of everything before she . . . she had her attack?"

"Yes." He set his glass in the sink. "I really can't believe she was murdered, Anastasia, much less poisoned. Maybe the police have simply got it wrong?"

I didn't figure Detective Lissy would waste his time looking for a murderer unless he had unambiguous evidence that a murder had been committed. "Did Corinne leave the table at any time?"

"She left to visit the ladies' room before dessert."

"How long was she gone?"

"Good grief, Anastasia, I wasn't timing her."

"Long enough to bump into someone and chat?" I persisted.

"Maybe ten or twelve minutes?"

Maurice smoothed a weary hand over his hair and I realized he must be exhausted. "Let's sleep on it," I said, handing him the extra pillow and a blanket I'd taken from the linen closet. The air-conditioning kept it chilly. "I even changed the bed for you."

That got a small smile before worry cloaked his face again. "Perhaps I should visit the police station now and get this straightened out."

"In the morning," I said. "When you're sober. With a lawyer."

Chapter 3

I wanted to accompany Maurice to the police station in the morning, but he refused.

"I'll be in and out in under half an hour," he said with a confidence brought on by a good night's sleep, a handful of painkillers with an oatmeal breakfast, a washed and ironed shirt (I'd tossed his shirt in the wash after he'd gone to sleep), and his white hair slicked back as usual, with a handful of my mousse. He complained the vanilla scent wasn't manly, but lodgers at the Graysin Motel can't be too choosy about their complimentary toiletries.

"Don't go without a lawyer," I said, already dressed in my dance clothes to teach my Ballroom Aerobics class. It was the only class at Graysin Motion that didn't teach competition-type or social ballroom dancing and, wouldn't you know it, it was our most popular class. I had a full studio every Wednesday and Friday at seven a.m., and on Tuesday and Thursday over lunch.

"That won't be necessary," Maurice said with a wave of his hand. "I'm innocent."

Rolling my eyes, I said, "That's not enough for Detective Lissy." I handed him the business card I'd dug up earlier. "Here. Take this. Drake is a high-powered criminal defense lawyer. He'll—"

"I am not a criminal!"

"He'll help you." My uncle Nico had sent Phineas Drake to rescue me when the police thought I killed Rafe. Drake made me nervous—he'd hinted that he could set up anyone I wanted as Rafe's murderer—but he got results. "He's expensive, though."

"Money isn't an issue." Maurice waved the card away and I jammed it into the key pocket of my spandex shorts.

I wished I could say, "Money isn't an issue." Could be that cruise lines paid more than I realized. "Good, then. Call me as soon as you're finished with the police, okay?"

Maurice smiled and kissed my cheek. "Thank you, Anastasia."

"Sure." I shrugged it off, embarrassed by his gratitude. "What are friends for?"

An hour and a half later, sweaty from the high-voltage class, I walked into my office to find Tav sitting at his desk. I smiled involuntarily at the sight of his dark head bent in concentration over a spreadsheet. Octavio Acosta, Rafe's half brother, had inherited Rafe's share of the business. Instead of selling out, he had elected to stay on as my partner, for a while at least, and he handled the numbers end of the business that I hated. In his "real" life, he owned an import-export company in Argentina and was spending a year in the States to set up an outlet or branch or outpost in the northern Virginia area. It kept him busy, and he didn't spend much time at his desk here.

"To what do I owe the pleasure?" I asked.

He looked up with a smile. His lean face with its strong nose and brows, dark eyes glinting with humor, and sensuous mouth was disturbingly attractive. His black hair was a bit longer than it had been when he arrived almost two months ago, curling halfway down his collar; maybe he hadn't found a good barber yet.

"Stacy. I looked into the ballroom, but you did not see me. You were leading the ladies around the room in a circle, doing a leg exercise of some sort."

His sexy Argentinean accent, so like Rafe's, made me tingle. "Tango lunges," I said. Nodding at the papers spread on his desk, I asked. "So, are we solvent?"

"Barely." His brows twitched closer together. "The trip to Blackpool took a big bite out of our cash on hand."

The Blackpool Dance Festival in England was the most prestigious international professional dance competition of the year. Couples competed by invitation only, and wins at Blackpool could significantly boost ballroom dancers' reputations and, thus, their bottom line via increasing numbers of students, endorsement deals, invitations to perform on *Ballroom with the B-Listers*, and the like. When Rafe got killed, I'd had to find a new partner quickly. I'd been lucky that Vitaly Voloshin had left his dance partner in Russia when he moved to nearby Baltimore to be with his life partner. We'd paired up, practiced like demons, and won trophies for our waltzing and quickstepping. Given that we'd had only a few weeks together, I was happy with the outcome and looking forward to next year's festival.

"We had to go," I told Tav.

"I know. But some belt-tightening measures are in order now."

I wasn't fond of belt tightening. I liked buying new

competition dresses, bling, and accessories. I plopped onto the love seat by the window, idly watching tourists crowding the sidewalks of Old Town.

"Possibly you could share a hotel room with someone at the Virginia DanceSport competition."

I wrinkled my nose with distaste. Rafe and I had shared a room when we went to competitions. Vitaly and I didn't bunk together, of course, so the studio's hotel bill for competitions had doubled. I sighed. "If I have to."

"There is a huge bridal show coming up," Tav said.

"Thinking of getting married?"

"*Por Dios*, no!"

His expression was comical, and I laughed. I realized I didn't know whether Tav had ever been married. We'd met under intense circumstances and gotten to know each other on some levels pretty quickly, but once we became coowners of Graysin Motion, a certain awkwardness had come in. Having learned my lesson about being involved with a business partner from the difficulties that resulted when Rafe and I broke up but still had the studio to run together, I was reluctant to become too close to Tav. Dating was out of the question, although something about him—his scent, his intensity—made me far too aware of him. Not that he'd ever asked me out, I thought with irrational pique.

"Why the interest in bridal shows, then?"

"I thought that Graysin Motion might purchase space and use the convention as an opportunity to advertise ballroom dance lessons. Encourage brides and grooms and their attendants to learn to waltz for their wedding receptions."

"We could even offer a gift registry, where people could buy the happy couple dance lessons," I said, enthused by the idea. "That's very clever, Tav." We'd always had a trickle of business from engaged couples hoping to shine on the dance floor at their receptions, but I'd never thought of specifically going after wedding business.

He grinned, teeth very white against his tanned skin. "Advertising is one of my gifts. Like soccer and—"

I stopped myself and him before I could speculate about his other possible gifts. "Did you hear about Corinne Blakely's death?"

"No. Who is she?"

I gave him the twenty-five-words-or-less summary of her career. "There's no one bigger in ballroom dance circles," I finished.

Tav looked a question at me, clearly wondering why I was giving him the life story of a woman he'd never meet.

"She died yesterday," I said.

"I am sor—"

"The police think she was murdered."

"Murdered?" Dismay clouded his brow. "Stacy, please do not tell me—"

"Maurice was with her when she died," I blurted. "He's at the police station now."

Running a hand down his face, Tav said, "That is all the studio needs—more publicity related to murder."

"I'm sure the studio won't be drawn into it," I said, hoping I was right. "Maurice will tell the police about lunching with Corinne and taking her to the hospital, and they'll thank him and wave good-bye."

The phone rang.

Happy for the interruption, I lunged for it. "Graysin Motion."

"Anastasia?"

I winced at the distress in Maurice's voice. "Are you okay?"

"Perhaps you could call your lawyer friend for me?"

*   *   *

I put in a call to Phineas Drake, but his secretary said he was in New York for the day. Asking her to have him call me as soon as possible, I said a hurried good-bye to Tav, who was headed into D.C. to look at spaces-to-let for housing his new store, and ran downstairs to shower and change.

Seeing the brick police building on Mill Street again made my tummy flutter nervously. Reminding myself that no one suspected me of anything this time, I climbed the shallow stairs and pushed into the crowded waiting room. I avoided eye contact with the people waiting to submit forms for background checks, get fingerprinted, or report crimes, and marched straight to the counter to ask the bored-looking officer for Maurice Goldberg. In the event, Maurice exited through a door to the left of the counter before the officer could pick up the phone to locate him.

"Maurice!" I hurried to him and gave him a big hug. He looked worried, but not like he'd been beaten with hoses, stretched on the rack, or forced to listen to Justin Bieber albums. "They're letting you go?"

"For the time being." He sounded like he thought the police would drag him from his bed at midnight and toss him into jail.

"Did they read you your rights?"

He nodded, a little dazed. "Just like on television."

Not good. Detective Lissy must consider him a real suspect.

"Let's talk elsewhere, hm?" He herded me toward the door; I knew just how he felt, since I'd been in his shoes.

We emerged, blinking, into bright sunlight and energy-sapping humidity. Old Town Alexandria is a lovely area with a fascinating history, but situated as it is, smack-dab against the Potomac River, the summer air is frequently heavier than a wet towel. By the time we'd walked the half block to where I'd parked my yellow Beetle, we were both sweating. I leaned my face into the stream of air-conditioning after starting the car, letting it dry my damp hairline.

"Home?" I asked, pulling away from the curb.

"I'd rather stop by Rinny's place, if you don't mind, Anastasia," Maurice said.

I darted a quick look at him. "Why?"

"I did some thinking while waiting for the police officers to interview me," he said. "And it crossed my mind that *if* Corinne were murdered, it might have something to do with her new book."

"Really?"

"She was laughing about it, but nervous, too, when we lunched. 'Maury,' she said, 'I've been keeping secrets for fifty years and it's time to speak up. I'm not getting any younger, you know. I could pop off any day.' She laughed like it was a joke, but look what's happened." Maurice tapped a nervous finger against his thigh.

"You think she was murdered over a book?" I couldn't keep the skepticism out of my voice.

"Stranger things have happened, Anastasia." The tension vibrating in Maurice's voice told me he was pinning his hopes on this new theory.

"I suppose so," I said, figuring it couldn't hurt to play along for a bit. "Which way?"

He gave me directions to Corinne Blakely's house off of the Mount Vernon Parkway. As we sped south with the Potomac glinting on our left, I asked, "What kind of secrets?"

"The usual," he said, with a ghost of his insouciant grin. "Infidelity, skullduggery, crimes of passion."

"Related to ballroom dance? You sound like you're describing the action on Tortuga Island."

"Ah, Anastasia. You find pirates in all walks of life." He pointed to the right and I turned, thinking the road he indicated would lead to a neighborhood. Instead, it turned out to be a driveway leading to a mansion—there was no other word for it—that occupied what Realtors called a "parklike setting" and had, I imagined, splendid views of the Potomac River from the front windows.

"Corinne Blakely lived here?" I cut the engine.

"She married well. And more than once. This house belonged to her first husband, who died only two years after they got married. Some tropical fever. His money came from hotels." Maurice unfolded himself from the front seat and strode toward the door, seemingly completely at home.

"Wait." I hurried after him, hampered by my strappy sandals. "What are we going to do—knock on the door, hope someone answers, and say we want to come in to—what?—search for a manuscript?"

"Corinne lived alone," he said, unperturbed by my gentle sarcasm. "There won't be anyone here, unless the housekeeper's around."

"So we're going to break in? That's so much better." I'd ditched the "gentle" and moved on to unadulterated sarcasm.

"I thought we'd use the key," Maurice said, producing one from his pocket.

"Wha—? How?" I eyed Maurice uncomfortably. He hadn't lifted the key from Corinne as she lay unconscious on the restaurant floor, had he?

"Tut-tut, Anastasia," he said, reading my expression. "I would never. No, I neglected to give this back."

"Give it back?" I gaped at him. "You used to live here? You and Corinne—"

"Were married for about ten minutes in 1964," he said.

I stopped at the base of four marble steps that led to the double front doors inset with stained glass. Maurice kept climbing. "You were married to Corinne Blakely?"

He looked over his shoulder at me. "I was twenty-two. She was twenty-four. I was her rebound relationship after Charles died. Or so she told me when she divorced me eight months later."

I kept staring at him. A flush warmed his tanned cheeks and he turned away to fumble with the key. "I never knew," I breathed.

"It's ancient history . . . as relevant as the Phoenicians and the Assyrians or some such. A few people knew, but it wasn't common knowledge. It was over so fast. . . ." He shrugged. The lock clicked.

I mounted the steps to stand beside him and he paused with his hand on the knob. "The police?"

"Yes, they know."

"That's why they're looking at you so hard. The divorced husband with a grudge."

"The divorce happened in the Dark Ages, and I never had a grudge against Rinny." Maurice sounded unusually testy. He crossed his arms over his chest. "We were too young. I was too young."

"Sorry. I didn't mean *I* thought you held a grudge, just that the police—"

"We stayed friends," he said, tacitly accepting my apology, "throughout her marriages. She shucked husband number six some twelve or fourteen months back. Constancy was never Rinny's strong suit," he said with a reminiscent smile.

"I'd think the police would be more interested in her last husband than in you," I said.

"He's a Hungarian count or Latvian baron or something. He returned to Europe after Corinne tossed him over." Maurice looked around. "Let's go in, Anastasia, before the neighbors start to wonder."

The nearest neighbor would have to use binoculars to spot us, but I didn't argue. "Let's get it over with," I agreed.

Maurice reached for the ornate doorknob, but the door swung inward before he could touch it.

Chapter 4

Maurice sprang back, bumping into me, and I almost toppled down the steps. Only my dancer's reflexes and core strength saved me. I regained my balance in time to see Maurice slip the key into his pocket as a beautiful young man appeared in the doorway, dark brows arching high and an expression of surprise on his face. Pale skin and silky black hair set off intensely blue eyes. He wore jeans and a rugby shirt, but looked like he should have been dressed in an ascot and spats, like a character from an Evelyn Waugh novel. Not that I'd ever read Waugh's books, but I'd seen the miniseries. The young man spoke, spoiling the effect with a blatantly mid-Atlantic accent and a scornful tone.

"Maurice! What the hell are you doing here?"

"We were just about to knock," Maurice lied. "What are *you* doing here, Turner?"

"I was staying with Grandmama when she—" He broke off, pressing his lips together as if overcome by grief.

"Thrown out of another school?" Maurice asked with

spurious sympathy. I looked at him; I'd never heard him sound so contemptuous.

"No," Turner spit. "It's summer break. Duh. Who's she?"

"This is Anastasia Graysin," Maurice said. "Anastasia, Turner Blakely."

"Nice to meet you," I said, extending my hand. "It's Stacy."

"Nice to meet *you*," he said, running appreciative eyes over my figure and holding on to my hand too long. A smile that would have been charming if he hadn't been so conscious of its effect curved his sculpted mouth.

I almost laughed; he couldn't have been more than twenty-one or twenty-two. I tugged my hand away forcefully and he jolted forward a half step. He covered it up by descending the stairs past us and walking partway down the driveway to pick up the newspaper. He returned, slapping it in one hand.

"What are you doing here, anyway?" His suspicious gaze tracked from me to Maurice.

"Last time I was here, Thursday night," Maurice said smoothly, "I left a pair of reading glasses. I was going to ask Mrs. Laughlin if she'd found them."

"I fired the judgmental old witch this morning," Turner said, stepping back into the foyer. Behind him I glimpsed a magnificent chandelier dangling with thousands of crystals, rounded walls painted a pale salmon, and a Chinese rug. "I've got to hit the road. Bachelor party for a buddy down in Virginia Beach tonight." He started to close the door without even a polite good-bye, but Maurice stopped the door with his hand.

"When will the funeral be?" he asked.

I heard the sadness in his voice.

Turner looked like he wasn't going to answer, but then

said, "Friday. Ten a.m. First Presbyterian." He shoved the door closed.

I resisted the juvenile temptation to call, "Nice to meet you, too," at the impassive doors. Instead, I turned and descended the steps. "Mrs. Laughlin?" I asked Maurice.

"The housekeeper," he said, keeping pace with me as we returned to the car. "She's been with Corinne for years. Decades. I can't believe Turner fired her before Rinny is even buried. She must be devastated. She's my age, at least, and it's unlikely she'll get another job. I hope Rinny left her enough to live on."

"You were pretty quick, coming up with an excuse for our being here," I said.

He smiled. "I'm lucky he didn't ask why we were there when he first opened the door. I would have stuttered and given the game away. Corinne didn't mention that he had moved back in with her. It must have been over the weekend, because he wasn't here Thursday night."

I almost asked, *Or Friday morning?* but didn't for fear of embarrassing Maurice. I was getting the distinct impression that he and the unconstant Corinne had been *close* friends. Friends with benefits, even.

"Why didn't you ask him about the manuscript?" I asked as I pulled back onto the Mount Vernon Parkway going north.

"He and his father are among the people who may not come off so well in Corinne's memoirs," Maurice said. "If Turner knew Corinne had a book deal, he'd probably do what he could to destroy the manuscript."

"Oh?"

"He's got a little problem with cheating," said Maurice, "which is why he's been to three colleges in as many years. His father, Corinne's son, Randolph, is addicted to painkillers. He broke his back in a skiing accident some years back and has had troubles with prescription drugs since then. I know Corinne's paid for a couple of stays in rehab programs, but Randolph can't seem to stay clean."

"A Charlie Sheen type," I said. "His dad's had no luck helping him, either."

Maurice looked at me blankly, apparently not a devotee of *People* magazine or gossipy entertainment shows.

"Never mind."

I mulled over the situation as Maurice stayed silent. He'd been lunching with Corinne Blakely when she died—possibly poisoned—and the police considered him a suspect. He was convinced the real killer was someone afraid that Corinne's book would expose a secret the murderer preferred to keep secret. That seemed far-fetched to me; I suspected that if Corinne was murdered, it was for a more concrete reason, like money. Pulling up in front of Maurice's house fifteen minutes later, I asked, "Who inherits Corinne's estate? Her son?"

Maurice shook his head. "No. She wrote him out of the will two years ago when it became clear his last stint at rehab didn't 'take.' She was afraid that if she left him all her money he would use it to feed his addiction and eventually kill himself. No, I think the bulk of her estate goes to Turner. At least, that's the direction she was leaning last time we talked about it."

"What about you?" I asked. "Will you inherit anything?" I was worried that if Corinne had left him a substantial bequest, the police would consider it motive.

He chuckled. "She used to joke about leaving each of her husbands something to remind us of our time with her. If she did, I'm sure it will be no more than a token, a memento."

"Okay." I glanced at my watch. "Look, I've got to go. Are you okay?"

Patting my cheek, he said, "I'll be fine, Anastasia. Thanks for springing me from the pokey. I'll see you this evening for the Latin class."

"You don't have to come if you don't feel up to it," I said. "I can call Vitaly."

"I'll be there." Maurice got out of the car. "Ciao."

I arrived late to the furniture store, where I had promised to help my sister, Danielle, pick out a new sofa. The old one had collapsed under her and her boyfriend, Coop, when they were, she alleged, simply watching *Jeopardy!* a couple nights ago. The store was a freestanding building on Lee Highway, surrounded by a gymnastics place, a restaurant, and an oil-change garage. Traffic whizzed by. Dani was pacing the concrete walkway in front of the store, curly red hair billowing around her, frown etching her pretty face.

"Sorry," I started as I came up to her, thinking her uncharacteristic anger was directed at me.

"Have you talked to Mom today?" she asked, ignoring my apology.

Ah, now I knew where her anger was coming from. She and our mother had had a difficult relationship since Mom chose to follow her passion for horses and dressage rather than stick around to be a wife and mother. Dad had given her an ultimatum—him or the horses—and she'd chosen the nags. I'd been fifteen when she left and I'd sorta, kinda, maybe understood her choice. By then, I'd been ballroom dancing for several years and knew I wouldn't be me if I couldn't continue. Danielle, a couple years younger, had never forgiven her.

"No, I haven't been home. Is she okay?"

Danielle snorted. " 'Okay.' That's one word for it."

I moved into the air-conditioned cool of the store and Danielle trailed after me. We waved away the saleswoman charging toward us like Yogi Bear after a pic-a-nic basket.

"She wants us to join her on a vacation," Danielle said, clearly incensed.

"So?"

"So, she's going to a dressage competition in Georgia and she wants us to meet her afterward on Jekyll Island. Her treat."

"Oh." The reason for Danielle's anger became plain: Jekyll Island was the site of our last vacation as a family, before Mom moved out.

"She wants to ruin our memories of our last vacation together," Danielle said, plopping down onto a brown plaid sofa. "Too hard." She popped up again and punched the pillows of a beige microfiber conversation pit.

"Not beige," I objected, drawn to a red leather sofa.

"Beige blends," she said.

"There's such a thing as too much blending." I admit I was biased; I'd rather go naked than wear beige or brown or any of the other "blendy" colors Danielle stocked her closet with. As a union negotiator, she thought a "nonthreatening" wardrobe helped her connect with the employees she was helping. I didn't think that perspective needed to extend to her living environment. "Don't you want something that pops?"

"Not really." Checking the price tag, she added, "You're not going, are you?"

"I don't know. I haven't even talked to Mom. It would depend when it is, I guess."

"Well, I'm not going."

"Did you tell Mom that?"

She bit her lip. "I told her I'd think about it."

I sighed. For a woman who dealt with confrontation day in and day out in her job, Danielle was strangely loath to lay things on the line in her personal life. "Well, if you said you'd think about it, why not think about it? It might be fun . . . a girls' weekend at the beach, mani-pedis, piña coladas, shell collecting."

"Daddy should be there." She put on a little-girl-lost face, eyes wide, mouth trembling.

Sheesh. Getting all maudlin wasn't going to help. "Dad? With Beryl, I presume?" His second wife, a woman he'd married five years ago, after Dani and I had already left home. "They could have a room that adjoined ours, and Mom and Beryl could compare notes while they had their toenails painted." I put on a New Jersey voice like Beryl's. "'Didn't you just hate the way Ronald tossed his socks near the hamper but never in it, Jean?'"

"Not like that!" Dani tried to suppress a laugh but failed. "You know what I meant."

"Yeah. You meant you want to turn time back a dozen or so years. Not possible, baby sister."

"I don't see why not," she grumbled.

I wisely left that unanswered. Instead, I distracted her by telling her about Corinne Blakely's death and Maurice's involvement.

"I can't see Maurice poisoning someone," she said.

"We don't know that she was poisoned," I cautioned, even though I had told her that poison was my guess for the murder weapon, since Maurice would have noticed a gun, knife, or garrote.

"Poison's a woman's weapon."

"How sexist."

"It is," she insisted. "I read it somewhere. Who does

Maurice think did it?" Crowding me onto an ottoman as she passed me, she fingered the fringe on a pillow.

"Someone whose secrets Corinne was going to reveal in her new tell-all memoir."

Danielle stopped examining furniture to look at me. "Really?"

I nodded. "But I think it might have been her grandson. He struck me as the kind of whiny rich kid who expects to have things—everything he wants—handed to him on a platter. Immediately."

"Was he at the restaurant?"

"Not as far as I know. Good point." Danielle's question made me think: Were there slow-acting poisons someone could have administered to Corinne earlier in the day/week/month that resulted in her death at the Swallow? My knowledge of poisons was severely limited. I knew better than to drink household cleaners or splash them in my eyes, and I thought oleander leaves were poisonous to animals—and maybe humans?—but that's where my expertise stopped.

"What about this?" We had wandered halfway around the store and I pointed at an olive green sofa with puffy cushions and a faint red stripe thinner than angel hair pasta. Not too bright, not too boring. Best of all, it was on sale. Dani sat on it, leaned back, and reclined with her feet hanging just off the edge.

"It's nice," she said, "but I don't think it goes with my Aegean Sunset walls."

"Maybe I should come over and see the apartment, now that you've off-loaded the broken sofa on Goodwill." I made a frame of my hand and pretended to peer through it. "It's been a while since I've seen the place; I haven't been over since you repainted."

"Sure," Dani said. "How about tomorrow night? Cooper left today for a business trip, some sort of security convention in Las Vegas—ha!—so I don't have plans any evening this week."

I never had evening plans unless I was teaching, so I didn't feel too sympathetic that she was dateless for a few days. I pointed out another sale couch, but she said, "I've got to think about it. This is the first store I've been to; I want to look in a couple other places."

I rolled my eyes but said nothing, used to my sister's habits. I was impulsive and made decisions about sofas or clothes or holidays on a whim, on intuition. Dani pondered things, researched products in *Consumer Reports*, and spent forty dollars in gas trekking around to eighteen stores in order to save ten bucks on something.

"Fine," I said. "Let me know when you want to go looking again. I'm getting ideas for when I can afford to replace Aunt Laurinda's midcentury atrocities."

"You know," Danielle said as we threaded our way back through the displays to the door, "her furniture might be worth money, like to a collector or something."

"I don't think they're legitimate antiques. They're just old."

"Retro," Danielle corrected me. "Collectible. Maybe you could make enough off of them to buy new furniture."

"It's worth a thought." We pushed through the glass door to the parking lot. "How would I find someone who would know if it's worth something? I don't think that Cari Something from the *Cash and Cari* show is likely to drop by, or the crew from *Antiques Roadshow*."

Dani tossed her hair and sniffed, knowing I was making fun of her love of do-it-yourself and home-makeover

TV shows. "Laugh if you want, but I've learned a lot from those shows. I'll find someone to give you an estimate."

"Really?" I hugged her good-bye. "Thanks, Dani." She headed toward her car and I called after her, "Think about it." I wasn't talking about the sofa.

Chapter 5

Between collecting Maurice from the police station, our field trip to Corinne Blakely's house, and the furniture-shopping expedition with Dani, I'd taken an extraordinarily long lunch. No biggie, I told myself, climbing the interior stairs to the studio at almost two o'clock. Our next class wasn't until four, and I'd be working until eight o'clock tonight with classes and a private lesson with one of the men who paid me to dance with him at professional-amateur competitions. Such students were a pro's bread and butter, and I was hoping to take on a couple more, since one of my best students, Mark Downey, had turned out to be an unbalanced stalker type.

When I opened the door into the studio hallway, the strains of "With You I'm Born Again," one of my favorite waltzes, drifted from the ballroom. Curious about who was here—I'd installed new locks not long ago and only a few people had keys—I paused outside the ballroom door. Vitaly Voloshin, my new dance partner, stood at the bar stretching. He had a lanky body and was one of those people who look totally unprepossessing at first glance; in fact, you wouldn't be surprised to hear he was a 7-Eleven clerk or video store manager, with his longish, strawlike hair, pale skin, and bony face. But when he stepped on a dance floor, he underwent an amazing transformation, becoming somehow elegant and electric. I couldn't explain it. He caught sight of me in the mirrors I'd had installed when we redid the room after the fire, and his face split into a grin. He loved smiling since his partner, John, had gifted him with dental work that turned his formerly tannish, crooked teeth into movie star–worthy choppers.

"Good. You is here. We can practicing. I have the new ideas for our waltz."

"We didn't have a practice scheduled."

Vitaly raised his brows. "So?"

"You're right. Give me a minute." I clattered back downstairs and threw on dance leggings, a T-shirt, and my dance shoes. He was waiting in the middle of the ballroom's hardwood floor when I returned, hand extended in invitation. He cued the stereo with the remote as I walked toward him, feeling myself drift into the dreamy, elegant mood of the waltz as the first notes floated around me. We moved slowly at first, then more swiftly as he whirled me into a turn series. I extended my limbs with each movement, knowing the pointed toe, the half twist of the wrist, and stretched fingers made the elongated and graceful lines that separated a so-so waltzer from a champion waltzer. Even without a flowing dress and an updo, I felt timeless, regal, like I was dancing at the court of some long-deposed or beheaded European king.

New songs came on, but Vitaly and I held the mood. People think that competitive dancers get to prepare a routine to a specific song, like they do on *Ballroom with the B-Listers*, but we really dance to whatever the competition organizers cue up. Vitaly's clasp was strong, his steps perfectly suited to mine, and we danced for at least forty-five minutes, stopping to perfect a pose or rework a turn, before I found Maurice's problems intruding on my thoughts. Vitaly felt my mind drift and cut the music in midphrase, frowning slightly.

"You is losing concentrations," he said.

"I know. I'm sorry. Let's take a break." I darted across the hall to the minifridge in the bathroom and returned with a bottled water for myself and a grapefruit juice for Vitaly. "You heard about Corinne Blakely?" I asked, handing him the bottle.

"*Da*." He drank deeply and swiped his mouth with the back of his hand. "Is tragic losing for dance world. She was—how do you say?—'only one of her type.'"

"One of a kind. Did you know her well?"

"*Comme ci, comme ça*." Vitaly waggled his hand in the international gesture for "so-so." "We are dancing together at exhibition in France."

"I remember that exhibition. What was it—two, three years ago?"

"She is having amazing control, is being very precisely," he said, "for a—"

He threw in a Russian word that I automatically translated as "old woman," "grandmother," or "ancient crone."

"Maurice was having lunch with her when she died. The police interrogated him."

Vitaly opened his eyes wide. "Is not possible!"

I didn't know whether he thought it was impossible that Maurice killed Corinne, or impossible that the police questioned him.

After another long glug of grapefruit juice, he added, "Is bad for business. Peoples is not liking dancing with murderers or where murders is happened." His eyes slid to the spot near the windows where I'd found Rafe's body.

"Maurice is not a murderer."

"You should proving." Vitaly's face lit up.

"Investigate? I don't think so." I shook my head, making my ponytail swish across my shoulders.

"But yes! You has found Rafe's killer. You can finding Corinne's."

"I've got a ballroom studio to run, students to recruit, expenses to slash, and classes to teach," I said. "I don't have time to play investigator. Besides, the police let Maurice go after talking to him this morning; chances are he's not even a suspect anymore."

My cell phone rang. I didn't recognize the number. "Hello?"

"Anastasia, you'll have to ask Vitaly to fill in for me at tonight's class." Maurice's voice was calm, but a twinge of tension, like a taut piano wire, hummed through it. "I've been arrested."

Chapter 6

A few frantic minutes and a couple of phone calls later, I had elicited a promise from Phineas Drake's law firm that a legal minion of some sort would be dispatched to Maurice immediately, even though the great man himself was on a train returning from New York City. Hearing the desperation in my voice (or having checked Maurice's financials and found that he could pay the firm's exorbitant fees), the aloof assistant patched me through to Phineas Drake's cell phone. I could hear the rhythmic clacking of the train as we spoke, and I visualized the bearded, bearlike man reclining in a seat, his size and girth discouraging anyone from sitting beside him.

"Stacy Graysin." Drake's voice boomed through the phone, and I could see Vitaly crane his neck to listen. "I didn't think I'd be hearing from you again so soon." He chuckled, a rich Santa-ish sound. I always had trouble reconciling his jovial exterior with his sharp and calculating mind.

I explained about Maurice's situation. "I don't know

why they've arrested him," I said. "I don't think he knew for sure."

When he spoke again, Drake's voice was all business. "If he's been smart enough to keep his mouth shut, it won't matter; we'll get him out of it, although it may be tomorrow, because it's too late to get him arraigned today. Allison is on her way. She's a chip off the old block."

I had no idea what "old block" he was talking about.

"For a while there, during her sophomore year at Yale, it looked like she was going to be a vet, but then she decided to follow in dear old Dad's footsteps and become a legal eagle."

"You have a daughter?" Somehow I hadn't pictured Drake as being married, much less having children.

"Six."

"Six daughters? Good heavens!"

"Three are lawyers like their pop, two are doctors like their mom, and one's a clockmaker."

I resisted the urge to pry further into the Drake family's situation. "So Allison can get Maurice out? Can she find out why they arrested him?"

"Absolutely. In fact, I can find that out with a phone call to the DA. Call me back in ten." He hung up.

Vitaly had been dancing from foot to foot in front of me, impatient to find out more. "What is happening?" he asked.

"The police have arrested Maurice for Corinne Blakely's murder, and I've arranged for a lawyer to represent him. Can you help me with the Latin class tonight?"

"*Da*. Of course." Vitaly nodded impatiently. "What can I doing to help Maurice?"

I smiled, touched by his willingness to help a man

he'd known only a couple of months. "That's very kind, Vitaly, but I can't think of anything right now, besides covering his classes and maybe working with his private students."

"Vitaly is doing," he said with the air of one making a heroic sacrifice. "I will even dancing with the hippies."

I didn't correct his English. One of Vitaly's conditions about working here had been that he wouldn't have to partner heavy women, even though one of them was one of our top two or three dancers. "Has it been ten minutes?" I looked at my watch. "Close enough."

Phineas Drake answered on the first ring. "They've got a pill bottle that apparently was the source of the poison that killed the Blakely woman," he said without preamble. "It's got Goldberg's fingerprints on it."

I gasped. Drake chuckled. He didn't seem worried about the damning evidence against Maurice. "Dozens of ways Goldberg's fingerprints could've gotten on that bottle," he assured me. "If that's all the police have ... *pfft.* We'll know more after we get a look at the autopsy report."

I hung up, feeling slightly queasy, and relayed the news to Vitaly. "He asked me to feed his cats," I added. I hadn't even known Maurice had cats, but he'd asked me to take care of Gene and Cyd "for a night or two" when he called about his arrest.

"Go, then," Vitaly said, flicking me away with his hands. "Vitaly is holding the port until you returning."

"Fort." I left.

Maurice's house was a Craftsman-style bungalow with a compact front yard planted with dark green ivy rather than grass. Pink, mauve, and white impatiens bloomed in red ceramic pots on either side of the door, which was

painted a dark purple. I wondered whether the color was
Maurice's choice, or if he bought the house like that. I
found the key under the rightmost pot, as Maurice had
said, and opened the door.

"Mrow!"

A silvery cat with darker gray markings came trotting
toward me, tail up, and began to twine around my legs. If
I hadn't known better, I'd have thought she'd been alone
for days rather than just the hours since Maurice's arrest.
"You must be Cyd," I said. "As in Cyd Charisse." I
stooped to scratch under her chin. The cat purred, inti-
mating that I could call her anything I liked as long as I
kept scratching. Another cat, bigger and darker, with
white markings like eyebrows over his green eyes, and a
white-tipped tail, jumped from a plant ledge to a console
table in the hall, knocking something off with a clink. I
squatted to stroke both cats and pick up whatever
Gene—named for Gene Kelly, Maurice had told me—
had knocked off.

It was a key. I was about to put it back on the table
when a thought came to me. It looked like the key Maurice had used at Corinne Blakely's house, brass-colored
and a bit larger than your standard house key. I weighed
it in my hand, thinking. Thought one: Finding the manuscript was important to Maurice. Thought two: Turner
Blakely had mentioned he was off to Virginia Beach, two
and a half hours away, for a bachelor party. He'd drink
too much, put the moves on the stripper—he was the
kind of guy whose friends would definitely have a stripper or two at a bachelor party—and crash at a friend's
house for the night. Thought three: This evening would
be a perfect time to search Corinne's house for the manuscript. There might not be another chance.

Dismissing thought four, which had to do with arrest,

trial, and imprisonment for breaking and entering, I fed the cats, locked up, and pointed my Beetle toward home. I'd have to postpone my debut as a housebreaker until after the Latin dance class.

Twilight stretched shadows across the yard and gave the unlit house a somewhat forbidding aspect when I arrived at nearly eight thirty. An accident on the parkway made the drive that had taken twenty minutes in late morning take three times that long. One of the joys of living in the greater D.C. area. I had plenty of time to question my impulsiveness on the drive, but I didn't turn around. If there was the slightest chance that the mysterious manuscript would help erase Maurice from the police's suspect list, then I had to do what I could to find it.

Getting out of my car, I climbed the steps to the front door and slid the key into the lock. I looked over my shoulder, feeling furtive, and saw nothing and no one except my yellow Beetle looking lonely on the circular driveway. I eased the door open. Darkness greeted me. I pulled out the small flashlight I'd had the forethought to bring along and clicked the "on" button. Nothing happened. I shook it and tried again. More nothing. *Shoot.* Next time I'd have to be forethoughtful enough to check the batteries before setting out on a house-searching expedition. I reminded myself that there were no nearby neighbors and felt along the wall for a light switch. My fingers touched a rheostat and I turned it slightly. The chandelier glowed to life, bulbs half-lit like fireflies surrounded by sparkly crystals.

I'd had time to develop a strategy on the drive, and I set out in search of an office. No way could I search every room in this mansion—I'd lived in apartment complexes that were smaller—so I'd decided to look in

Corinne's office and her bedroom. Then I'd leave, even if I hadn't found the manuscript. On the ground floor, I poked my head into rooms filled with antique tallboys and silk-covered sofas too fragile to sit on, a dining room table long enough to seat the Redskins' starting offense and defense, oil paintings in heavy frames, and a kitchen with an oversize farm sink and cabinet-front appliances. I suspected most of the parlors, drawing rooms, music rooms, and sitting rooms—or whatever they were called—went largely unused. Nothing looked remotely like an office.

I climbed the curving staircase to the second floor, my footsteps muffled by the expensive-feeling carpet lining the steps. A wide hallway extended on either side of me, and I went right. The first room I looked in was a bedroom, but the room across from it, which must face the backyard, was an office, complete with desk, file cabinet, and typewriter. Finally! I made my way across the room mostly by feel and fumbled with the drapes, pulling the cord to close them. Only then did I return to the door, find the light switch, and flick it on, illuminating a Tiffany table lamp.

I made straight for the desk, the sight of the old Smith Corona electric typewriter making me hopeful. No stack of manuscript pages sat beside it, however, and I could find none in the drawers. Sighing, I turned to the wooden file cabinet and opened the top drawer. Financial records. Investments. Insurance. The second drawer held what looked like personal correspondence, each file folder labeled with a name. Riffling through the first folder, marked AMELIA ADAMS, I found letters dating back to the mid-twentieth century. Corinne must have saved every letter she ever got. Fascinating for a biographer, but not so useful to me. The rest of the folders in the drawer, alphabetically filed, held similar contents.

I checked the time. I'd been in the house eighteen minutes. The low buzz of adrenaline that had been keeping me pumped was beginning to wear off, and I felt jumpy and tired. What if Turner Blakely had car trouble and didn't make it to the bachelor party? He could be home any moment. What if some nosy neighbor got curious about my Volkswagen and called the police? They could be surrounding the house right now. Once the thought had entered my mind, I couldn't get rid of it. Giving in to my paranoia, I crossed to the window and drew one fold of the drapes aside a smidge. Nothing moved in the backyard. Feeling silly, I returned to the file cabinet and opened the bottom drawer.

No sign of a manuscript here, either, but one of the folders was labeled BOOK AGENT, and another bore the name of a publishing house. I didn't have time to read all the legal documents in either folder, but I copied down the agent's name and phone number, as well as the name of the woman who'd signed the letters from the publisher; her title was executive editor and vice president. Slipping my one puny page of notes into my pocket, I checked to make sure I had my useless flashlight, and returned to the hall. I glanced toward the door at the end of the hall, the one I figured led to Corinne Blakely's bedroom. The half-open door beckoned me, an invitation, but my nerves were fried, and I felt uncomfortable about invading the dead woman's bedroom. Ransacking her office was bad enough; I couldn't make myself paw through her bedside tables or peer under the bed for a manuscript I was beginning to think must be already with her agent or editor. I turned toward the stairs.

I found myself speeding up as I neared the stairs; I

was jogging by the time I reached them and started down. I took them two at a time, holding on to the banister, eager to reach the foyer, the front door, and freedom.

That might be why I didn't notice the woman just to the left of the bottom stair, holding a fireplace poker in a stance that would have done Mark McGwire proud, looking like she planned to slam me over the fence, until I practically bumped into her.

Chapter 7

I let out a stifled scream.

The woman took two steps back and raised the poker higher. "You stay here while I call the police," she said in a surprisingly deep voice that belied her looks. She was short, plump, and eighty years old if she was a day. Thinning white hair crinkled around her seamed face, and a pair of modern, red-framed bifocals perched on her Roman nose.

"I don't think so."

I sprinted toward the front door but didn't get two steps before the poker cracked against my ankle. She hadn't been able to put much force into the blow, but it stung like the dickens and made me stumble. I righted myself and had a hand on the door handle when a wheezing sound made me turn. The old woman had sunk onto the lowermost stair and had one hand pressed to her chest as she drew labored breaths.

Oh, damn. I hovered on the threshold, pulled in two directions. On the one hand, my Beetle, escape, and freedom beckoned me. On the other, if the old woman was having a heart attack or a stroke, I couldn't leave her to die. I could call 911 once I was on the road, my practical side said. She could be dead by then, my more compassionate side pointed out. *Aaagh.* I took one step onto the veranda, then turned back with a muffled curse and ran to the woman.

Her eyes widened as I approached, but I knelt beside her and said, "I'll call for an ambulance." I fumbled for my cell phone.

The woman, a line of pale blue ringing her lips, said, "Pills. Purse. Kitchen." Her voice got weaker with every word.

I raced to the kitchen and saw a purse that hadn't been there earlier sitting in the middle of the granite-topped island. It was about the size of a book, with a rigid bottom so it sat upright, dual handles curving upward. Snapping it open, I dug through it, locating the pill bottle without trouble, since the purse held only a thin wallet, keys, a glasses case, and a tin of breath mints. I dashed back to the woman, unscrewing the bottle as I went and tipping some pills into my hand.

Giving me a grateful look, she plucked a tablet from my palm and tucked it under her tongue, closing her eyes.

"Should I call nine-one-one?"

A slight head shake answered me. I hovered near her, shifting from foot to foot, my fingers bouncing on the phone's keys, until the blue tinge disappeared and her breathing came more easily. "I'm so sorry I scared you," I said.

"You're a peculiar kind of thief," she said, eyes snapping open, voice more robust.

"I'm not a thief!"

The old woman peered over the tops of her glasses. "Of course you're a thief. You broke into this house."

"As far as that goes," I said, rearing back, "you broke in, too."

"I did not." She glared at me. "I live here."

"Do not. Corinne Blakely lived here, and she died." We eyed each other with mutual suspicion.

"I worked for her for nigh on fifty years. Half a century." Sorrow weighted her words.

"You must be Mrs. Laughlin!"

"How did you know that? We haven't met, have we?" She scanned my face in the way people do when they're afraid they ought to recognize you but can't quite dredge up a name. An extra anxiety wrinkled her brow: the anxiety of an aging woman afraid she was losing it.

"No. I was here earlier today with Maurice Goldberg and he mentioned you."

Mrs. Laughlin relaxed a tad and let me help her to her feet. "Maurice is a good man. He was good for Corinne, the only one of her husbands she shouldn't have divorced."

"Did you know them all?"

"All except the first one. He passed before I came here to work."

"You came from England?" The faintest trace of an accent had been nagging at me, but now I placed it.

"Canterbury."

"I go to Blackpool every year. I love England."

She allowed herself a tiny smile. "You must be a ballroom dancer."

I offered her my hand. "Stacy Graysin. Maurice teaches at my studio."

Mrs. Laughlin shook my hand, her grip firm, although her skin felt as thin as tissue paper. "I could use a cuppa. Why don't we sit in the kitchen and you can tell me what you're doing here, if it's not thieving."

I trailed her back to the kitchen, where she filled a stainless-steel teapot and put it on the range. I perched on a bar stool drawn up to a breakfast bar. "What are *you* doing here?" I asked. "I thought Turner said . . . you didn't work here anymore." I opted not to say the F-word—fired.

"That twit fired me this morning," she said with an affronted sniff. "About ten minutes after he found out dear Corinne had passed. I worked here for more than twice as long as he is old, and he turns me off with no notice." She didn't sound too upset. "I was going to quit; he stole that pleasure from me. I did tell him I wouldn't work for a spoiled, cowardly adolescent like him for twice what Corinne was paying me."

"I'll bet he liked that." I accepted the china cup she handed me and breathed in the fragrance of Earl Grey.

"Not by half," she said with a reminiscent smile, seating herself beside me. "He hollered and carried on and ordered me out of the house on the spot. That's why I came back now: I knew he'd be out, and I wanted to collect my things and a few mementos Mrs. Blakely intended me to have." She nodded toward a couple of suitcases and boxes near a door that I guessed might lead to the housekeeper's quarters.

"Do you have someplace to live?" I felt a tug of concern for the old woman whose knuckles were swollen with arthritis in the kitchen's clear light.

"Bless you, I'm going back to England to live with my sister Abigail," she said. "She's got a snug little cottage in Cornwall and has been after me for years to retire and set up house with her. Now"—she leveled a stern look at me from pale blue eyes—"perhaps you'll tell me what you're doing here."

I liked Mrs. Laughlin and couldn't believe she'd had

anything to do with Corinne Blakely's death, so I told her about Maurice being arrested and about the manuscript Corinne was working on. "I don't suppose you know where it is?"

She was shaking her head before I finished the question. "No. I know about the book, of course. She talked about it constantly these past few months, and used to ask me if I thought she should include this happening or that anecdote, but as far as I know, she hadn't actually written the thing yet. She was waiting for a contract. 'There's no point doing it on spec, Mrs. Laughlin,' she said to me more than once. She did have an outline, though, which she revised every day. 'Should I put in the bit about Greta Monk?' she'd ask, or 'I don't think I'll use the story about Frederick Winston . . . poor old Freddy.'"

Mrs. Laughlin sipped her tea. "Sometimes I thought it would be best if she didn't get a contract, because then she'd have to write the book, and I didn't know what she'd focus on once it was finished. I had one of my feelings—that when she typed 'The End' on the last page, she'd be at her end, too. A foolish worry, as it turns out." She stared into the amber liquid in her cup.

I tried to imagine what it must be like for her at eighty-whatever to have lost the woman I suspected was her best, if not only, friend, her employer, and her home all at once.

"You wouldn't believe how worried some people were about what she was putting in the book," Mrs. Laughlin went on. "My, my. I can't tell you how many times one person or another cornered me in the kitchen if they were over for dinner, or asked me on the phone, if I answered it, exactly what she was including. I gave them all the same answer: 'You'll have to ask Mrs. Blakely.'"

Interesting, I thought. If Danielle or one of my former dance partners or boyfriends told me they were writing a memoir, would I be worried? Okay, maybe a little bit. Danielle certainly knew a few things about my love life that I'd just as soon my parents never knew, and Andrew might reveal the story of how we raised the money to enter our first serious ballroom dance competition, but I couldn't see myself taking any drastic steps to protect those secrets. Just how big did a secret need to be to inspire someone to want it kept under wraps "at all costs"? A question to ponder later.

"I can help you carry your stuff to your car," I said, beginning to worry about Turner Blakely returning. If he wasn't spending the night in Virginia Beach, he could come driving up anytime. Even though he was probably whooping it up with his about-to-be-married buddy, I couldn't help worrying. A flat tire or a headache or a falling-out with a drunken friend might bring him home early.

"That's very kind of you."

I helped her down from the stool and hefted two boxes. She led the way through a back door to a detached four-car garage that held only an aging Volvo station wagon. I slid the boxes into the back and returned to the kitchen for the suitcases. When I'd loaded those, the cargo area of the Volvo was less than half-full. "Is that all?" I asked doubtfully, thinking it sad that the accumulation of fifty years would take up so little room.

"Other than the few things I mean to gather," she said, walking briskly back toward the house.

I caught up with her. "I'm afraid Turner will come back."

She made a derisive noise. "That sot? He's been taken up for drunk driving three times already; he can't afford to be pulled over again. No, he'll stay over with his chum in Virginia Beach. That one's another with more money than sense." She stalked into the house, if a woman who bore more than a passing resemblance to Tweety Bird's Granny could be said to stalk.

I followed her through the mansion, fascinated by the items she chose and the stories associated with each one. I carried the things she indicated. "That pillow," she said, pointing to an ornately embroidered throw pillow on one of the couches. "I made that for Mrs. Blakely when she turned forty. What a party we had that weekend." In the dining room she pointed at a framed photo. "That's me and Mrs. Blakely and Fred Astaire. They were very close at one time; he said she was the best dancer he ever led onto a dance floor. Ginger Rogers supposedly took a pet when she heard that."

I eyed the black-and-white photo as I picked it up. It was a casual snap of the three of them, taken in front of this house. Corinne Blakely was young and lovely, holding windswept blond hair back with one hand. Mrs. Laughlin was laughing up at a middle-aged Fred Astaire, who had an arm draped around her plump shoulders. "She lived a lot of ballroom dance history," I observed.

"She *is* ballroom dance history," Mrs. Laughlin said, taking the photo from me and passing a sleeved forearm over the glass. She held it as we continued through the house, acquiring a small landscape painting, an old-fashioned pincushion shaped like a strawberry, a pair of earrings—"she was wearing those the night the baron proposed"—and a competition gown of turquoise satin and chiffon, heavy with rhinestones and trimmed with feathers. I recognized it.

"She wore that when she and Donald—that's Donald

Stevenson, one of her early partners—performed on *The Ed Sullivan Show*," Mrs. Laughlin said.

"I've seen the footage," I said, carrying the plastic-wrapped gown high in one hand so it wouldn't drag on the ground. "It belongs in a museum."

Mrs. Laughlin glared at me. "She said she wanted me to have it. She and Lavinia and I worked on it together, oh, decades ago, before Lavinia had her accident and turned to designing full-time."

"Lavinia Fremont?" She was a famous and successful competition gown designer, the same vintage as Corinne Blakely. I bought gowns from her; in fact, she was working on my and Vitaly's costumes for the upcoming Virginia DanceSport competition.

Mrs. Laughlin nodded and headed back toward the kitchen. "They were best friends," she said. "Mrs. Blakely was very good to Lavinia after the accident, invested in her design business."

I vaguely remembered hearing about a tragedy or scandal involving Lavinia Fremont some decades ago, but I couldn't summon up the details. I'd ask Maurice. "Aren't you worried Turner will miss some of these things?"

She shook her head so her fluffy white hair danced. "A pillow? A pincushion? The boy is oblivious to anything whose value can't be totted up by a bank."

"The painting?" It had left a bare rectangle of lighter paint where we unhooked it from the wall. Something about the luminous colors and quiet serenity of the scene made me suspect it was valuable.

"Maybe," she admitted with a tight smile. "But I don't care. It'll be on its way to Cornwall tomorrow, and I'll be following it immediately after the funeral. He may suspect I took it, but I don't see that he can do anything about it."

I supposed I ought to object to aiding and abetting a thief, but I found I didn't care. If the painting meant something to Mrs. Laughlin, I was glad she could have it. We exited through the back again and finished loading the Volvo. I told the housekeeper that I'd see her at the funeral, and watched as she backed out carefully. Then I made sure the back door was locked—I didn't want real thieves ransacking Corinne Blakely's house—and trotted around to the front. Clouds had drifted in, obscuring what little light the stars and new moon provided, and the wind blew in fitful gusts. I locked the front door, too, fumbling the key a bit in the dark, and was just descending the steps when headlights swept into the driveway.

Chapter 8

I froze. Turner Blakely! I was so screwed. My choices were try to brazen it out or dive into the bushes adjacent to the stoop. If I tried to run for it, he'd see me. I dived.

Stiff holly leaves pricked me and scratched my face, and crushed juniper let out a fresh piney scent. The drop was only four feet or so, and I landed on my feet but pitched forward onto my knees. Damp soil caked my hands. Concentrating on being still, I tried not to think about the spiders or other creepy crawlies that might lurk in the greenery. I couldn't see Turner or his car from my vantage point, but I heard the motor cut off, the door slam, and footsteps. A man's figure came into view, pausing beside my Beetle. He stopped to look into the passenger-side window, then straightened and looked around. After a moment or two, he started toward the house.

Watching him walk, I knew it wasn't Turner. As a dancer, I'm very aware of how people move, and this man didn't move like Turner. His stride was longer, his balance better. Besides, I noted as he mounted the stairs, this man was taller than Corinne's grandson. Looking over his shoulder when he reached the door, he reached for the knob and jiggled it in vain. I was glad I'd locked it.

The man rattled it harder, cursed, then pulled something from his wallet and had at the door again. Lock picks, maybe? I wondered whether he was one of those opportunistic thieves who read the obituaries and burgle dead people's homes. The *skritch* of his tool against the door sounded loud in the stillness. A moment later, a faint snap elicited another curse and something fell to the ground almost noiselessly. As the man bent to pick it up, a gust of wind snatched it and tossed it into the bushes, right at my feet.

Ack! I tried to shrink back without rustling the bushes. Luckily, the wind was blowing hard enough to clack the branches together, so it covered, I hoped, any sounds I made. The burglar swore loud and long this time and crossed the wide stoop with a heavy tread, coming straight toward me. There was something familiar about his voice. . . .

I didn't have time to figure it out as I concentrated on looking small and bent my head forward so my white face wouldn't glimmer. I held my breath, praying the man wouldn't want whatever he'd dropped badly enough to brave the holly to look for it. Labored breaths sounded from only a couple feet away, and the man muttered to himself, "Shit . . . flashlight . . . no one . . . find it."

When the footsteps moved away again and no beam of light shone into my face, I took that to mean he wished he'd brought a flashlight and didn't think anyone would find whatever he'd dropped, so it wasn't worth searching in the bushes. The *tink* of metal against glass moments later, followed by a shaking sound, told me he was trying to raise the window. I found myself hoping he'd get in, so I could seize the opportunity to escape.

Instead, he descended the stairs two at a time and I stopped my breaths, afraid he'd decided to search for what he'd dropped after all. The footsteps moved away, however, and soon I couldn't hear them. Was he leaving? I listened hard. No, I didn't hear a car start up. Glass shattered somewhere around the back of the house and I realized he'd broken a window. Now was my chance. Still on all fours, I crawled forward a couple of feet, wincing as a holly leaf scored my cheek. A second later, that pain was forgotten as something jabbed into my palm. I closed my lips over the "Ow!" and it came out as a muffled, "Urmf."

I picked up the thin, flat item, figuring it was the tool the burglar had dropped, and slipped it into my pocket. Rising to a half crouch, I shouldered my way through the remaining shrubs, saw no one on the expanse of lawn and driveway in front of me, and broke cover, doing my best gazelle impression until I thudded against my car. Scrambling around it, I flung open the driver's door, sat and inserted the key in one motion, threw the car into reverse because the burglar's dark sedan had me blocked in from the front, and backed down the drive faster than I'd ever backed up in my life.

As my rear wheels spun onto the pavement of the main road, I flicked on my headlights. They grazed the burglar's car, glinting off the Mercedes hood ornament. What kind of burglar drove a Mercedes? A really successful one? I didn't have time to think about it as horns honked to complain about my precipitate arrival onto the Mount Vernon Parkway. I straightened the wheel and stomped on the gas, waving apologetically to the car behind me. I was halfway home before it crossed my mind to call the police and anonymously report a burglary in progress.

Safely home, I poured myself a healthy glass of Chianti and eased my hand into my pocket to see what the burglar had dropped. Pulling it out with two fingers, I found one-third of a credit card, snapped off so the hard plastic formed a cutting edge. This was no professional burglar, I decided. Even I knew you couldn't pop a dead bolt with a credit card. Holding the card under the counter light, I made out the last few letters of the burglar's name: LIDO.

I caught my breath. Putting together the voice I'd heard with those four letters gave me the man's identity: Marco Ingelido. Why in the world was the man who owned the most successful chain of franchised ballroom dance studios in the business, Take the Lead with Ingelido, trying to break into Corinne Blakely's house the day after she was murdered?

Chapter 9

I rose early Thursday morning to do a private lesson with a student who was preparing for his first ballroom dance competition. We would compete in the bronze division as a professional-amateur couple. He was a fiftyish, divorced man who initially signed up for a dance class to meet women, but found himself liking it so much he decided to try his hand at competition. He liked to practice early, before work, so we were finished shortly before eight o'clock. He left for a day in cubicle-ville and I went downstairs to shower and dress.

The ringing phone yanked me out of the shower just as I turned off the taps. Grabbing a towel, I trotted to my bedside table to answer, hoping it was Maurice calling to say he had been released.

"Stacy?"

It was my mom's voice, clear and a bit reserved, as always. Mom was not one to show a lot of emotion. "Hi, Mom."

"Have you talked to your sister?" She also wasn't much of one for beating around the bush or wasting time with small talk. I conjured an image of her thin, angular body and graying red hair. From the whuffling horse sounds behind her, I knew she was standing at the wall phone in her small barn, probably wearing old jodhpurs and rubber boots for mucking out. Bird, her twenty-two-year-old gelding, whickered behind her; I'd learned to ride on him and would recognize his "voice" anywhere.

"Hi, Bird. Yes. She told me about your invitation. Sounds like fun."

She sighed. "I'm glad you think so. Danielle clearly wasn't enamored of the idea, even though it'll be my treat."

"It's the Jekyll Island thing. It'll bring up a lot of memories of our last vacation, all of us together."

From her silence, I knew she hadn't previously made the connection. "That was years ago," she finally said, as if old memories didn't carry much weight. In my experience, sometimes they carried the most weight.

"Yeah, well."

Another silence fell. I finally broke it. "What dates did you have in mind?"

She told me and I checked my mental calendar. "That should work. It's the weekend after the Virginia State DanceSport Championships. Count me in."

"Thank you, Stacy." She hesitated. "And if you could talk your sister into it, I'd be very grateful. I hate it that things are so awkward between us."

"Have you told her that?"

"Of course not."

Of course not. I hung up a few minutes later, mentally shaking my head. My mom could practically read a horse's mind, could communicate with the big beasts telepathically, but she had no clue what her own daughter was thinking. I'd do my best to talk Dani into the vacation, because it would be fun for all of us.

I headed upstairs to work on choreography for a husband-and-wife amateur team who were competing at the Virginia state competition with the Graysin Motion team. I worked in the small studio at the back of the house, liking the view of my tiny courtyard from the studio's window. I'd worked up most of a samba routine for the pair when someone knocked on the doorjamb and spun me around.

Tav stood there, newspaper in hand, a less-than-thrilled expression on his face. "You did not think I would be interested in the fact that Maurice was arrested?"

"It made the newspaper?"

He flipped through a couple of pages and read, "'Alexandria police announced the arrest of Maurice Goldberg, a ballroom dance instructor with Graysin Motion, for the murder of Corinne Blakely, his former wife and also a professional ballroom dancer.' It goes on to give details about her career."

"Well, that sucks."

"As you say." His mouth quirked up on one side. "Have you talked to Maurice? Is he okay? Does he have legal representation?"

I smiled, wanting to hug Tav. Even though he was worried about the studio's reputation, he was concerned about Maurice, a man he barely knew. "I got hold of Phineas Drake and he took Maurice's case."

"Do I need to worry that Drake will frame me for the Blakely woman's murder?" He looked over his shoulder in an exaggerated way and I laughed. He was well aware that Drake had offered to set someone up for Rafe's murder when the police thought I did it.

"I don't think so. As I understand it, Corinne had five other husbands; I'd think any of them would make a bet-

ter murderer candidate than you, well, except the one
who died. And she was apparently writing a tell-all memoir that was making a variety of people nervous, according to her housekeeper."

"When did you talk to her housekeeper?" Tav asked.

"Last night." I bent to grab my water bottle and my
notes, hoping he wouldn't dig any deeper.

"She happened to drop by the studio?" he asked in a
politely skeptical voice.

"I might have stopped by Corinne's house," I muttered.

"Stacy—"

"Okay, I got the key from Maurice's house and went
to Corinne's to find the manuscript," I said all in a rush.
"Maurice thinks someone murdered her to keep her
book from getting published. I thought I'd find it and . . ."
What had I planned to do if I'd come across the manuscript? ". . . and turn it over to the police." Well, I
might've.

He didn't berate me for my stupidity. "Did you find it?"

I shook my head. "No. Mrs. Laughlin—the housekeeper—thinks she hadn't written it yet, that all she had
was an outline."

"Can one get a contract on a book that is not even
written?"

"How would I know?" I remembered that I had the
names of Corinne Blakely's agent and editor. "But I
know how we can find out." I ran downstairs to retrieve
the phone numbers from my dresser. I didn't realize Tav
had followed me until I turned and saw him standing in
the doorway, surveying the rumpled pink sheets—I
wasn't much of one for making my bed—the litter of
jewelry and cosmetics on the dresser, and a periwinkle
bra draped over the chair. Something in his eyes made

me sure the thought uppermost in his mind didn't have to do with my untidiness.

Blushing slightly, I brushed past him, too aware of his warm male scent, saying a bit breathlessly, "Here's the number."

I thought for a moment he was going to reach for me, but then he stepped aside with a quiet, "Pardon," and followed me to the kitchen—much safer territory— where I picked up the phone and dialed a New York City number, holding the phone out a little so Tav could hear. I had to wade through two layers of assistants before the agent picked up the phone. "Angela Rush," she said with a brisk New York accent.

When I asked my question, she laughed. "We sell non-fiction books all the time off no more than a chapter outline and a marketing plan. It's all about the *platform*."

"Platform?"

"The author's credentials. Her fame, or notoriety as the case may be. How hot is her topic? How likely is media attention? And, darling, Corinne Blakely was hot. What with the popularity of *Ballroom with the B-Listers* and the International Olympic Committee about to vote on ballroom dancing—excuse me, DanceSport—as an Olympic event, and her charisma, well, let's just say we had a *major* deal in place. Her death is a tragedy for the arts community in America."

And a tragedy for Angela Rush's pocketbook, I suspected. "So you don't even have an outline?"

"Oh, I have one of those." Ms. Rush's voice turned cagey.

"You do? Can you fax it to me?"

"I'm afraid not." She didn't sound remotely sorry. "We're still going forward with the project, and I don't want any details leaking before publication. This book is going to be an *NYT* bestseller. I have an instinct for these things."

Excuse me? How could she go forward with a memoir when the memoirist was dead? "How—"

"We've been in contact with someone we're sure can do justice to the book," Ms. Rush said coyly. "Now, if you'll excuse me, I've got a meeting at FSG."

Tav and I stared at each other for a moment after Ms. Rush rang off. "Well, that raised more questions than it answered," I finally said.

"Indeed."

Conscious that Tav was still standing close enough to listen in, close enough to make my skin flush with a desire I had no intention of giving in to, I moved toward the sink and poured myself a glass of water, adding a couple ice cubes for good measure.

"Perhaps if you shared this information with the authorities . . ." Tav suggested.

"Detective Lissy could chisel the outline out of Ms. Rush. My thought exactly. Great minds think alike." I smiled.

Tav's answering smile suggested that our two great minds were thinking alike on an entirely different topic. "Stacy—"

The doorbell rang. I started, jolting cold water onto my shirt. "Coming!" I headed toward the front door and opened it to see Maurice.

"Maurice!" I hugged him hard. After a startled moment, he returned the hug. "You're free."

"For the time being," he said. He looked as immaculate as ever in a crisply ironed button-down shirt and tan slacks, and smelled like he'd just stepped out of the shower. I remembered spending a half hour in the shower after being hauled down to the police station for an interview. It must be a thousand times worse to actually spend the night in jail.

"That very competent young lady you sent got me released on bail first thing this morning. Then she and her father—he seems like a force to be reckoned with—grilled me more intensely than the police." A faint smile showed he appreciated their thoroughness. "I'm meeting with them again Friday evening, after they've had a chance to check on a few things. Will you come with me?"

"Of course," I said, dragging him into the hall. "Have you had breakfast?"

"Food would be appreciated," he said.

Tav walked in from the kitchen and Maurice's white brows soared as he looked from me to Tav. "We just called Corinne Blakely's literary agent," I said.

Tav shook hands with Maurice. "I am glad the police released you," he said. "I would like to talk more, but I have an appointment I cannot miss. Please be assured that I will do whatever I can to help prove your innocence. Although Stacy has a head start on that task." With a grin, he left, saying he'd catch up with us later in the day, and reminding me about the bridal fair that started tomorrow.

Dragging Maurice into the kitchen, I started putting together some French toast while I told him about looking for the manuscript, talking to Mrs. Laughlin, avoiding Marco Ingelido, and tracking down Angela Rush. As the egg-soaked bread sizzled on the griddle, Maurice poured himself a cup of coffee and sat at the kitchen table. "You're amazing, Anastasia," he said. "I can't believe you searched Rinny's house last night alone."

I shrugged. "What are friends for? I'm only sorry I didn't get anything useful."

"Maybe you did," he said. "Didn't you say she had an electric typewriter?"

"Yes, a Smith Corona. So?"

"So, you wouldn't realize this, probably never having operated anything as antiquated as a typewriter, but those typewriters had cartridges that snapped into the machine to provide ink. The keys struck the tape and transferred letters to the paper."

My interest in typewriter mechanics was limited at best. I put a plate of French toast in front of Maurice and set a syrup bottle beside him. "So?"

"So, the keys leave an impression on the ribbon. The last . . . I don't know—twenty? fifty?—pages Corinne wrote will be on the cartridge."

"We could reconstruct her most recent outlines," I said, finally catching on. "But how do we get the typewriter? Turner's probably back from his stag party by now."

"I'll think of something," Maurice said. He ate breakfast with appreciative murmurs and looked at his watch. "Don't you have the Ballroom Aerobics class to teach?"

My gaze flew to the clock over the stove. Ten to eleven. "See you later," I said, racing toward the stairs and taking them two at a time up to the studio.

Chapter 10

Students were already starting to trickle in, and I greeted them as they lined up in the ballroom. The hour flew by and I felt invigorated by the exercise. The tension of the last couple days drained out of me as I led the class.

Vitaly came in as the students left and immediately asked about Maurice. "Has he breaked out of the jails?"

"They let him go, yes."

"Vitaly is glad. I will helping prove his innocence." He thrust his chin up, looking like a gladiator about to enter the arena.

"I'm sure he'll appreciate that, Vitaly," I said. "Tav said he'd help, too, so between us we ought to be able to come up with *something*." I told him about Marco Inge-lido breaking into the mansion, sure that Vitaly had come across Ingelido at some point during his career.

Vitaly wrinkled his nose and sniffed. "Ingelido is ask-ing me if I want to own a Taking the Lead with Ingelido studio. I laugh in his face."

"Tactful."

"His methods is a joke ... is only fitting for the sociable dancers, not for competing."

"Well," I said, "ballroom dancing is becoming a much more popular social activity. The numbers of dancers have grown a lot in the last five years." I bent to pick up a stainless-steel water bottle one of the women had left. "If Ingelido's methods help—"

Vitaly, facing the door, drew in his breath with a hiss. "Speaking of the devils—"

I spun around to see Marco Ingelido on the threshold, surveying the ballroom with an expression that hovered between appreciative and assessing. In his early sixties, he was beginning to put on weight around his middle, but was still a good-looking man, with thick, dark brows over deep-set eyes and an aquiline nose. He'd been balding for years and had finally shaved his head, telling people that if it was good enough for Kojak, it was good enough for him. He'd been moderately successful as a professional ballroom dancer but gave up competing five or six years back, shortly after I started winning, to concentrate on expanding his business.

"I heard you two partnered up," he said, his gaze going from Vitaly to me. "Anya dump you, Voloshin?"

Vitaly bristled. "I am moved to Baltimore and Anya is not wishing to leave Russia," he said.

"And of course we all know what happened to your partner, Stacy," Ingelido said. "I don't think I've seen you since Rafe died. Didn't I hear something about you being arrested for his murder?" Malice gleamed in his dark eyes.

I chose to ignore his question. "Can I help you with something, Marco?" I asked, convinced his showing up like this was not a coincidence. Not after last night.

"You can give me what you found last night," he said, his voice flat. "At Corinne Blakely's."

"I don't know what you're talking about."

Ingelido smiled coldly. "My son-in-law is a cop. He ran your license plate for me."

Oops. "I saw you break into Corinne's house," I said. Two could play the intimidation game.

"Your word against mine."

"Hm, I think your credit card says otherwise."

He thinned his lips, clearly wishing he'd taken the trouble to retrieve the snapped credit card. "I didn't come here to quarrel with you. I can't imagine what Corinne had on you—you're so young—but I know you were after her manuscript. I want it. Or"—he held out a placatory hand—"I want your assurance that it's been destroyed."

"What is Corinne having on you?" Vitaly asked, eyes bright with curiosity.

Ingelido hesitated, then finally said with an air of great honesty, "We were lovers. I was in my late thirties. Corinne was . . . older. I was between wives, so it's only . . . embarrassing. I'd just as soon not have the affair publicized. We were discreet at the time. I don't know why she decided to go public with it now." His voice was a growl of frustration.

"How did you know she was going to write about you?" I asked.

"She told me!" He paced like a trapped tiger: three steps away, three steps back. "I had the impression she was giving everyone she was writing about 'fair warning.' That's what she called it when she told me."

"I didn't find the manuscript," I said, feeling a twinge of sympathy for Ingelido. "And her housekeeper said she never wrote it, that she only had an outline."

Ingelido's chest expanded as he took a deep breath and held it. He blew it out. "That's that, then." His shoulders sagged with relief. I debated telling him what I'd learned from Angela Rush, but before I could say anything, he said, "This is a nice little studio you've got here. If you signed on with Take the Lead, we could turn it into a profitable enterprise. My franchisees are seeing a twelve percent return on their investment in the first year and up to thirty percent in the second year."

"I'm perfectly happy with my income now," I said.

His smile said he knew I was lying. "If you change your mind . . ."

"She won't changing her mind," Vitaly said. "Stacy and Vitaly is buildings most successful studio on East Coast."

I appreciated his positive thinking and shot him a smile.

"An ambitious goal," Ingelido said in a voice that suggested he thought we'd have more chance of winning a Nobel Prize. "If—"

Before he could finish the thought, Maurice entered the ballroom, stopping abruptly at the sight of the other dancer. "Ingelido," he said in a cold, un-Maurice-ish voice.

"Goldberg," the other man replied, equally cool.

The temperature in the room went down to levels a penguin would enjoy, and Vitaly and I glanced at each other, wary of the animosity between the two men.

"Shouldn't you be making license plates or something? I read that you'd been arrested. I debated sending a congratulatory note to our men and women in blue."

"To paraphrase: 'Reports of my incarceration have been greatly exaggerated,'" Maurice said. "Sorry to disappoint."

"Ah, well." Ingelido loosed a dramatic sigh. Giving Maurice a considering look, he added, "You and Corinne went back decades. She must have known where all your skeletons were buried."

Maurice flinched almost imperceptibly, and I was startled to see fear skate across his eyes before he banished it. An uneasy thought crossed my mind: Could Maurice have something to hide?

He rallied. "At least my skeletons—if I had any—are decently buried. Some of yours are still walking around, hm?"

Ingelido flushed red and then paled. "I have no idea what you're talking about. Let me know if you want more information about the franchise opportunity, Stacy." He handed me a business card with the stylized, top-hatted logo of Taking the Lead with Ingelido, and left.

Vitaly followed on his heels, exclaiming, "I am late for meeting John."

Left alone with Maurice, I raised my brows and asked, "What in the world was that about?" Before he could answer, I said, "You can tell me while I work. I've got to clean the bathroom." Since our bottom line was a little shaky, we saved money by doing the cleaning ourselves. It wasn't too onerous, but I looked forward to the day we could hire a janitorial service again.

Maurice followed me to the powder room and watched as I liberated cleanser, a sponge, and rubber gloves from the under-sink cabinet. I squirted cleanser under the toilet rim and motioned for Maurice to start talking. "Marco Ingelido is a cad," he said. "He hurt Corinne very badly some years ago. She was in love with him—why, I'll never know, except she had unfortunate taste in men—"

"Present company excepted."

A slight smile eased his frown. "Thank you, Anastasia. Anyway, Corinne loved him and he threw her over for Marian, the woman he's married to now."

"Is that what you meant when you said his skeletons were still walking around?" I looked up from scrubbing the sink to see a crease appear between his brows.

"He has a niece, Sarah. Sarah Lewis. She's a photographer ... must be almost thirty now. Marco dotes on her. They've always had a close relationship, much closer than your average uncle and niece. Anyway—"

"He had an affair with his own niece? How very Woody Allen of him. No, that was his stepdaughter, wasn't it?" I wrinkled my nose, sloshed the brush around the toilet, and flushed away the foamy water. I'd had a crush on my cousin Tom when I was fifteen or so and he was nineteen. We'd sneaked a few kisses (okay, it was really several hours' worth of nonstop, volcano-hot kissing) during a family reunion at a lake in the Poconos, and I'd had a hard-to-explain case of bristle burn that made my chin, lips, and cheeks raw. We'd returned to our separate states and Tom had moved on to an eighteen-year-old girlfriend before we got too serious, but I'd moped about him for several months. I sighed at the memory.

"He—"

Clicking noises from the hall approached quickly. Moments later, Hoover skidded to a stop with a woof. He wedged his head between Maurice's leg and the door-jamb, nearly knocking Maurice over as he wriggled into the small bathroom. I patted his heavy head as Mildred Kensington's voice fluted, "Hoover, you bad dog. How many times have I told you it's not polite to interrupt someone in the loo?"

Hoover ignored her, nosing at the minifridge's door in an attempt to open it. "Hello, Mildred," Maurice said, backing out of the bathroom doorway.

"Maurice! Oh, I came as soon as I heard. Thank goodness you've been released." She threw her plump form at him and embraced him, almost knocking him off his feet. He steadied himself with a hand against the wall.

She released him, her eyes bright. Dabbing at them with a lace hankie she pulled from her sleeve, she said, "It makes me so emotional. To think of you cooped up in a prison cell with no room to *dance*."

I could think of a lot worse things about being imprisoned than that, but I didn't mention them. A slurping sound brought all our heads around, and we saw Hoover lapping happily from the toilet. Thank goodness I'd already flushed the cleanser down. He looked up when Mildred shrieked his name, slobbering on the toilet seat and tiled floor. So much for my clean bathroom.

"Hoover, dear, that's a nasty, nasty habit," Mildred scolded. "How many times have I told you that?"

The Great Dane's tail thumped against the fridge. Stripping off my gloves, I joined the others in the hall, and Hoover followed me.

"It was kind of you to stop by, Mildred," Maurice said, "but—"

"Oh, I didn't just stop by. I've come to tell you that I'm starting a legal defense fund for you." Mildred beamed. "I've already put out collection jars at many of the businesses around here, with that lovely photo of us from when we competed at the Emerald Ball a couple of years ago. And I've sent an e-mail to all my correspondents, explaining the situation and asking for donations."

Maurice looked appalled. "Mil—"

"Oh, no, you don't have to thank me." She held up a

beringed hand sparkling with diamonds, rubies, and platinum. "You know you're so much more than a dance instructor to me, Maurice, and I couldn't sleep at night if I didn't do what I could to make sure you don't end up *incarcerated* for life. Or worse. Do they have the death penalty in Virginia?"

"Indeed they do," Maurice said grimly. "One of the guards 'joked' that when I got convicted and put on death row, I could be known as 'dead man waltzing.' Apparently the phrase 'dead man walking' refers to a condemned prisoner on his way to be executed."

"That's horrible!" I said.

"We'll have to make sure it doesn't come to that," Mildred said, patting his arm. "Don't you worry. I'm all over this like stink on excrement, as my grandson says."

When I choked back a laugh, she twinkled at me. "Well, that's not exactly how he says it. Come on, Maurice." She hooked her arm through his. "I'm taking you to lunch. It's a wonder you didn't waste away on that nasty prison diet."

"I was only there one night," he said, letting himself be dragged away.

"Perhaps Hoover could stay here with you, Miss Graysin?" Mildred called over her shoulder. "For some reason they don't appreciate him at Giuseppe's."

Imagine that. "Sure."

They exited through the door by my office. Hoover sat in front of the closed door, cocking his head. When it didn't reopen, he raised one great paw and scratched at it, looking over his shoulder to invite me to let him out.

"Sorry, buddy. You're stuck with me for the moment."

He stared at me disbelievingly. When it dawned on him that Mildred wasn't coming back immediately, he threw up his nose and let loose with a mournful *whoo-wooo-ooo*.

"I think I have some peanut butter crackers in my drawer," I said, coaxing him into my office. He snarfed down the six crackers, snuffled around the desks, then clambered onto the love seat, resting his head against the back of it so he could see out the window.

Maurice and Mildred returned more than two hours later. Hoover leaped off the couch at the sound of their footsteps on the outside stairs and dashed to the door to greet them. The three of them crowded into the office moments later, Mildred looking distinctly disgruntled.

"That Turner Blakely is a nasty young man," she announced.

"Did you run into him at the restaurant? What did he do?"

"It was my idea," Mildred admitted, patting Hoover as he nosed at her hand. "When Maurice filled me in on your search—so brave of you, dear—I thought up a wonderful scheme for getting the typewriter cartridge from Corinne's house. 'Tell Corinne's grandson you want the typewriter for sentimental reasons,' I told Maurice. 'Tell him it's special to you because Corinne used it to write you letters.'"

"I thought it was worth a try," Maurice said, "but Turner turned me down flat. His insurance adjustor was there, and someone to fix the broken window—"

"Courtesy of Marco Ingelido," I put in.

"—and an alarm company representative to install a security system, so he was distracted."

Mildred took over. "Even so, he told us quite nastily that we were trespassing and that he wouldn't give Maurice the time of day, never mind anything from Corinne's house. 'My inheritance,' he called it."

Maurice shrugged. "It was a long shot anyway."

I made commiserating noises, and said, "The agent may yet come through with the outline." *Fat chance.*

"It's best not to rely on other people's efficiency or memory," Mildred said wisely. "Things get done better and faster if you do them yourself. We're off to Maurice's now to come up with a new plan," she added. "Ta-ta. Come, Hoover."

I wondered briefly how Hoover would get along with Gene and Cyd, Maurice's cats, but decided it wasn't my problem. "Keep me posted," I called after them.

My watch said it was closing in on three o'clock. I didn't have to be back in the studio until time to teach a tango class at six thirty. Now would be a good time, I decided, to kill two birds with one stone.

Chapter 11

I took the Metro yellow line from the King Street station to Gallery Place, changed to a red line train, and got off at the Woodley Park station, not far from Lavinia Fremont's small boutique. In addition to designing ballroom dance costumes, she did one-of-a-kind special-occasion dresses and the occasional wedding gown. Vitaly and I needed new costumes for the upcoming Virginia State DanceSport Competition, and Lavinia had already started on them. I'd called to make an appointment for a fitting and figured I'd work in a few questions about Corinne Blakely.

Walking the few blocks from the Metro station to Lavinia's made me glad I'd grabbed a hat on my way out the door. Mature trees arching over the root-heaved sidewalk cut some of the sun, but enough of it got through to make the sidewalk sizzle. Lavinia's design studio was tucked into a row of shops that formed the ground floor of what started out as a girls' school before an enterprising developer converted the buildings into trendy lofts. Lavinia had one lavender satin-and-chiffon gown in the narrow display window, its bodice encrusted with sequins.

Pushing through the glossy black door, I entered the cool of the shop. Bolts of fabric lined one wall, and a citrusy scent drifted from a glass bowl heaped with apples, pears, and lemons set on a high table cluttered with sketchbooks, pencils, shears, pins, and snippets of cloth.

"Coming," Lavinia called from somewhere in the back. She emerged moments later, while I was flapping my blouse to circulate some air-conditioning to my sweaty tummy. She was dressed all in black, which I might have taken as a statement of mourning for Corinne, except Lavinia always wore black. Today's version was a narrow dress that fell to her ankles, cinched at the waist with a gray–and-silver sash that hung to her knees. Her hair, an unlikely auburn for a woman of seventy, swung in a razor-cut bob around her thin, lined face. "Lovely to see you again, Stacy," she greeted me, moving forward stiffly with hand outstretched. "The dress is ready to try. And you said something on the phone about needing an exhibition costume?"

"Yes." Her fingers were long, her palm cool against mine when we shook.

"Good. Then we can be creative. No need to please a bunch of rigid judges." When she crossed the room to sort through bolts of fabric, her skirt swished from side to side, giving glimpses of the prosthetic foot that made her gait a bit stiff. "With you and Vitaly both being so blond, we need a strong hue that will contrast with your coloring, but not overwhelm you. Not this," she said, moving aside a bolt of cream satin, "or this." She pushed past a pale yellow velvet I quite liked. "I'm thinking maybe this red"—she pulled out a bolt of dark red fabric—"or this green. With flesh-colored inserts—or maybe midnight blue?—and stones. Lots of rhine-stones."

She passed me, thin arms laden with bolts of fabric, and laid them on the cutting table in the middle of the room. "But first, let's try the other dress." With a gait that was surprisingly graceful despite the limp, she disappeared into the back and emerged a moment later, holding a hanger high. I could vaguely make out the shape of the carnation-colored dress under a plastic bag. Unzipping the bag, Lavinia freed the dress, removed it gently from the hanger, and passed it to me. I ducked into the tiny changing room outfitted with only a couple of hooks and a curtain instead of a door.

Slipping out of my clothes, I carefully dropped the new gown over my head and smoothed it into place. I loved the way the salmon pink made my skin glow and set off my blond hair. It was a strong color and would be distinctive on the dance floor without being harsh or garish. I brushed aside the curtain and stepped out for Lavinia's inspection.

"Hm." She pinched a fold of fabric at my waist. "You have lost weight."

"Maybe a pound or two," I admitted.

Her deft fingers inserted a couple of pins.

"I was so sorry to hear about Corinne Blakely," I said. "I know you two were friends for a long time."

She hesitated, her face hidden from me as she bent to measure the distance from the floor to the hem in several places. "She was my best friend for many, many years," she said, straightening. True sorrow lined her face.

"How did you meet?"

She draped a spangled length of tulle several shades lighter than the dress around my shoulders and stepped back to survey the effect. "I grew up on a ranch in Montana, but I was always more interested in dancing and fashion than cattle or corn. I ran away to New York when I was seventeen, convinced I'd be starring in Broadway shows within minutes of my arrival."

"That was brave of you."

" 'Stupid' is the word you're looking for. Anyway, I was doing telephone sales selling newspaper advertisements by day, auditioning every chance I got, and taking acting and dancing classes at night. I shared a one-bedroom apartment with three other gals and lived off canned tuna and peanut butter. The building super was out to get in my pants, and the rats outnumbered the tenants three to one. I'm pretty sure they were better fed, too." She gave a grim little smile. "But I was too proud to go home, take up again with William Denney, who'd been hoping to marry me since we were in junior high, and live out my days as a Montana rancher's wife."

I turned to face the mirror, in obedience to the pressure of her hand on my shoulder.

"Too much," Lavinia announced, removing the scarf. "We'll keep the neckline simple."

"Okay."

"Anyway," she continued, "one night I went to a tiny dance studio in the Village that a friend had mentioned. I'd heard a big-shot producer was casting an off-Broadway musical that required waltzing, and I was determined to impress them with my dancing ability, since my singing voice was only so-so. Well, I walked up four flights of stairs to this studio, and was huffing and puffing by the time I got to the top. I was a smoker in those days. We all were—it's how we kept our weight down. When I got to the top, there was Corinne, dressed in an aqua gown and elbow-length gloves, twirling with her partner. She looked like a princess or a fairy queen. Titania, maybe, if I remember my Shakespeare correctly, or Queen Mab. I was captivated.

"Halfway through the piece, Corinne broke away from her partner with a few choice words about his dancing—she could cuss like a ranch hand, even though she looked so dainty—and said that someone who had never waltzed could dance more gracefully than he did. Before I knew what was happening, she grabbed my hand and pulled me out onto the dance floor. People—there must have been eight or ten students standing around, most of them older than Corinne and me—were laughing, and Corinne's partner was sulking, and I wanted to sink through the floor. But then I got caught up in the music and the rhythm and let myself dance. That was it for me; from then on, it was ballroom dancing or nothing."

"Did you get the part?" I asked.

A reminiscent smile lit her face. "I did, actually. But the show folded after only a couple of performances. I ditched my telephone sales job and studied ballroom dancing with Corinne and a couple of others. What a time that was. Think *Rent* set in the sixties, with booze and cigarettes instead of drugs, and without the AIDS, and you get a feel for how close we were—those of us who were serious about ballroom dance—and how passionate about our art. Corinne and I became roommates and best friends. We did everything together—double-dated, went to competitions, taught dance. She even came out to Montana with me one Christmas." Lavinia laughed at the memory. "I don't think she'd ever seen a cow in person before. Anyway, competitive Latin dancing was just coming into its own in the early 1960s and I fell in love with it. My partner, Ricky Marini, could have made it in the movies—he was easily as good as—and much better-looking than—Astaire or Kelly. Together . . . we set the dance floor on fire."

Her focus was past me now, past the display window with the lavender gown, past the view of the busy street outside, all the way back to the 1960s. "We were the best. Absolutely the best. Corinne and her partner were good, but not as good as Ricky and I were. The four of us were invited to the first Professional Latin Championship at Blackpool. Nineteen sixty-four, that was." She tucked a strand of auburn hair behind one ear and rubbed her fingers together like she wished she had a cigarette. The sun slanting through the window deepened the lines and hollows of her face in a mean way.

"What happened?" I asked softly.

"To make a long story short—it's too late for that, isn't it?—the four of us were coming out of a nightclub in the wee hours of the night before the competition started. A man jumped us. Corinne screamed. I barely caught sight of him before something slammed into my leg and I fell. The guy took off and Ricky chased him. He didn't catch up with him, though.

"At the hospital, the doctors said my leg was broken. I couldn't dance in the competition. I was devastated. So were the others, Corinne especially. She kept saying, 'This was your championship, Lavvy. This was your time.'"

"Did she win?"

"Corinne and Donald? No. The winners were a married Swiss couple named Kaiser. I'm sure worrying about me distracted Corinne and Donald and cost them their chance at the title, too."

"How awful." I looked at the seventy-year-old woman in front of me, imagining her as a young twenty-something anxious to set the world on fire with her ball-

room dancing, excited about competing overseas. She'd
been beautiful, I was sure, with glowing auburn hair and
the lithe, athletic figure she still had to some degree.

"Change," she ordered, unzipping the pink gown.

I shrugged out of it behind the curtain, draped it over
the hanger, and quickly donned my own clothes.

"Yes, well. It got worse when my leg got infected. The
doctors couldn't get it under control, and eventually they
had to amputate below the knee." She moved away from
the dressing room and I heard the *ka-thump*, *ka-thump*
as she unrolled the fabric bolt on the cutting table. Her
voice was brisk as she said, "My dancing career was over,
of course. Prosthetics in those days were nothing like
they are today. I keep up with that, you know; I read the
articles about what they're able to do for our soldiers
who lose limbs in Afghanistan or Iraq and I'm just
amazed. The technology these days is wonderful."

I popped out from behind the curtain, tucking my
blouse in. "Did they ever catch the guy?"

She shook her head. "No. The police never caught up
with him. Their theory was that he was attempting a
mugging and panicked, that he hit my leg by accident."

"You didn't agree?"

"I wasn't sure. Corinne always maintained that he'd hit
me on purpose. And then in the nineties, when that awful
Harding person arranged for someone to injure Nancy
Kerrigan, hoping to keep her from skating in the Olympics, I began to think about it again. It sounded just like
what had happened to me, although of course the Blackpool Dance Festival was not a sporting event on a par
with the Olympics, at least not as most people viewed it.
That was thirty years after the fact, though, and I didn't
spend much time thinking about it. I'd made a name for
myself as a designer by then—Corinne and her first hus-

band loaned me the money to get started and supported me while I went to school and then did an apprenticeship with a fashion house in Paris—and I had almost convinced myself that the attacker had done me a favor. One can work as a designer, you know, for far longer than one can be a competitive athlete of any sort."

"Absolutely," I said, as if my reassurance mattered to her one little bit.

She gave me a wry look, acknowledging my intent, I thought, and picked up a sketchbook. Her pencil whisked over the page and a dress began to take shape. I peered over her shoulder.

"I should not have burdened you with my sad history," she said, concentrating on the page. "It's not something I think about normally. Just with Corinne's death . . ."

"It's like part of your history has died," I said.

"That's it," she said, arching thin brows. "Ricky died years ago—lung cancer—and Donald passed away four or five years back. Now it's like I'm the only one left who knows that part of my story. Memory is a slippery thing, Stacy. When we're young, we're sure that things happened as we remember them, that our recollection is true. As we age . . . well, I think most of us trust our memories less and, maybe, if we're honest, admit that 'truth' depends on one's perspective. Now my memory of that time is the only truth left. It's a strange feeling."

I didn't answer, feeling completely incapable of saying anything worthwhile in the face of her nostalgia and grief. I thought I understood a little of what she was saying, though, since I'd had similar feelings since Rafe's death. After a respectful moment, I said, "You know, the police arrested Maurice Goldberg for Corinne's murder."

Lavinia's pencil clattered to the floor. "What?"

I picked up the pencil and handed it to her. "They've released him for now and he's got a good lawyer, but—"

"That's ridiculous," she said angrily. "Maurice! Why, he's the best thing that ever happened to Corinne. I let her have what-for when she told me she was divorcing him, but she'd made up her mind."

"You knew her better and longer than anyone," I said. "Did she have any enemies that you know of?"

"Not before she started writing that memoir," Lavinia said. "The police asked me the same thing."

"So there was no one . . . ?"

She hesitated, doodling some background around the sketch. "Well, Greta Monk won't be grieving about Corinne's death."

"Who's she?"

"She calls herself a patroness of the arts," Lavinia said in a tone that conveyed what she thought of such pretension. "She and Corinne ran a dance scholarship charity for several years. It dissolved when Corinne caught her embezzling."

"I never heard about that."

"The board kept it hush-hush, made a deal where Greta repaid the money and avoided prosecution. Something like that. Anyway, the timing of Corinne's tell-all couldn't have been worse for Greta, because she's in line for a position on the board of trustees of the Kennedy Center, something she's been lobbying for for *decades*. A scandal now would mean she could kiss that good-bye."

"And Corinne was including the embezzlement story in her book?"

"She was never happy that Greta got away with it in the first place."

Hm. And if what Marco Ingelido said was right,

Corinne would've made a point of "warning" Greta that she had a starring role in the upcoming book.

"There." Lavinia thrust the sketchpad toward me.

The dress was perfect: tight through the bodice, with off-the-shoulder straps and a skirt that floated away from the body like mist. "It's divine."

"I'll work something up for Vitaly." The suggestion of a grin erased years from her face. "That man! Can you pick the pink dress up Sunday afternoon? I know you're dancing on Monday, but I can't have it any earlier."

"Sure," I said, straightening. "Thank you, Lavinia."

"Of course, Stacy. Always a pleasure."

I left, shutting the door carefully behind me to keep the air-conditioning in. Turning to wave as I passed the display window, I saw that the seat by the drawing table was empty.

Chapter 12

Danielle lived in a block of apartments west of me, in a quiet area off of Taney Road. The complex was spread over several tree-lined streets and consisted of rectangular, yellowy-tan brick buildings so alike that Danielle had once tried to get into her apartment well after midnight and found herself confronting a pissed-off man holding a baseball bat. She'd been in the wrong building. She never admitted it, but I thought too many margaritas might have been a factor. Parking in the lot outside her building and double-checking to make sure it *was* her building, I trotted up the stairs to her second-floor apartment and rang the bell.

"Come in!"

I pushed open the door, saying, "Good grief, Dani, this is D.C. Don't you keep your door locked?" I stood in the two-foot-square foyer delineated by faux-wood flooring to distinguish it from the attached living room, which had the kind of pale brown carpet apartment managers think won't show dirt or damage. There was a gaping hole where the sofa had sat against the far wall, and the walls themselves were a deep aqua green that made me think of mermaids for some reason, instead of the boring taupe they'd been last time I visited.

"This is a safe neighborhood." Her voice came from the kitchen and I tracked her down. She sat on the vinyl floor surrounded by images torn from various decorating magazines and looked up when I came in. With her red hair in a ponytail and no makeup, she looked about fourteen.

"I am not, not, not going through home fashion magazines," I said. I've never been much of one for obsessing over fabric swatches or room layouts or the kind of makeovers they show in such magazines. Dani, though, has always loved poring over the pages, even as a teenager, when the most she could hope to talk Dad into on the redecorating front was a new bedspread for the room we shared.

"Just look at this. . . ."

I scrunched my eyes closed as she held up a page with a jagged edge where she'd torn it out of some magazine.

"Fine." She sounded disgruntled but not surprised. Rising from her cross-legged position, she preceded me back to the living room, nudging magazines out of her path as she went.

We spent forty-five minutes rearranging furniture and talking about possible color combinations before her phone rang and she trotted to the bedroom to answer it. I sat in the worn recliner I'd been urging her to get rid of so she didn't have to match her new couch to its beige-and-maroon-striped upholstery—*ick*—and picked up an open photo album from the end table. It took me only a second to realize I was looking at pictures from our last family vacation to Jekyll Island. Mom's invitation had obviously started Dani on a trek down memory lane.

Flipping through the pages, I paused at a photo of me and Dani and Nick crouched over a dead jellyfish on the beach, the backs of our legs covered with sand. We'd been arguing about whether the creature was dead or whether we should "rescue" it. Nick's idea of rescuing it was to put it in the bucket and keep it forever, despite Mom telling him it would die in the car halfway home, and she wasn't having a bucket of water sloshing around in the backseat, anyway. Dani wanted to return it to the ocean. I was convinced it was already dead and said so repeatedly. In the end, we scooped it up on a shovel and plopped it back in the water, on the off chance. As I looked at more photos, I saw signs of parental tension I hadn't noticed at the time. In all the family photos, Mom and Dad were at opposite ends, with us three kids between them. We had plenty of photos of Dad reading on the beach or showing Nick how to snorkel, and Mom building sand castles with me or inspecting a butterfly with Dani, but no pictures of the two of them together. I hadn't thought anything about it at the time, but Dad had slept in the hammock outside, saying he wanted to enjoy the stars, while Mom had the bedroom to herself.

I felt tears welling and sniffed them back. We'd gone through a couple of hard years after Mom left, but we were fine now. If this album proved anything, it proved that we weren't by half as happy as I'd thought we were while Mom was still living with us.

"It was a great vacation, wasn't it?" Dani said quietly from behind me.

"It was fun. I'm not sure it was as fun as we thought it was, though, at least not for Mom and Dad."

"What do you mean?" Danielle bristled.

I pointed out what I'd seen in the photos, the tension between our folks, but Dani wasn't buying it. She was annoyed with me for daring to suggest that the vacation she had convinced herself was perfect in every respect hadn't been. Taking the album from me, she slapped it closed and slotted it onto a bookshelf. There was a moment of awkward silence before I said, "So, I think a white sofa would really look good against that aqua wall."

"Are you insane?" Dani asked, reverting to normal. "White? Do you know how hard that would be to keep clean?"

We spent the rest of the evening drinking strawberry daiquiris from a frozen mix Dani had left over from a party several months back, and discussing her sofa options. I even broke down and looked at some sofa photos in her decorating magazines. Jekyll Island didn't come up again.

Chapter 13

Friday morning found Tav and me setting up a Graysin Motion table at the expo center for the bridal fair. There wasn't much setting up for us to do, in truth, not compared to some of the other vendors. Florists had colorful, pungent displays of corsages, bouquets, and flower arrangements bursting with carnations, orchids, roses, lilies, and a host of blooms I couldn't identify. Bakeries had multitiered cakes on display, some with layers canted at strange angles and iced in every color imaginable, although white predominated. My favorite stood twelve tiers high and looked like a sunset, with tangerine, pink, and yellow layers decked with fresh flowers in the same colors. Mannequins from wedding dress stores wore gowns with skirts wider than Marie Antoinette's, slim sheaths, and mermaid-style skirts that belled at the bottom like an upside-down champagne glass. Jewelers displayed rings in glass cases. Deejays and bands played discs that showcased their talents and added a festive sound track to the buzz of a thousand brides-to-be, grooms, mothers, wedding planners, and heaven knew who else.

Dani and I had attended a bridal fair like this one soon after I got engaged to Rafe. Before I found out he was cheating on me. Before I broke it off. Before he died. I'd strolled from table to table, sampling cakes, sniffing bouquets, and generally brimming over with excitement that I was going to be a bride, a wife. Watching the excited brides-to-be flitting from display to display, I wondered sadly how many of them would never walk down the aisle, at least not with the man they were currently engaged to.

"Weddings are big business," Tav observed as he fanned a handful of Graysin Motion brochures across the table.

"The biggest." I propped up a life-size, 3-D cardboard image of Rafe and me that had been used to advertise our presence at a fund-raising exhibition a couple years back. "Have you ever been married?" I asked impulsively.

Tav straightened, looking handsome enough to pose for one of the tuxedo ads plastered in the space next to ours. "Once. A long time ago."

"Really?" I don't know why I was surprised. "What happened?"

"She decided she did not want to be married. It lasted seven months. We were both twenty, far too young to get married."

"Are you still in touch with her?"

He shook his head. "Last I heard, she was working for a television producer in Australia. You?"

"Nope. Rafe's as close as I ever got, and you know how that turned out."

"My brother was a fool," he said.

I didn't know how to respond to that, so I set the foot-shaped cutouts on the floor in front of our table in a simple waltz sequence. A young brunette who might have been of Indian or Pakistani extraction watched me. "Are you her?" she asked, pointing with her chin at the 3-D stand-up.

"Uh-huh."

"I'm not that flexible," she said dubiously.

In the photo, I had my left ankle on Rafe's shoulder, right leg extended behind me as he dragged me. "That's the paso doble," I said. "Probably not what you had in mind for your wedding. The waltz is much easier. Want to try?"

She shook her head and hurried past.

"We will get clients from this," Tav said, noting my disappointed expression. "That dress was an inspired choice."

I smoothed the deep orange skirt of the gown I used to wear for international standard competitions. Cut almost to the waist in back, with crisscross straps, it was eye-catching. I'd worn my hair up, like for a competition, but gone easy on the makeup, skipping the false eyelashes that I wore to compete.

"Orange stands out," I agreed.

We weren't as mobbed as some of the bakery or wedding dress vendors, but a steady trickle of people stopped by to take brochures. Several couples actually signed up for lessons, prompted by Tav's smooth patter. One or two embarrassed couples even gave it a go, using the cutouts on the floor and my encouragement to guide their first tentative steps.

Shortly before lunchtime, a bride who looked close to my age stopped in front of the table, dragging her fiancé to a halt beside her. "Drew, doesn't this look like fun?"

His expression suggested he'd rather wrestle alligators. "I don't know, Hailey. . . ."

"C'mon." The woman laughed. "It can't be that hard."

"It's easy," I assured him, holding out my hand. "I'll show you."

"I've never danced," Drew said, backing away.

"Even someone who has never danced before can learn to waltz. Look." I turned to Tav with a mischievous twinkle. "Tav will demonstrate."

He looked taken aback but came around to the front of the table.

"But he's a dancer," the groom-to-be objected.

"Not even close," Tav said. "Football is my game."

"He's my business partner," I said, "not my dance partner. Here, we'll show you." I grabbed Tav's left hand and raised it to the proper position, then laid my other hand across the back of his shoulder, arching my back.

"Did I not mention once that learning to dance in front of a crowd does not appeal to me?" he whispered. He didn't sound angry, although the look in his eyes promised retribution. His breath against my ear made me shiver.

"Think of it as growing the business." I smiled up at him and felt his hand tighten against my back. We hadn't been this close since we agreed to be partners and I'd given him an impromptu lesson in my kitchen. With his nearness creating a fog in my brain, I remembered why I'd kept my distance. Dancing with Tav undermined my determination to keep our relationship strictly business.

Faking a composure I didn't feel, I talked him through a few steps, for the benefit of the watching couple. He moved gracefully, with the balance of an athlete. That didn't surprise me greatly, because I knew he had played soccer seriously in college and now played with a league in D.C. a couple of times a week. Too aware of the mus-cled strength in his chest and thighs where they touched mine, I whispered, "There's supposed to be more space between us."

"Where is the fun in that?" His smile was devilish, and his hold tightened.

Resisting the temptation to melt against him, I ended the "lesson." The engaged couple applauded when I stepped back and dropped into a curtsy.

"See? Easy." I smiled as they let Tav sign them up for a series of lessons. My stomach growled, and I motioned to Tav that I was going to grab something to eat in the concession area. *I'll bring you something*, I mouthed.

Serpentining through the maze of tables, booths, and displays, I made for the concession area and the tantalizing aroma of hamburgers and onion rings. I couldn't afford to eat either one—Vitaly would kill me if I gained an ounce—but I could bask in the smell without worrying about weight gain. In the row adjacent to the roped-off concession area, with its rickety tables and folding chairs, I spotted a photographer's booth with a poster-sized photo of a bride and her father sharing a private moment before the ceremony. I stepped closer to examine it, and read the photographer's sign: SARAH LEWIS PHOTOGRAPHY.

The name seemed familiar ... with a start, I realized she must be Marco Ingelido's niece, the one Maurice had mentioned. Curious, I studied her as she spoke with a potential customer and what looked to be the bride's parents. I could see a faint resemblance to Ingelido in the sweep of her cheekbone, the aquiline nose, and something about the eyes. Dressed casually in jeans and a shirt with the sleeves rolled up, her dark hair in a loose braid, she looked like she'd be more at home photographing wildlife in the Galapagos than persuading a wedding party of twenty to all smile at once.

On impulse, I crossed to her and introduced myself as the bride and family left. "Aren't you Marco Ingelido's niece?" I asked. "I was chatting with your uncle just yesterday."

"Nice to meet you." She smiled easily; she was attractive in an athletic, outdoorsy way. "You know, I've photographed you before."

"You have? When?"

"I freelance for dance magazines at ballroom competitions. I also do a lot of publicity photos for people in the business, as well as recital photos for dance studios. In fact, I prefer that to this"—she gestured to the bridal fair chaos—"but weddings pay more bills. Let me know if you need photos—you've got a new partner, right? I heard your former partner died suddenly. He called me once, wanting to know my rates for doing recital photos. He never got back to me, and I didn't understand why until I heard about his death. I'm very sorry."

"Thanks." I bit the word off, infuriated to think that Rafe had been going ahead with his plans to broaden the studio's offerings and put on a recital behind my back. I'd wanted to build Graysin Motion's reputation as a world-class ballroom dance studio; he'd wanted to rake in the bucks with tap for tots and beginning ballet classes, to become a recital mill like Li'l Twinkletoes. If he hadn't already been dead, I'd've killed him.

Sarah gave me a funny look. "Sorry," I apologized. "My mind drifted. Vitaly and I *do* need some publicity shots—do you have a card?"

She handed one over. "It seems strange," she said. "Two prominent ballroom dancers dying so close together, and both murdered, from what I hear."

I was pleased she'd brought up Corinne so I wouldn't have to find a way to work her into the conversation.

"It's sad. The deaths aren't related, but even so. Your uncle mentioned Corinne yesterday. I guess they used to be close?"

"So family rumor has it," Sarah said, her face closing down a bit. "It was before he married Aunt Marian—at least thirty years ago—so I don't know much about it. I heard him and my mom going at it once, and Corinne's name came up, but I didn't pay much attention. One doesn't think of older relatives *that* way, does one?"

My mind flashed to Uncle Nico and conversations I'd heard between my mom and dad about Nico's womanizing. *Ew.* One certainly didn't want to think of one's relatives that way, especially not the Uncle Nicos. Trying to blot from my mind the image of Uncle Nico with one of his much younger model-type girlfriends, I blurted, "Marco seemed okay with Corinne's memoir not getting published, now that she's dead, I mean."

"I didn't know she had a book coming out." Sarah looked no more than mildly interested. "I'd've thought he'd be pushing for it if he was in it. He's always looking for publicity, especially for Take the Lead with Ingelido. He's become a workaholic in his old age, my mom says."

Her mom must be Ingelido's sister. Sarah certainly didn't sound as if she cared about what Corinne might have had to say. Well, why would she? She was single, if her ringless finger was anything to go by, and even though the uncle-niece thing was a bit icky, they were both consenting adults. It looked to me like Ingelido had a lot more to lose if the affair became public than Sarah Lewis did. "So, you never wanted to be a ballroom dancer yourself?" I asked. "Even with a ballroom dance champion in the family?"

She laughed. "Uncle Marco tried hard to turn me into a dancer, as a matter of fact. But I've got the proverbial two left feet. My sister was better than I was, and our brother was better than both of us. Now she's a stay-at-home mom of four kids who complains she hasn't been out dancing since her first pregnancy, and Zach married a born-again type who doesn't approve of dancing, among other things. Poor Uncle Marco." She shook her head in mock sadness.

"I'm sure he got over it." She seemed completely unself-conscious talking about him, not guilty or furtive, like I'd have thought if she'd had an affair with him. Still, many and many an affair started on the dance floor. Stories of pros and students hooking up, or pros with other pros (regardless of marital status), abounded in ballroom circles. "Well, thanks," I said, pinging her card. "I'll give you a call."

"Nice to meet you, Stacy." She turned to greet an engaged couple in their fifties, hovering nearby as they waited for us to finish.

Still thinking about Ingelido's relationship with his niece, I bought a limp Caesar salad for me, with fat-free dressing and sans croutons, which really made it a heap of Romaine lettuce leaves, and a burger and fries for Tav. I snitched two of the fries on my way back to our table.

Tav was seated at our table, checking e-mails on his phone. "Thanks," he said when I handed him the burger.

Between bites of salad, I told him about talking to Sarah Lewis, then backed up and filled him in on my conversations with Marco Ingelido and Lavinia Fremont. "I was hoping Lavinia could point me toward someone in Corinne's past who might really have something to lose if the book got published, and she named Greta Monk." I explained.

He eyed me thoughtfully. "Avoiding prosecution for a

crime would be a strong motive. But is there not a statute of limitations?"

"I don't know. I also don't know how long ago the embezzlement—alleged embezzlement—happened. I can ask Phineas Drake about the statute of limitations. Maurice is supposed to meet with him this afternoon and he wanted me to go with him." I realized I still hadn't talked to Detective Lissy about what Angela Rush had said. "Oh, and I need to call Detective Lissy."

Since no bridal couples were fighting for the opportunity to sign up for ballroom dancing lessons just then, I whipped out my phone and dialed Detective Lissy's number. It was still in my cell's memory from when he'd been trying to pin a murder on me.

He came on the line with a weary, "Yes, Miss Graysin?"

I told him about locating Corinne's literary agent, Angela Rush (although I didn't mention searching the Blakely house), and suggested that he might want to get a copy of whatever the literary agent had of Corinne's book.

There was a lengthy pause when I stopped talking. "Detective Lissy?"

"Miss Graysin—"

I imagined him folding in those too-red lips.

"I've been doing this job for—"

"Yes, I know, twenty-seven years." He might have mentioned that two or eight times while investigating Rafe's murder.

"—and I assure you that I don't need your help. In fact, if you wanted to help, you could have refrained from aiding and abetting a suspect."

"I let a friend sleep at my place for a night. That's hardly aiding and abetting," I said, rising to pace around our tiny display area. I bumped the stand-up of Rafe and me and we teetered. I steadied us. I realized that arguing with Lissy was not going to help Maurice's case. "Look, Detective Lissy, I know you know how to do your job. It's just that I've talked to a few people—"

Lissy groaned.

"—and it seems to me that Corinne Blakely stirred up a lot of old . . . animosities when she set out to write her memoir. Lots of people, it seems to me, had much better motives for killing Corinne than Maurice did. Why, he doesn't even have a motive."

"That we know of. Yet. Moreover, he had means and opportunity, which are much more important. Now, it seems to *me*, Miss Graysin, that you should stick to dancing and let me do the investigating."

I tried to rush in a question before he could hang up. "What were the means, exactly? I mean, how did she d—"

He hung up, leaving me staring at the disconnected phone. "Well!"

Tav gave me a quizzical look. "No success with your favorite police detective?"

"You'd think he'd be grateful for a little citizen involvement," I said, flouncing back to my chair. It's easier to flounce in a satin ball gown than in, say, a pair of jeans. "The police are always asking people to get more involved, to join neighborhood watches and all that."

"Ungrateful. That is what they are." The corners of his mouth dented in, in a way that told me he was holding back a smile.

"You're laughing at me!"

"Never." He shook his head unconvincingly.

"I've got to help Maurice." I was prepared to get mad at Tav if he objected.

"Of course you do," he agreed. "It is one of the things I most appreciate about you—your loyalty to your friends."

"Really?"

"Really."

"Appreciate" didn't light me up as a verb choice—I'd have preferred "like" or "find attractive"—but I felt a warm glow nonetheless.

A managing mother-of-the-bride type sailed up just then, hapless daughter in tow, so we turned back to the business of convincing people that ballroom dance could change their lives. Or, at the very least, that it would impress the heck out of their friends and family when they performed a graceful waltz or foxtrot at their wedding reception.

Chapter 14

Late afternoon found me trapped in traffic on I-66, trying to drive into Crystal City, where Phineas Drake had his offices, to get to the meeting Maurice had asked me to attend. I'd planned on zipping home to change first, reckoning that traffic going toward the city should flow pretty well on a Friday afternoon, but an accident had snarled things up, and I didn't have time to go home after leaving Tav to man the fort at the bridal fair.

As a result, I walked into Drake's conference room twenty minutes late, traffic-frazzled, wearing the orange gown. I attracted quite a few stares and whispered comments as I crossed the marble-floored lobby and rode the elevator to the twenty-sixth floor. When the elevator door opened on the offices of Drake and Stoudemire, the hum of conversation, phones ringing, and keyboards clicking, muffled by plush carpeting, told me plenty of lawyers were still at work at past six on a Friday. Drake's well-trained receptionist didn't blink an eye at my attire, merely leading me to the small conference room with a wall of glass looking over the Potomac and into D.C. I didn't feel quite so out of place when Drake rose to greet me and I saw he was wearing a tuxedo, complete with tartan bow tie and cummerbund.

"I see you got the memo about formal wear for this meeting," he greeted me, smiling behind his mustache and bushy brown beard streaked with silver. He looked more like a modern-day fur trapper or logger than a lawyer. He had a barrel chest and a rounded stomach, and his hand completely swallowed mine when we shook. "I don't suppose you're going to the bar association gala this evening?"

I laughed. "No, just coming from a bridal fair."

Drake's brows soared. "Should I wish you happy?"

"Heavens, no. Graysin Motion bought space at the convention to entice brides and grooms to learn to dance before their big day."

"I don't know why we didn't think of doing that sooner," Maurice said. He was on the far side of the table, back to the windows, and wore his usual navy blazer and crisp shirt. He gave me a welcoming smile, although he looked tenser than usual.

"Tav has some good promotional ideas. Where's your daughter?" I asked Phineas Drake as we sat. My orange skirt billowed around me and I smoothed it down. "I thought she was handling Maurice's case."

"We'll be working on it together," Drake said. "She's flying to Bermuda as we speak, a working flight with one of our corporate clients. Now." His tone turned businesslike. "I've counseled Maurice that it's not in his best interest to have you here. I recommend against it."

I must have looked hurt, because he continued. "You're not subject to privilege. You can be compelled to testify."

"Since I don't plan to admit to killing Rinny, it's not going to be a problem," Maurice said. "I want Stacy here."

"Very well." Drake opened a folder that lay on the gleaming wood table in front of him. "Before you arrived, Stacy, I was telling Maurice that I got a copy of the autopsy report this afternoon. It seems Ms. Blakely died from a myocardial infarction." He paused.

"A heart attack?" I looked from Drake to Maurice, confused. "Then why ... ?"

Drake looked pleased, as if I'd come up with the response he was looking for. "Not so fast. The MI was caused by an overdose of epinephrine, apparently ingested in a capsule that was supposed to contain Ms. Blakely's heart medication. Epinephrine raises blood pressure and increases heart rate, which triggered the heart attack."

"Rinny took a pill soon after I arrived at the restaurant," Maurice said, leaning forward with his forearms on the table. "She had a minor heart attack four years ago and has been on medication since. She dropped the bottle and it rolled under the table. I crawled under there to get it for her."

"An excellent way to account for your fingerprints on the pill bottle," Drake said, nodding approvingly. "We'll find someone on the restaurant staff who remembers seeing you retrieve the bottle." He made a note.

Maurice continued, as if he were thinking aloud. "If the epinephrine was in the capsule, it proves I couldn't have killed her. I never left the table after I arrived; I didn't have the opportunity to doctor the capsules." Relief softened the tightness in his jaw.

"Not so fast," Drake said, raising a cautionary finger.

"You were at Ms. Blakely's house last Thursday, you said. Did you have access to the medicine cabinet at that time?"

Maurice's silence answered for him.

"On top of that, the police have a record of you buying an epinephrine-based product at the Walgreens nearest your house two weeks ago. Not enough to start your own meth lab, which is, of course, why you can't buy those meds now without signing for them, but certainly enough to send Ms. Blakely's ticker into overdrive." His look invited Maurice to explain.

"I had a cold! I bought some decongestants."

"He did have a cold," I said, remembering a sniffling Maurice. I'd sent him home from one class so he could rest.

"The police are testing all the capsules in Mrs. Blakely's bottle," Drake continued, "to see if any others were tampered with. I guess that will tell us how quickly someone wanted her dead."

"It sounds like a pretty iffy way of killing someone," I said. "What if she didn't take the doctored pill? What if she noticed that someone had tampered with it?"

"Perhaps the killer didn't have a specific time line," Drake suggested. "He or she could afford to wait until Ms. Blakely ingested the poisoned pill. And who looks at their pills before they take them? I take a handful each morning—blood pressure, cholesterol—and I certainly don't examine them. I spill 'em out and pop 'em in." He mimed dumping pills in his hand and tossing them in his mouth. "At any rate, our job's to prove that Maurice here didn't do it, and the killer's made that an easier task for us."

"How so?" asked Maurice.

"Anyone with access to Ms. Blakely's house during the time period since she last refilled her prescription—

hopefully a month or so ago—could conceivably have put the epinephrine in the capsule. The DA will have a much harder time of hanging this on you," he said with grim satisfaction, "with such a large window of opportunity for, I imagine, a healthy number of folks."

"What about Turner?" I asked. "Her grandson. He lives at her house now, and he's going to inherit everything, right?"

"Oh, believe me," Drake said, eyes narrowing, "I've got an investigator prying into every corner of young Mr. Blakely's finances and lifestyle as we speak. And into the housekeeper's. She had unparalleled access to the prescription bottle."

"Mrs. Laughlin wouldn't do anything to hurt Rinny," Maurice said. "They've been together for nearly fifty years."

"The same could be said of many married couples until the wife snaps one day and puts a bullet into hubby dearest, or he loses it and has at her with a poker. In my experience, living with someone for a long time makes you less tolerant of their . . . foibles, shall we say? . . . than more tolerant. You can leave the toilet seat up only so long before it's wood-chipper time."

I could see that being a criminal defense attorney gave one a cheery outlook on humanity.

"So what do I do now?" Maurice asked, fingers twiddling with a loose button on his blazer sleeve. I gave him a sympathetic look.

"Nothing," Drake said. "Go to work, go home, don't talk to the media, and absolutely don't talk to the police unless I'm present. The ball's in my court. I'm working on getting a copy of Ms. Blakely's will so we can see who else might have had a financial motive. I've also got someone finagling the memoir outline from the literary agent. I don't think you have much to worry about, Maurice."

Maurice crinkled his forehead. "But a jury—"

"I don't believe in juries," Drake interrupted. "Nice people, most of 'em, I'm sure, but unpredictable. No, the best way to keep a client out of jail is to make sure he never sees a jury. And that's what I aim to do in your case. Now, if you'll excuse me, I've got to meet up with the missus at the bar association shindig before she bids on a time-share in Fiji or some such at the silent auction." Smoothing his vest over his considerable paunch, he ushered us from the conference room.

Maurice had ridden the Metro to the meeting and was happy to accept a ride home with me. Rush-hour traffic still snarled the streets, and I resigned myself to a long commute. Glancing at Maurice's profile, I asked, "Do you feel any better about the situation now?"

His mouth twitched in a "not really" way. "I'm less concerned about ending up in the pokey with Drake on the case," he conceded, "but Rinny's still dead, isn't she? And the murderer is still out there." He gazed through the side window as if hoping to spot the killer in the semi idling beside us, or in the van leaking rap music in front of us.

"Do you know Greta Monk?" I asked, giving him a brief account of my visit with Lavinia Fremont.

"Poor Lavinia." He sighed. "She was an amazing dancer . . . so light on her feet you'd have thought she was a piece of dandelion fluff tossed by the wind."

"Very poetic."

He reddened and said sheepishly, "Well, she was a born dancer. Maybe not as technically proficient as Corinne, but with a musicality that set her dancing apart.

It was a crime—literally—when she lost her leg. Although she's achieved a lot with her design business."

"She said Corinne and her husband helped her get set up."

Maurice nodded. "Indeed. I've often thought Corinne felt guilty about Lavinia."

I took my eyes off the road to look at him—no big deal, since I-395 more nearly resembled a parking lot than a highway. "Really? Why on earth?"

"Because the trip to England was her idea. She'd had a bee in her bonnet for a long time about winning at Blackpool, and she's the one who talked Lavinia and Ricky into accepting the invitation to compete. Lavinia was more of a homebody; I don't think she'd have gone if it hadn't been for Corinne."

"Corinne presumably didn't force her to go at gunpoint. It sounded to me like Lavinia was pretty keen on competing at the dance festival." Traffic stuttered forward a half block, and a motorcycle cut through the line of cars, making me wonder whether I shouldn't trade my Beetle in for one of those cute scooters that came in fun colors, like pink. I looked down at the gown I was wearing and gave up on the scooter idea; exposure to wind, rain, and smog wouldn't be good for my competition wardrobe.

"As you say," Maurice agreed. "As to Greta Monk ... well, she's a piece of work. I think she studied ballet once upon a time, but she didn't have what it took to get on with a professional company. Then she took to ballroom dance, but ..." He shrugged. "I will say this: She seemed aware of her limitations as a dancer and switched to 'patronizing' the arts, rather than trying to be a performer, not long after she married Conrad Monk. He encouraged her to chair fund-raising events and the like, and when she and Corinne started talking about putting together a foundation to award scholarships, he put up a big chunk of change."

"If her husband was well-off, why would she embezzle from the foundation, if she did?" I asked.

"Don't ask me," Maurice said, a hint of asperity in his voice. "Why do those pretty, rich young actresses shoplift? It's not always about the money."

The cars in front of us shot forward like water from a pipe that was suddenly unclogged, and I stepped on the gas, thinking that Maurice might be right. The Lindsay Lohans of the world certainly let us know that some thefts must be motivated by the adrenaline rush that accompanied the risk, or the thrill of getting away with something. I'd never been that way myself, but I'd had a friend in high school who was constantly shoplifting a lip gloss here or a CD there. And it wasn't because she couldn't afford to pay for them. She used to bring the items to school and brag about how she stole them. I'd stopped hanging out with her after she stole a tank top from Target while I was with her. I'd been petrified when she pulled it out of her purse in the store parking lot, laughing about how easy it was.

"If you want to talk to Greta," Maurice said, "she'll be at the Willow House battered-women's shelter fundraiser tomorrow. It's a Mardi Gras–themed party on a Potomac cruise. Greta organized it."

"Isn't Mardi Gras in February?"

"Would you want to go on a river cruise here in February?" He gave an exaggerated shiver.

There'd be ice on the river; temps would dip into the twenties; gusty winds would rock the boat. "I guess not."

"I've got tickets, if you want them. Greta strong-armed me into buying them. Corinne and I were going to go, but now . . . The *Plantation Queen* launches at four; she's an old-fashioned paddleboat."

"I'll still be at the bridal fair," I said.

"Let me man the booth at the fair," Maurice said. "I'd welcome a day to sit and schmooze with brides-to-be and their lovely mothers. I'll bet I can sign up more ballroom students than you did today; the key is charming the mothers. Everyone's oohing and ahhing over the beautiful bride and her sparkly ring, and the mother gets less attention than the bride's purse or hairdo. A few kind words, a graceful compliment, and voilà—the mother convinces the whole wedding party they need to learn to foxtrot."

"No bet," I said with a laugh. "Okay. You've got it."

We pulled up in front of Maurice's house and he opened the door. I put a hand on his arm. "You okay?"

"Dandy," he said.

I eyed him with concern.

"No, really, Anastasia." His face grew serious. "I'm okay. Sad about Corinne's death and not happy that I'm a suspect, but I'm not going to drink myself into a stupor or sit around and mope. I'll make myself some dinner, maybe pop 'round to the Fox and Muskrat for a pint, and turn in early. Corinne's lawyer is reading her will tomorrow at eight, and I've been asked to attend. Can't think why. She can't have left me more than a token." His brows drew together briefly. "Want to come with me?"

"I don't know. . . ." His request took me aback, but the eagerness in his eyes seemed to suggest he could use some moral support. "Would they let me?"

"I don't see why not. Good!" he said, as if it were settled. "It'll be over and done with in time for me to get out to the bridal fair before the expo center doors open."

I agreed, reluctantly, to attend the reading of the will with him, and we arranged to meet in front of the lawyer's office shortly before eight. "You'll get a chance to meet Corinne's other husbands," he said with a hint of a mischievous smile. "Make sure you tell me that she went downhill after divorcing me."

"Not a doubt of it," I said. "See you in the morning."

Chapter 15

Corinne Blakely's lawyer was a gentleman about Maurice's age, with uniformly black, suspiciously stiff hair draped across his head. The toupee covered the tops of jutting ears and brushed his collar in the back. With his lined face, and dark-framed reading glasses perched at the tip of his nose, he looked a little like the King of Rock and Roll might have looked if he were still alive. Elvis: the golden years. Fortunately, the lawyer wore a pin-striped suit and not a spangled white jumpsuit. Standing at the head of the conference room table, he shuffled papers in an expandable file, glancing at his watch and then the door approximately every forty-five seconds.

Maurice and I stood in the back right-hand corner of the room, having arrived too late to get one of the twenty-four chairs drawn up to the oblong table. People lined the walls as well, and I guessed there must be eighty people present, mostly men. Interesting. I recognized only a few of them. Turner Blakely sat at the lawyer's right hand, reclining in his leather chair, sunglasses obscuring his eyes. Hungover, maybe? Mrs. Laughlin sat midway down the table on the side opposite Turner, dabbing at her eyes with a utilitarian hankie. Lavinia Fremont sat beside her, occasionally patting the housekeeper's hand. She looked tired, and older than when I'd seen her Thursday. Standing against the far wall, abreast of the lawyer, Marco Ingelido stood with his arm around a fiftyish blonde I took to be his wife. When he caught sight of me, he raised his brows and tried to stare me down, apparently not thinking I belonged there. I held his gaze until he looked away.

I was about to mention it to Maurice when a tan man in his mid-sixties squeezed in beside me, all heavy gold jewelry and expensive golf attire.

"Goldberg," the newcomer greeted Maurice. He had an unfortunately high-pitched voice that made him sound like a munchkin, and wore a salmon pink shirt that clashed viciously with raspberry trousers.

"Lyle," Maurice said in a resigned way.

"I'm Stacy," I said, offering my hand.

Lyle shook it, looking from me to Maurice, brown eyes sparking with curiosity. "Lyle Debenham," he said. "It looks like they've been selling tickets to this shindig," he observed. "It's a packed house."

"How did you know Corinne?" I asked when Maurice didn't say anything.

"I was Mo's replacement." Lyle chuckled.

It took me a minute to realize "Mo" was Maurice.

"Husband number three," Maurice said dryly.

"She always said she was going to leave each of us something to remember her by," Lyle said, apparently unperturbed by Maurice's cool manner. "What do you suppose it'll be? Old Goudge"—he tilted his head toward the lawyer—"wouldn't even give me a hint. I thought about not coming, but I had nothing better to do this early—tee time's not till nine forty-two, so here I am. You're not related to Corinne, are you?"

"No," I said.

"For what it's worth, old man," Lyle said, leaning across me to address Maurice directly, "I know you didn't have anything to do with offing our mutual ex-wife. Not your style."

"Decent of you," Maurice said, a bit more warmth in his voice.

"Wasn't me either," Lyle volunteered. "I was at my grandson's graduation in Alabama this past weekend. He's going on to med school so he can take care of his old grandpop in my declining years. Didn't get back here until Thursday. Hamish, though . . ."

I followed his gaze to where a cadaverously thin man sat at the table, arms crossed over his chest.

"A little bird told me he never gave up on getting Corinne back, that he continued to send her a bouquet of tulips—"

"Her favorite flowers," Maurice put in.

"—every week of her life. He made a total ass of himself at the wedding when she married the count."

"He's a baron," Maurice said. He scanned the crowd. "I don't see him here."

"Not worth making the transatlantic trip," Lyle said. "I heard he's close to bankruptcy, that his shipping business has taken some big losses the past couple of years."

Before Maurice could respond, the lawyer cleared his throat with a loud "Ahem."

My watch showed exactly eight o'clock. A sense of anticipation upped the energy level in the room. Peering over his glasses at us, the old lawyer said, "It is a relief to see that so many of you could avail yourself of the invitation I extended to be here this morning, in accordance with Corinne Blakely's expressed wishes. There appear to be quite a few people here whom I did not invite and who are not mentioned in the will. . . ." He scanned the room with a disapproving gaze.

I squirmed as his eyes seemed to linger on me. Was he going to kick me out?

"But we shall get on with it, regardless."

A communal exhalation told me I wasn't the only noninvitee here.

"For those of you who don't know me, I am Jonathan Goudge, and I had the honor of Mrs. Blakely's trust and confidence for nearly half a century. It is my privilege to carry out the last task she entrusted to me, the reading of her will and the distribution of her assets."

Goudge had a sonorous voice that almost put me to sleep as he read through the opening paragraphs of legal mumbo jumbo in a measured way. Corinne seemed to have left mementos—a letter opener, a brooch, a sterling tea set, and the like—to many, many people. Some recipients teared up, some frowned, and some left the conference room after their inheritances were announced. Lavinia Fremont started to sob when the lawyer read that she was to receive all of Corinne Blakely's clothes, including a collection of vintage evening wear and competition gowns, plus one hundred thousand dollars to preserve and display the gowns as she saw fit. The bequest was "in memory of the friendship that has meant more to me than any other during my life." I shivered at the naked loss on Lavinia's face and said a prayer of thanks for my sister, who was my dearest friend. Lavinia rose, with the help of the man behind her, and made her way out of the room, face buried in the handkerchief Mrs. Laughlin had handed her.

The lawyer paused momentarily in his reading, until

Lavinia had cleared the door and attention returned to him, and then read that Mrs. Laughlin was to receive a pension from the estate for the duration of her life, and was to be allowed to select such mementos as she pleased from the house where she had served so long, excepting only those items specifically left to other people.

Turner Blakely jerked his head up. "Anything she wants?"

Leveling a reproving look at Turner over the top of his glasses, the lawyer reiterated, "'Any such mementos as she pleases.'"

"A memento would be something small, right? Something valued under, say, a hundred bucks?" Turner refused to give up, and seemed unaware of the disgusted looks aimed his way.

"The term 'memento' has no specific definition as to size or value," Goudge said.

I grinned inwardly, thinking of the items Mrs. Laughlin had already spirited from the house. She hadn't been greedy; she'd selected things for their sentimental value, not their money value. I smiled at her and she lowered her right eyelid in the suggestion of a wink as Turner subsided into sulky silence.

Maurice gripped my arm tightly when the lawyer began. "'And to my former husbands, I bequeath . . .'"

I stood up straighter, feeling Lyle come to attention, too.

"'To Baron Klaus von Heffner, my sixth husband, I leave my collection of classical albums, because music soothes the savage beast.'"

A few titters rose from the crowd and I arched my brows at Maurice in a "what does that mean?" way. He shrugged, looking as puzzled as I was.

"'To Jeffrey Washington, my fifth husband and dear

friend, I leave the 1953 Packard Caribbean, in memory of our road trips.'"

A good-looking African-American man who seemed to be in his early fifties smiled and raised a hand. "Thank you, Coco, wherever you are," he said. "We had some good times."

"He looks a lot younger than Corinne," I whispered to Maurice.

"Her husbands got successively younger," he said. "I believe there was a twenty-two-year gap between Corinne and Washington."

The lawyer continued, his voice a bit louder, to be heard over the hum of low-voiced conversations. "'And to my fourth husband, Hamish MacLeod, I leave five thousand dollars with the hope that he will spend it on tulip bulbs to replenish the earth's supply of tulips, since he lavished so many of them on me.'"

The thin man at the table stiffened. Was Corinne making fun of him or thanking him? I wondered. Mac-Leod seemed equally uncertain as he pressed his lips into a thin line, shoved his chair back from the table, smacking into the knees of the people standing behind him, and lurched to his feet. "I was intended by God as Corinne's only true husband," he said with a soft Scottish burr. His gaze swept the room as if daring anyone to dispute it. The man and woman sitting on either side of him inched their chairs away. "What God has joined together, let no man put asunder."

"Didn't he realize several men had already been sundered from Corinne before he married her?" I asked in a low voice.

Maurice snorted and, when he got control of himself, said, "He's a minister, originally from Edinburgh. He relocated to California years ago, and Corinne met him when he officiated at a friend's wedding."

"That was the end of me," Lyle put in, unabashed about eavesdropping and apparently bearing Corinne no ill will for dumping him for the skeletal pastor. "She took one look at him and wham! Of course, he had a bit more meat on him back then. Looks like he's been starving himself since Corinne left him."

I was about to reply when I noticed a latecomer sidle through the door to stand against the wall, slightly behind Mr. Goudge. Detective Lissy! *Uh-oh.* What was he doing here?

MacLeod sank back into his seat, the crowd quieted again, and Goudge resumed reading. Corinne had left Lyle a share in a country club, news he greeted with a fist pump. "That's my gal!" Beaming, he said good-bye to Maurice and me, then scooted out the door in a flash of salmon and raspberry.

As the lawyer intoned, "'And to my second husband, Maurice Goldberg . . .'" I looked at Lissy. He stood yardstick straight, too-red lips pressed together, something in his bearing making me think of a cat about to pounce on an unsuspecting mouse.

"'. . . I give the Andy Warhol portrait of myself. He knows why.'"

"Ah, Rinny." Maurice sighed, so quietly I don't think anyone heard him but me. He was looking toward the front of the room, but I got the feeling he was seeing something from long ago.

Turner Blakely whipped around, searching the room for Maurice. When his gaze landed on him, he blurted, "That painting's worth millions! It should be part of my inheritance."

Jonathan Goudge put a hand on Turner's shoulder. "Mr. Blakely, please." His tone told me he wasn't very fond of Corinne's grandson.

The young man angrily shrugged the hand away. "Isn't it the law that you can't profit as a result of murdering someone, or something like that? Then Goldberg can't have the painting, since he killed Cor— my grandma. The police arrested him! That would be profiting from murder."

By now, every eye in the place was fixed on Maurice, and you could have heard a piece of swan's down land on the polished tabletop. Maurice had stiffened beside me, and although I ached to proclaim his innocence loudly, I knew I'd just be drawing more unwanted attention to us. Help came from a completely unexpected quarter.

"Mr. Blakely." Detective Lissy's voice, dry and pedantic, broke into the silence. "I have a few questions for you about last weekend, when you're done here." Lissy eased his jacket aside to reveal the badge hooked over his belt, and a couple of gasps erupted from the crowd. Lissy's gray eyes met Turner's bloodshot ones for a moment. Interesting. Even though Detective Lissy had been happy to arrest Maurice, it seemed like he wasn't young Mr. Turner Blakely's greatest fan either. That made me feel marginally more positive about Lissy. The assembled inheritors began murmuring, and heads bobbed from Lissy to Turner to Maurice, like they were watching a three-way tennis match.

"What the hell . . . ?" Turner's neck flushed red.

Goudge interrupted him to finish reading the will. The gist of the remaining pages was that Turner Blakely inherited everything that hadn't already been given to someone else, with the proviso that he take care of his father,

Corinne's son, Randolph. "The rest of this is mere legalese," Goudge said with the smile of one who is proud of his legalese. He flapped the pages. "My firm will be sending notifications to each of you, and the inheritors who could not be present, to inform you of when and how your inheritances will be made available." He bestowed a slight smile on the room and walked with a stately step to the door, acting like all his will readings were attended by accusations of murder. Maybe they were.

"Let's get out of here," Maurice muttered, breaking for the door. I followed in his wake, feeling some trepidation when Detective Lissy moved to intercept us as soon as we exited the conference room.

"Congratulations on your inheritance, Mr. Goldberg," Lissy said with a tight smile. "Or maybe not. I'd say a multimillion-dollar painting supplies the one thing missing from our case against you: motive."

"He had no idea she was leaving him anything more than a memento," I said, the good feelings I'd been having about him since he put Turner Blakely in his place evaporating instantly.

"And you know this how?" Lissy asked. "Because he told you so?" He whisked his jacket-covered forearm over the face of his watch to polish it.

"Anastasia." Maurice put a calming hand on my shoulder. "I've got a booth at a bridal fair to man," he told Lissy. "If you'd like to chat, give my lawyer a call to set up an appointment." With a quick kiss on my cheek, he walked off, leaving me facing Detective Lissy.

I took advantage of the moment. "Did you get the outline from the literary agent?" I asked.

"Not yet," Lissy said. "The agent is insisting on a court order." His gaze lingered on Turner Blakely, who was one of the last people out of the conference room.

"You can tell he's got a temper," I said, "and he seems desperate to get his hands on every penny of Corinne's estate."

"Is that your idea of subtlety, Miss Graysin?" Lissy asked, returning his gaze to my face.

It was, actually. "You must have your suspicions, too," I said, "since you're here to interrogate him."

"On a totally different matter from the murder," Lissy said crushingly. "I'm satisfied we arrested the right man for that. And the bequest he received today is just one more nail in his coffin. Excuse me." He walked away, headed for Turner Blakely.

I wished I could overhear what the two men were talking about, but my watch told me I was going to be late for the salsa class if I didn't hustle, so I trotted to the door and down the stairs fronting the gracious Georgian home that served as the law firm's offices to my car.

The rest of the day passed quickly as I taught the salsa class (a popular one, since several nightclubs in the area catered to salsa enthusiasts), conducted private lessons with a couple of clients getting ready for a competition, and practiced with Vitaly for an exhibition for members of the Olympic committee and the public to promote ballroom dancing as an Olympic sport. We, along with other prominent members of the DanceSport community, were participating in the exhibition and luncheon on Monday. Corinne had organized it, I remembered sadly.

While we danced, Vitaly tried hard to talk me into adopting a rescued puppy. He and his partner, John, volunteered with an anti–puppy mill organization.

"John and I is adopted a boxer puppy," he said, dipping me low as we rumbaed. "We is naming her Lulu."

"Cute." I spun out and leaned away from him at an acute angle as he held my hand and braced me.

"Her littering mates needs homes, too," he hinted.

Stroking my hand down his face in a simulated caress, I said, "No. I can't take care of a puppy. I'm too busy. I travel too much. It wouldn't be fair to the dog."

He sighed and released me as the music ended. "If you are knowing anyone who would liking a puppy . . ."

"I'll point them toward you," I promised, turning off the stereo system. I turned and caught him smiling at himself in the mirror to admire his teeth. His grin widened when he saw me watching him. "Oh," I said, "I talked to a photographer who would be willing to do some publicity shots for us. Is that okay with you?"

"*Da*. We is needing." He tugged a Johns Hopkins sweatshirt over his head.

"Her name is Sarah Lewis. She's Marco Ingelido's niece."

Vitaly curled his lip. "I hope she is being better photographer than he is dancer."

I merely hoped she'd be able to shed a little light on her uncle's attitude toward Corinne and the publication of her memoir.

Chapter 16

Danielle and I arrived at the Alexandria dock at Union and Cameron streets, just north of the Torpedo Factory, minutes before the *Plantation Queen* was due to sail with the Willow House party aboard. I'd dithered about whom to take with me, considering Tav before deciding that he might think I was asking him for a date, which, of course, I wouldn't have been, since our relationship was strictly business and my urge to dance with him stemmed solely from my belief that he should know how to dance if he was part owner of a ballroom studio, and not because I liked the feeling that tingled through me when he took me in his arms, and the way he smelled, and . . . I stopped my unruly brain and thought about asking Vitaly, who would be fun to have around for the dancing, and even Mom, because we didn't do too much together these days. I finally decided to ask Danielle whether she'd go with me, because I knew she'd get a kick out of doing a little sleuthing on Maurice's behalf, and because, well, seeing Lavinia's tears over Corinne's death made me think I ought to spend a little more time with my sister and best friend.

Danielle had enthusiastically agreed, explaining that Coop was giving chess lessons that evening to some local middle-schoolers and she was at loose ends. She rang the doorbell as I was spritzing on a light floral perfume. I wore a frothy cocktail dress with a tight bodice and floaty skirt that came to midthigh. My Grecian-look gold sandals perfectly set off the swirls of white, peach, and gold in the fabric, and my hair bounced loose against my shoulders. I opened the door to Danielle, who had on a staid navy blue dress with a cropped jacket and matching navy blue pumps.

"You've got to lose the jacket," I said the moment I set eyes on her. What I really wanted to say was, *You look like you're going to a funeral*, but I bit my tongue, figuring she wouldn't take it well. "And I've got some shoes you can borrow that don't look like they came out of Great-aunt Laurinda's closet."

"My outfit is perfectly—"

"No, it isn't." I dragged her in, pushed her down on the sofa, which let out a poof of dust, and ran to my room for a pair of high-heeled silver peep-toes with rosettes. While there, I grabbed two long strands of silver set with sparkly crystals. Danielle had shed the jacket by the time I came back, revealing spaghetti straps that showed off her toned arms and lovely neck.

"Here." I thrust the necklaces at her and crouched to slip the sandals on her feet. "Voilà! Cinderella," I said, stepping back to survey the effect. She wore her red hair twisted into a loose chignon and it looked dramatic against the navy and silver of her dress and jewelry. "And we didn't even need a fairy godmother."

"Hmph," Danielle said, but she crossed to the full-length mirror in the hallway and surveyed her reflection with a pleased smile.

We walked the few blocks to the waterfront, slightly hobbled by our impractically high heels on the uneven brick sidewalks, to find the boarding process almost complete. The *Plantation Queen* rode low in the water, three stories—or decks, I guessed—of pale blue accented with lacy white ironwork along the decks. Enclosed cabins with large windows on three sides took up most of the space on the lower and middle decks, but the top deck was an open observation platform only partially shaded by an awning. Twin smokestacks rose from the upper deck, flaring at the top. A huge red paddle wheel dripped water at the stern, with two gulls perched on one of the unmoving slats. A young man in a jaunty sailor outfit that looked more like a costume than serious naval attire took our tickets with a smile. "Come aboard. You almost missed the boat, ladies, and that would have been a shame."

His admiring gaze traveled over both of us, but lingered on Danielle. Tossing cheap Mardi Gras beads over our heads, he offered each of us a hand up the unsteady metal gangway. Four feet wide, it was about fifteen feet long, with a corrugated sort of surface designed to prevent slipping, but not ideal for stiletto heels. My heel caught in one of the indentions, and the crewman saved me from falling by grabbing my upper arm. I thanked him, he smiled, and we made it safely up the rest of the gentle incline to the lowest deck. The paddle wheel began to churn moments after we were aboard, and the *Plantation Queen* slid away from the dock toward the center of the Potomac.

Laughter drifted from all the decks, and waiters circulated with trays of champagne. Dani and I each snagged a glass and wandered toward a stairway, or whatever you call it on a boat, to climb to the upper level, where a trio conjured up images of Bourbon Street on a saxophone, trumpet, and clarinet. Well-dressed men and women laughed and flirted and talked as the late-afternoon breeze stirred artfully casual hair and sheer silk and chiffon dresses. Actually, the breeze was turning to windy gusts, and several women had to hold their dresses down.

"The beautiful people," Dani whispered.

"This is the life," I agreed, turning my face up to the sun and letting the wind sift through my hair. Taking a sip of the champagne, I held it in my mouth a moment, letting the bubbles tickle my tongue, before swallowing. I closed my eyes and felt, rather than saw, the sun disappear behind some clouds.

"So which woman is this Greta person?" Dani asked, always more task-focused than I.

Reluctantly, I opened my eyes and scanned the crowd. "That one," I guessed, pointing discreetly to a woman who was a little too blond, in a mint silk sheath that was a little too tight, and who was working a little too hard at being vivacious and charming. Rings glittered on her gesturing hands, and her unlined face testified to the skills of a good plastic surgeon, making it hard to guess her age. She held herself gracefully erect with a dancer's posture, though, which made me think she might be Greta Monk. I was sure of it when she moved on to another clump of partiers, greeting them like a hostess and exchanging small talk for a few moments before stepping aside to consult with a man wearing a chef's toque.

"So, what's the plan?" Danielle asked. "Cruise up to her and ask whether she poisoned Corinne Blakely?"

"I think something less . . . 'in your face' would work better," I said, nibbling at the cuticle on my index finger.

"Great." Danielle looked at me expectantly.

"I haven't come up with anything yet," I admitted,

tracking Greta Monk as she moved toward the stairwell. She began to descend.

"Well, we need a plan," Danielle said, brows twitching together. "We could—"

"I think I'll wing it." I thrust my glass at Danielle and hurried to catch up with Greta, brushing against a middle-aged waiter and making him bobble a tray of full champagne glasses. "I'm so sorry," I said, catching the rim of the tray so it didn't tip. I craned my neck to see around him, but Greta had disappeared.

"No problem, miss," he said with a tired smile that said he'd rather be home watching *Everybody Loves Raymond* reruns than dodging tipsy passengers on a paddleboat.

"I'm not drunk," I assured him.

He gave me a "yeah, right" look and stepped aside so I could slip by him. I descended the stairs as quickly as possible, given my four-inch heels, and paused at the bottom, scanning the crowd for Greta. The paddleboat was lurching a bit now as the stiff winds kicked up some whitecaps, and I spread my legs wider to keep my balance. I didn't spot Greta, but my eyes lit on a photographer snapping a smiling foursome against the rail, and I recognized Sarah Lewis. Hm, that woman got around. She turned and saw me as Danielle emerged from the stairwell and thrust my champagne glass at me.

"Lost her, huh?" Dani said at the same time Sarah Lewis, after a brief hesitation while she dredged up my name, said, "Stacy, right?"

"Hi, Sarah," I said, momentarily giving up my search for Greta. "Done with the bridal fair? Oh, this is my sister, Danielle Graysin. Dani, this is Sarah Lewis. She's a photographer."

They made "nice to meet you" noises before Sarah

answered my question. "You know what they say: A paying gig in the hand is worth more than potential wedding contracts in the bush." Sarah shrugged. "I left some brochures on my table at the bridal fair." She gestured with her camera, an expensive-looking model with a fat lens that didn't bear much resemblance to my seventy-dollar point-and-shoot camera. "Let me get a picture of the two of you. They'll be for sale when we dock—all profits to benefit the women's shelter."

Danielle and I obligingly moved to the rail and leaned our heads together, smiling when Sarah said, "Say, 'Support your local battered women's home.' Great. Gotta go photograph some more donors. I'll catch you later." She moved off, khaki vest and sensible deck shoes contrasting with the colorful, less practical garb of most of the female guests. I explained to Dani who she was.

"Kinda weird to run into her again, don't you think?" she said.

"I don't know. She's a photographer. Her uncle's got connections and undoubtedly knows Greta Monk, who probably hired her. I don't think it's all that strange."

"Hmph." Dani sounded unconvinced. She stood on tiptoe to peer over my shoulder. "Look, there goes Greta." I whirled to see the event organizer chatting with a couple in front of her as she stood in line at a buffet table near the opposite railing.

"Come on." I maneuvered through the crowd and snatched up a chilled plate from the buffet table, filling it randomly as I worked my way toward Greta Monk, who had exactly two shrimp and a celery stick on her plate. She was still chatting with the older couple when I came up behind her.

"Isn't this a lovely party, Dani?" I said loudly to my

sister, who cringed in embarrassment. "So well organized!"

Greta turned with a smile stretching her thin lips. Her taut skin made it difficult to place her age—anywhere from fifty to seventy, I'd guess. "Why, thank you," she said. "I'm Greta Monk, and I put this party together for Willow House. Such a worthwhile cause."

"Why, my goodness." I put a theatrical hand to my heart. "Greta Monk. Corinne Blakely was talking about you just the other day. Isn't it a shame what happened to her? Maurice Goldberg was just too broken up to attend tonight, so he gave me and my sister their tickets." I gestured Dani forward, and she gave Greta a smile while shooting me a look that promised retribution.

"Really?" Greta's smile faltered slightly at the mention of Corinne. "And you are . . . ?"

"Oh, where are my manners?" I didn't know why I'd adopted the persona of a dithering Southern belle; it must have been the power of suggestion emanating from the gracious old boat, or the Dixieland music filtering from the cabin. "I'm Stacy Graysin, and this is my sister, Danielle. I own a ballroom dance studio."

"Pleased to meet you," Greta said automatically, looking anything but. "Did you say Corinne mentioned me? In a good way, I hope." She forced a chuckle, but the nervous look in her eyes told me she was anxious to know what Corinne had been saying.

"Oh, of *course*," I reassured her. "Something about how you're going to be on the Kennedy Center board of trustees, and a dance scholarship fund. I didn't really catch it all, but if the scholarships are merit-based, I've got a student or two who might qualify."

Greta pressed a napkin to her lips. "There's no . . . That was a long time ago. I don't know why Corinne . . ."

Composing herself, she said, "Corinne and I administered a fund years ago—*years* ago. I don't know why she'd bring it up now. Who was she talking to?"

"That's too bad," I said, ignoring her question. "About the scholarships, I mean. And about Corinne."

"Hideous," Greta agreed. "Corinne and I were like sisters. When I heard the news . . ." She shuddered. A fat pink shrimp slid off her plate and splotched her dress before dropping to the deck. "Oh!" She rubbed at the spot with her napkin, looking far more upset than the slight mark deserved.

"But isn't it wonderful that her book will still be published?" I said brightly. "She lived the early days of ballroom dance competition in America, and it would be such a shame if her memories were lost forever!"

"What?" Greta's plate fell and shattered on the deck. A passing server swooped in to begin picking up the shards.

Inspiration struck and I babbled on. "I'm really looking forward to reading the manuscript."

"How did you—"

"Corinne was worried that someone was out to steal the manuscript—wasn't that silly? But you know how she is. Was. So she gave it to Maurice Goldberg for safekeeping. She and Maurice have known each other for*ever*, you know. Anyway, he gave it to me to take to the publisher in New York when I go up next week for an . . . an appointment. He didn't want to risk losing it in the mail." The lies were stacking up, and I counted on Greta's being too much distressed at the news that the manuscript had survived Corinne to scrutinize my story too closely.

Danielle gave me a narrow-eyed gaze that said she thought I was insane. I ignored her.

"Where— What are you . . ." Greta started. "I'd be interested in—"

"Everything okay, Greta?" A powerfully built man in his mid- to late sixties with crew-cut gray hair had come up behind Greta Monk. He was only a couple of inches taller than she was, and was too stocky to look elegant in the off-white linen suit he wore with the jacket unbuttoned to show a shirt that matched Greta's dress. He slipped an arm around her shoulders, giving me and Dani an inquiring look from hard eyes.

"Oh, Conrad. No, nothing's wrong, except I dropped my plate. So clumsy of me. Excuse me; I've got to wash this off." She slipped out from under his encircling arm and hurried to the cabin door, which was propped open by an urn brimming with begonias.

Conrad Monk nodded brusquely and followed his wife.

Controlling herself until the pair was out of earshot, Danielle rounded on me. "Have you lost your friggin' mind? What was that all about?"

I wasn't sure myself. I'd gone with the impulse of the moment, as I was all too prone to do. "I thought Greta might let something slip if she thought the manuscript was still around. If her husband hadn't come up—"

"Did it slip your mind that the last person to have that manuscript got murdered?"

It had, actually. Not that I'd forgotten Corinne was dead, but I hadn't put two and two together. "We don't know she was killed because of the memoir," I said.

Danielle snorted.

"We don't. Maybe her son or her charming grandson offed her for the money. That's a much stronger motive, actually." I finished my champagne.

"Well," Danielle said after a moment, calming down

a bit, "if you wanted to make Greta nervous, I think you succeeded. The moment you mentioned the scholarship fund, she turned green."

The pitching of the boat in ever-building waves was making me feel a bit green. "Maybe she was worried about the weather." I nodded toward the dark clouds piling up against the western horizon. "I think her beautifully organized fund-raiser is about to get rained out."

On the words, the clouds spit a few raindrops at us. People descended from the upper deck, practically tumbling over one another as they came down the ladder and sought shelter in the glassed-in cabin area. A jagged blast of lightning zinged across the sky, and Danielle grabbed my arm. "Let's get inside."

Hurrying across the deck, I felt the boat slow and begin to turn. Moments later, an announcement sounded over a crackly public address system. "Ladies and gentlemen, we are sorry, but we must curtail today's cruise and return to the dock." The phrasing sounded like Greta Monk's, but the broadcast was so staticky I couldn't tell whether the speaker was male or female. Danielle and I crammed ourselves into the cabin area, which smelled like too many damp people crowded into too small a space. Only a lucky few had seats. An elderly couple sat holding hands on the far side of the room, orange life jackets strapped around their party attire. Most people seemed unfazed by the choppy water and the lightning, laughing and chatting as they tried to keep drinks from sloshing over whenever the boat lurched unexpectedly. A summer squall on the Potomac didn't carry the same panic factor for boats as a hurricane in the Atlantic.

"I'm going to get more champagne," Danielle said, eyes scanning the crowded room for a server. She must have spotted one, because she'd moved off before I could tell her I didn't want any.

Truth to tell, my stomach was lurching a bit with the boat's wallowing motion, and I was a teensy bit worried that the champagne I'd already drunk would reappear. My head began to throb from the heavy scents of perfumes, shrimp, and cigars in the moist air, and the overly loud jazz emanating from the brass trio that had been playing on the observation deck, but who had also sought refuge in the cabin. If I had to stay cooped up in here a moment longer, I was going to throw up. Two long strides brought me to the door, and I was through it in a heartbeat, taking in great gulps of fresh air.

I felt better almost immediately and found that the rain wasn't coming down hard enough to bother me. The misty wetness actually felt good on my bare arms and face, although I didn't imagine it was improving my dress any. Sheltered by the cabin's slight overhang, I noted that I wasn't the only one who preferred the elements to the crowded cabin. A couple huddled together against the far railing, holding the man's jacket above them to keep off the rain. A solitary man stood at the bow, looking toward the fast-approaching dock. Another announcement crackled over the PA system; I thought it might have something to do with disembarking.

With my stomach settling, I drifted toward the stern, drawn by the rhythmic slap of the paddle wheel slats against the water. As I approached the edge of the cabin I heard voices, low-pitched, apparently arguing. I slowed, not wanting to interrupt. Whoever the speakers were, they must be pressed up against the back of the cabin, the only wall that wasn't glass, just around the corner from where I now stood. I was about to back away, allowing them their privacy, when I heard a single word: "Corinne."

I stiffened. It was a man's voice, but I didn't recognize it. An unintelligible murmur followed, and I found myself creeping closer to the end of the cabin, hoping they wouldn't come around the corner to find me flattened against the wall, eavesdropping. The wind died for a second and I heard a woman's voice. Greta?

"... don't know. Corinne never—"

The man's voice cut her off. "We can ... Turner won't—"

Frustrated by catching only snippets of the conversation, I inched farther along the wall, just as the boat turned, plunging a bit as it came crosswise to the waves. It jolted me against the wall with a solid thud. Knowing the whispering couple must have heard the bump, I decided to reveal myself before they came looking for me. I'd brazen it out and act like I was just out for fresh air, attracted by the paddle wheel, which, I realized, had the merit of being true. I straightened my spine and stepped forward, glancing casually over my shoulder as I passed the end of the cabin, hoping to see the whispering pair.

No one huddled against the back wall. Realizing they must have gone around the far side of the cabin, I spun on my heel and slipped on the wet deck. One knee smacked into the deck, and I let out an exclamation of combined pain and frustration. By the time I regained my footing and limped around the cabin, there was no one in sight. A seagull perched on the flat roof fluffed his feathers and cocked his head at me. "*Ki-yi-yi*," he jeered.

"Oh, stuff it," I said.

The *Plantation Queen* had maneuvered into the small harbor area by now, and revelers began to stream from the cabin as the captain brought the boat alongside the dock. I looked for Danielle, but didn't see her in the press of people. I'd meet up with her on the dock, I decided. It seemed like half an hour, but was really only ten minutes or so before the crew secured the boat against the dock so it bumped against tires, and maneuvered the gangway into place. Despite crew members urging people to descend the gangway slowly, to watch their step, the crowd surged forward like teenage girls pushing into a Taylor Swift concert where the seating was up for grabs.

I moved forward with the crowd, going with the flow. I was on the outer edge of the gangway, watching my feet to make sure my heels didn't catch as they had when I boarded. So I didn't see whose elbow jabbed me in the side, knocking me off balance so that I teetered for a moment on the edge of the plank before plunging into the murky Potomac.

Chapter 17

I barely had time to snatch a breath before I splatted into the water, fanny-first. The scummy water closed over my head. I kicked hard for the surface and felt one sandal drift away. *Damn*, I thought, as my head popped out of the water and I took a breath. I liked those sandals. Excited voices called from the gangway, the boat, and the dock, and a waving array of hands reached down to me. Oil slicked the water with rainbow colors, and fast-food wrappers, cigarette butts, and other trash floated around me. The ick factor outweighed any fear of drowning. I could swim and I was only feet from the shore . . . it wasn't like I was in danger, except maybe from the hull of the *Plantation Queen*, which loomed a little too close for comfort.

Taking two strokes toward the dock, I reached up and grabbed for a helping hand at random, feeling a strong hand close over mine. A second man grasped my other arm and the two hauled me straight up from the water until my torso fell over the dock. I suspected I looked more like a half-drowned muskrat than a seductive mermaid as I sat up and slicked soggy hair off my face. "Thanks," I gasped.

A bearded crew member, the braid on his sleeve suggesting he might be the captain, hurried over. "Are you all right, miss?"

"Fine," I said, "although I've lost a shoe."

He gave my remaining sandal a disapproving look. "Those heels are dangerous. Not suitable for boating. It's not surprising that you tripped."

From my dock-level perspective, I had a great view of a lot of feet, and almost all the women wore shoes just as impractical as mine. I shot the captain a look and got to my feet, pulling off my sandal so I stood barefoot on the dock. I thought about telling him that I hadn't tripped, that I'd been pushed, but thought better of it. I'd sound like a crazy lady. There was no way I could prove someone deliberately knocked me into the water, and I had no clue who it was anyway. I accepted the towel someone handed me and wrung out my hair before draping the fluffy white cotton around my shoulders.

"Stacy!" Danielle skidded to a halt beside me. "I was still on the boat. . . . I saw you fall. Are you okay?" Her pretty features twisted with worry and she hugged me, disregarding my soggy state. "Your dress!"

I looked down at the sodden silk clinging to my curves. "I think it's a goner."

"Come on. Let's get you home."

The captain, probably relieved that I hadn't uttered any of the words small-business owners most dread— "sue," "fault," or "lawyer"—gave me a smile and promised me a free trip on the *Plantation Queen* anytime I wanted. I thanked him and looked around at the diminished crowd as Danielle dragged me away. I didn't recognize anyone. Whoever had pushed me was long gone.

The rain had quit as suddenly as it started, and the sun had reappeared, turning the puddles and soaked earth into a soil-scented steam bath. Danielle signaled for a taxi, but I told her I'd rather walk. She gave in after a brief argument and we started back toward my house. I carried the lone sandal in one hand and left a trail of drips all the way home. The sidewalk's warm bricks felt good against my bare feet.

"You might need a tetanus shot," Danielle said as I unlocked my front door. "There's no telling what was in that water."

"They gave me one when I got shot," I said, stripping to bra and undies in the foyer so I wouldn't drip all over the hardwood floors. The scar on my left arm was still livid and I ran my fingers over it, remembering the terror I'd felt when facing a murderer with a gun. Danielle fetched a garbage bag and I reluctantly balled the dress up and stuffed it in. "I liked that dress," I said.

"How did you slip, anyway?"

I headed for my bedroom and a warm shower, Dani trailing me. "Someone pushed me."

"What!" Danielle settled on the bed while I disappeared into the bathroom, stripped, and got in the shower.

Warm water sluiced over me, washing away the film left by the murky Potomac. "I said someone pushed me," I yelled over the water's pounding.

"Are you sure? There were a lot of people trying to get down the gangplank at the same time. Maybe someone bumped you by accident."

I stayed silent, ninety percent sure the elbow in my ribs had been deliberate. After a moment, Danielle continued, "Well, if it wasn't an accident, who was it?"

I'd given that some thought on the walk home. "Greta or Conrad Monk," I suggested, "or Sarah Lewis. I don't think I knew anyone else on the boat." Getting out of the shower, I turbaned my hair in a towel and wrapped another one around myself. I walked into the bedroom.

"I knew you shouldn't have made up that story about having the manuscript," Danielle said with gloomy "I told you so" satisfaction. "Someone's already trying to bump you off."

"Oh, please. No one tried to kill me. There were dozens of people around and the water wasn't that deep and I was six inches from the dock. If someone had wanted to kill me, he or she would've done better to toss me off the boat in the middle of the Potomac and hope I couldn't swim."

Danielle's silence conceded my point. Ducking into the closet, I got dressed and reappeared in shorts and a T-shirt. "What are you going to do now?" Dani asked.

"Dry my hair."

She threw a pillow at me. "Then what?"

"I don't know." I'd had enough investigating for the day, to tell the truth. I changed the subject. "Have you thought any more about Mom's invitation? I told her I'd go."

Danielle looked at me as if I'd volunteered to be part of a firing squad tasked with shooting her.

"Mom really wants you to come, too," I coaxed. "We'll have a good time. Don't you remember what fun we had shell collecting? And how we got up in the middle of the night to watch the sea turtles hatch and make a dash for the ocean?"

"I remember *Dad* waking us and walking us down to the beach. He let me carry the flashlight."

"Mom was there, too. She tried to scare away the herons eating the baby turtles by waving her arms and singing that Jim Croce song."

"'Bad, Bad Leroy Brown.'" An almost-smile lit Dani's face briefly. "It didn't even faze those herons."

I let the subject drop, not wanting to push too hard and have Dani decide she wasn't coming. Sometimes, not getting a "no" was progress.

Chapter 18

Sunday noon found me on the road to the Hopeful Morning Rehabilitation Center, Maurice seated beside me in my yellow Volkswagen Beetle. I'd called him mid-morning to see how his day at the bridal fair had gone, and we'd ended up discussing my unplanned dip in the Potomac and the murder. Visiting Randolph Blakely, Corinne's son, had been Maurice's idea. "She got together with him every Sunday for brunch," he said. "Maybe she said something to him the weekend before she died that would help us figure this out."

Accordingly, we were driving through Maryland horse country on our way to the rehab center, flashing past gently rolling hills and pastures featuring leggy Thoroughbreds. When Maurice told me to turn, I initially thought he'd made a mistake, because the property in front of us looked more like the home of a successful horse trainer than a medical facility of any kind. Stately trees lined the long driveway, and outbuildings and barns surrounded the sprawling brick house fronted with a wide veranda. I was about to ask Maurice whether he was sure we were in the right place when I spied a discreet sign almost enveloped by a honeysuckle bush that read, HOPEFUL MORNING REHABILITATION CENTER.

"Wow," I said, parking between a Mercedes and a BMW. "This is nicer than some resorts I've been to."

"Keeping Randolph here cost Corinne more than ten grand a month," Maurice said.

"Ouch. I guess they'll be sending their bills to Turner now."

The scents of honeysuckle and roses twined around us as we crossed the veranda. Bees buzzed lazily from flower to flower, and classical music drifted from a window above us. The facade of gracious living continued inside, with an Oriental rug on the marble-tiled floor and a crystal chandelier dangling from the ceiling. A young woman in khaki slacks and a black polo shirt with the center's name embroidered over her left breast directed us outside when we asked for Randolph Blakely. She pointed to a flagstone path that led away from a set of French doors opening off what looked like a dining room. "His quarters are down that path. First building on your right."

Maurice thanked her and we exited through the French doors. I realized as we walked that the buildings I'd thought were sheds were really little cottages. I had no knowledge of addiction treatment centers, other than what I'd learned from a thirteen-year-old ballet friend who'd been sent to a residential facility in Arizona when diagnosed with anorexia. "I guess the . . . patients aren't locked in?" I asked Maurice. I knew my friend had been strictly watched.

He shook his head. "Randolph's in a transitional program now, designed to help people who have undergone the initial detox and treatment phases. The transition program is supposed to help them adjust to living on their own and rejoining society. He can come and go as he wants, according to Corinne, but she said he hasn't set foot off this property in the ten months he's been here."

We knocked on the door of a blue bungalow that looked like something out of a Beatrix Potter book, complete with white shutters, white picket fence and gate, flowering shrubs, and nameplate on the door that said, HOLLYHOCK HAVEN. I just knew the other cottages had names like Rose Retreat and Sunflower Sanctuary.

"Gag me," I muttered as the door swung inward. "Too cutesy."

The man who stood in the doorway, a questioning look on his face, did not fit with the cottage. Instead of being plump and cheerful, he was heavy in a way that made me think of a burlap bag filled with wet cement, and had a waxy complexion that spoke of illness. Gray-blond strands of hair were combed straight back off a face lined beyond its fifty-some years. I saw little trace of Corinne or the handsome Turner in his features, although his eyes were the same intense blue. He'd shaved unevenly, and a quarter-sized patch of whiskers bristled to the right of his chin.

"Maurice?" Puzzlement and perhaps a bit of alarm flitted across his face. "What are you doing here?"

"Hello, Randolph," Maurice said. "It's been a while."

"Years." Corinne's son did not seem inclined to invite us in.

"I came to tell you how sorry I am about your mother. I didn't know if I'd see you at the funeral?"

"Who are you?" Randolph ignored Maurice and fastened his gaze on me.

"Stacy Graysin," I said, offering my hand. "I'm a ballroom dancer like your mom and a friend of Maurice's. I'm very sorry about your mother's death."

"I doubt you're like her," he said. His tone was ambiguous, and I wasn't sure whether he meant to slam Corinne or me. Looking from me to Maurice, he sighed. "I guess you can come in. I don't have anything to offer besides tea or water, though." He backed away so Maurice and I could slide past him.

The home's interior and decorations—heavy on chintz, doilies, embroidered pillows, and ruffled curtains—told me the place had come furnished. Only a flat-screen television and a laptop computer on an ottoman looked like they might belong to Randolph. He went ahead of us with the gingerly movements of a man in pain, and I remembered Maurice had said his painkiller addiction began when he injured his back. He led us into a kitchen so determinedly cheery that I expected a singing Snow White to pop out at any moment.

"Sit."

Maurice and I sat at the round oak table while Randolph filled a teapot and put it on the stove. Lowering himself into a chair, he said, "So, to what do I owe the honor?"

His tone and gaze were both sharper than when he'd opened the door, and I thought it wouldn't do to underestimate Randolph Blakely.

"How are you doing?" Maurice asked.

"Do you mean am I sober? Clean?" Randolph's gaze mocked Maurice, and I saw a little of Turner in the way his mouth curled up at one side. "Yes. If you mean am I grieving over my mother's death, then no, not particularly. She wasn't much of a mother." He said it matter-of-factly, and I found his lack of emotion somewhat eerie.

I saw Maurice fighting to control his reaction to the

slur on Corinne and jumped in with, "Have the police been out to see you?"

Randolph's gaze slid to me. "As a matter of fact, they have," he said, "although I'm not sure what business it is of yours."

"Um . . ."

Before I could think of a reply, Maurice said, "Did Corinne visit you as usual last Sunday?"

"She thought coming out here once a week made up for all the times she was gone when I was growing up." Grievance seeped from Randolph like gas from a sewer pipe.

I wanted to say, *You're fifty-plus years old; get over it already*, but I held my tongue. I thought I'd read somewhere that addicts had a habit of blaming others for their weaknesses. "Did she say anything about the memoir she was writing?" I asked.

The teakettle *shree*-ed and Randolph pushed himself up to remove it from the burner. "She was always going on about her precious manuscript," Randolph said, plunking a teabag into a mug and hefting the kettle in a silent question. Maurice and I shook our heads and he poured the steaming water, slopping some of it onto the counter. "She wanted my blessing on the chapters that dealt with me and my illness, as she called it."

"Did she show them to you?" Maurice asked. I shot him an approving look.

"Just talked about what she was going to write," Randolph said. "How she was too young when I was born, unprepared for motherhood. How when my father died she was 'cast adrift, emotionally untethered.' Those are the phrases she used. How she tried to provide me with loving stepfathers—of which you were the first," he told

Maurice, stirring a teaspoon of honey into his tea and rejoining us at the table. "Too bad she divorced you before I was old enough to remember you. Judging by the others, you were probably the best of the lot."

Wow, the acid bottled up in this man would etch granite. Maurice looked shell-shocked, so I asked, "Did she mention anything else about the book? What she might be saying about other people she knew?"

Randolph's eyes narrowed. "Wait a minute . . . are you saying you think she was killed because of something she wrote?"

Maurice and I exchanged glances but didn't say anything.

"That's rich." Randolph gave a phlegmy chuckle, like bubbling mud.

"You disagree?" I asked. "Several people seem nervous about what might have been in her book; one even broke into her house trying to get hold of the manuscript."

"Really?" He looked mildly interested. Downing half his tea, despite the fact that steam still curled from it, he licked his lips. "Who?"

I hesitated a moment, but then decided there was no harm in telling him. "Marco Ingelido. I guess he almost became one of your stepfathers."

He furrowed his brow, the wrinkles looking like grooves drawn in Play-Doh. "The guy who started the dance studio franchise? He was never one of Mother's 'special friends.'" He gave the last words a falsetto twist, and I could hear Corinne explaining her lovers to her young son as "Mommy's special friends."

"He said they were an item," Maurice put in, leaning forward so his forearms rested on the table.

"Absolutely not." Randolph shook his head. "Mother despised him, even before he opened those cheesy studios and 'dumbed down' ballroom dance, as she put it."

"Why?" I asked. Had Marco Ingelido lied to me for some reason, or was Randolph lying now? Or perhaps he wasn't as tuned in to his mother's love life as he thought he was.

"Who knows? Mother could hold a grudge like no one else." His fingers, strangely long and thin for his bulky build, tapped rhythmically against the mug.

Maurice shoved his chair back from the table as if wanting to distance himself from Corinne's son and his negative view of his mother. "If you don't think Corinne was murdered because of her memoir, who do you think did it?"

"That's easy." He looked down into his mug, but not before I caught the glint of malice in his eyes. "My only offspring, the fruit of my loins. Turner."

I gasped and I could tell my response pleased Randolph.

"You're accusing your own son?" Maurice asked, incredulous.

"One of the things they teach you in these sorts of places"—he waved a hand to indicate the greater Hopeful Morning Rehabilitation Center—"is to see clearly, to give up illusions and excuses and live honestly. Well, I've found it's easier to live honestly if one doesn't have to deal with one's family too often. Ergo, my present living arrangements." A wry smile twisted his lips. "Distance—physical and emotional—helps with honesty, too. I've had a clear-eyed view of Turner for some time now. I gave up on him the third time he was expelled for cheating."

"Corinne never gave up on you," Maurice said, anger and repulsion warring on his face.

"More fool she."

Ten seconds went by before I managed to say, "Do you have a particular reason for thinking Turner did it? Did he say something to you, do something suspicious?"

"I haven't seen or heard from him since I came to Hopeful Morning almost a year ago. I just know what he is. And I know Mother was concerned about his debt load and his lifestyle."

A lawn mower started up outside, its buzz cutting into the room. Glancing through the window on my right, I spotted a young woman watering potted begonias in the "haven" next door. She waved when she caught me looking, and I smiled in response. I wondered what addiction had brought her to Hopeful Morning. I'd suddenly had enough of the hopeless Randolph Blakely. I rose. Maurice jumped to his feet as if he'd been waiting for a signal to depart. When Randolph stayed seated, Maurice and I made for the front door to show ourselves out. As we walked under the arched doorway that led to the hall, Maurice turned back. "Where were you this past Tuesday?"

Randolph got up and put his mug in the sink. With his back to us, he said, "I didn't kill Mother." His voice was muffled and I wondered whether he was crying. But when he turned to face us, his eyes were clear. "I was here. I'm always here. I don't even have a car."

Unsatisfied and unsettled, I tugged at Maurice's hand and we left, shutting the door to Hollyhock Haven quietly behind us. I wondered whether we were closing Randolph in or closing the world out. It didn't matter. The woman from the cottage next door was watering flowers in the front yard, and she gave us a big smile. I saw she wasn't quite as young as she'd looked from the window—maybe in her mid-thirties. Fine, light brown hair wisped around her face, and she shoved it off her forehead with her wrist.

"It's so nice that Randolph's getting so many visitors these days," she said in a breathy voice, stepping closer to us and pouring water on a thirsty-looking rosebush. "For a long time, it was just his mom, on Sundays, but now it seems like every time I turn around he's got more folks stopping by. It's good to see him rejoining the world, as it were. So helpful with . . . well, you know . . . when you've got a good support group. I'm very lucky that my husband and my friends have all stuck by me." She paused, as if inviting us to ask about the reason for her presence at the rehab center. When Maurice dropped his gaze to the path and I just stared at her, completely unaware of the etiquette for these sorts of situations, she said, "I'm going home next week and I know everything's going to be fine. I'm going to be fine."

"Great," I said, a shade too heartily. "I'm sure Randolph will be fine, too, especially now that his friends are gathering around. Who all have you met?" Maurice winced almost imperceptibly beside me, and I wondered whether I was being too blatant, but the woman looked happy to gossip.

"Oh, I haven't *met* any of them, not if you mean been formally introduced. People here are cautious about 'boundaries,' you know." She made air quotes with her fingers, sloshing water out of her small watering pot, and twisted her face in a way that told us what she thought of boundaries. "But I figure the blond woman must be a girlfriend—although she wears a wedding ring. Naughty, naughty."

I exchanged a look with Maurice and he shrugged, clearly as clueless as I was.

"And the painfully skinny gentleman—his uncle, maybe? The man didn't look old enough to be Randy's father. Or I suppose he could be a friend or former business partner. They didn't really act like they were family, now that I think about it. Of course, some families are awfully stiff around one another, aren't they?" Her bright gaze invited us to agree with her.

I nodded. "When did you see them? Were they together?"

Maurice nudged me with his elbow, but I stood my ground, trying to figure out who the man and woman could be.

"Oh, I've never seen them together. The woman's been here a few times that I've noticed. I saw her last, oh, this past Monday? I've only seen the skinny man once, and that was Saturday. I remember because I was just coming back from therapy and Dr. Neston had told me he thought I was *ready*. Ready to leave, ready to rejoin my family." Her eyes lit up at the memory. "Well, I was so excited that I was skipping down the path, and I bumped right into the gentleman as he was coming through Randy's gate. I apologized, of course, and said something about what a beautiful day it was. He mumbled something about it being too hot—he had a lovely accent—and kept going."

A thin *beep-beep* sound cut through her recital. Setting down the watering pot, she tapped a button on her watch and said, "It was lovely talking to you, but I've got to go. Group!"

"Good luck with . . ." I wasn't sure what to wish her good luck with—returning home? Beating her addiction? I petered out awkwardly, but she seemed to know what I was saying and gave me a brilliant smile.

"Thanks."

The woman returned to the cottage and Maurice and I set off briskly down the path, not discussing the woman's revelations, me out of a completely unrealistic fear that Randolph would overhear us. Maurice, I suspected, because he was still embarrassed about the way I'd encouraged the woman to gossip. Maurice kept pace with me easily and we both breathed sighs of relief when we entered the air-conditioned cool of the main building. We saw no one as we crossed the foyer, exited through the front door, and climbed into my Beetle. Cranking up the engine and the AC, I reversed out of the parking lot and spun gravel from beneath the tires as I turned into the long driveway. I had to wait for a bus to pass before I could make the turn onto the main road.

The AC sucked up some of the bus's diesel exhaust and I coughed. A thought hit me. "Just because Randolph doesn't have a car doesn't mean he was stuck here in the boonies," I said, pointing at the bus.

"Too true, Anastasia," Maurice said. "And it crossed my mind that if Corinne visited him last Sunday as usual, he could have substituted the doctored pills for the ones in her purse without ever having to leave the grounds."

"You're right." I looked at him with respect. "Do you think he did it?"

Sadness weighed down Maurice's face. "There was certainly no love lost there," he said. "It has always distressed Corinne that she didn't have a better relationship with Randolph. I think that's partly why she went out of her way to help Turner, to be part of his life."

"Do you think Randolph knew about Corinne's will, or could he have expected to inherit her estate?"

"Corinne said she discussed it with him a couple of years back," Maurice said, rolling down his window to let fresh air and the scent of mown hay into the car. "She said he took the news well, seemed grateful even."

"Hm." I had doubts about how grateful anyone would be at hearing they *weren't* going to inherit tens of millions. A Machiavellian thought struck me. "Would he do it to help his son? Kill Corinne so Turner could inherit? He knew Turner needed money."

Maurice looked at me, aghast. "That's an awful thought, Anastasia."

"Who do you suppose his visitors were? Did you recognize the descriptions?"

"That woman was too nosy," Maurice said disapprovingly. "I don't know if we can trust anything she said."

"We've no reason not to," I pointed out. "I haven't got a clue about who the blond woman is, but it sounded to me like the skinny man with the accent might be that man at the will reading—"

"Hamish MacLeod." Maurice nodded.

"Why would Corinne's third husband—"

"Fourth."

"—be visiting Randolph?"

"I have no earthly idea," Maurice admitted. "Although it's possible that they had some sort of relationship. Randolph was still living at home—he must have been in his late teens—when Corinne married Hamish. He lasted longer than most of us, too; they were married for almost eighteen years, if I remember correctly."

We drove on in silence until we had almost reached Maurice's house. When I pulled to the curb, he reached over to squeeze my hand. "Thanks, Anastasia. It doesn't seem like we learned much, but I appreciate your help." He looked tired and beaten down, not his usual energetic, full-of-vim-and-vigor self. Grief and worry were taking a toll.

"Maybe we learned more than we realized," I said with a "keep your chin up" smile. As Maurice plodded toward his front door and I drove off, I vowed to look more closely at Turner Blakely. If his own father thought he was capable of murder, I wanted to learn more about how and why he'd moved in with his grandmother mere days before she died.

Chapter 19

Rather than drive home, I pointed the Beetle toward D.C. and Lavinia Fremont's shop. I needed to pick up the dress I was wearing for the Olympic exhibition tomorrow; she'd said it would be ready today. It being Sunday, I found a parking spot without too much trouble and passed a gaggle of well-dressed people emerging from the Baptist church a block from Lavinia's place. Some of the women wore hats decked with flowers or feathers or grosgrain ribbons, and I wondered idly why virtually no one wore hats anymore.

The shops around Lavinia's were quiet on a Sunday, and a "closed" sign hung on Lavinia's door. A sheath wedding gown in a rich cream had replaced the lavender ball gown in the window.

"Why did hats go out of fashion?" I asked Lavinia when she opened the shop's door to my knock. Her red hair was pulled back into a club of a ponytail, emphasizing the hollows under her eyes and her sharp nose, and she wore a sheer black blouse over a black cami and skinny cropped pants. I thought she looked more tired than she had on Thursday, and I wondered whether grief was causing her to lose sleep.

Her thin brows arched upward, but she said, "Because they take up too much room in the closet. Shoes and purses are bad enough, but hats meant hatboxes for storage, and even two or three of those boxes—pretty as they were—could eat up all your closet shelf space."

"I never thought of that."

She nodded. "I still have a couple of my favorites, but they're in a storage unit. Why do you ask?"

I explained, and she laughed, offering me a cup of herbal tea. I declined, saying I needed to get home, and she at once fetched my dress from the back. Unzipping the plastic cover, she revealed the luminous pink satin sparkling with rhinestones. "Did you want to try it again?"

I shook my head. "No. I trust you."

Smiling, she rezipped the bag and accepted my credit card. Swiping it, she asked, "How is Maurice? I hope the police are not still bothering him about . . . I saw you both yesterday at the lawyer's, and I meant to talk to Maurice, but after hearing about Corinne's bequest, I . . . well . . . I hope Maurice doesn't think I'm one of those who believe he could possibly . . ."

"I understand completely." I laid a sympathetic hand on her arm. "And I'm sure Maurice does, too. It's hard for him, as you can imagine, but he's got a really good lawyer. I've been talking to some people, too, hoping to uncover some information the police might have overlooked."

"You're a good friend, Stacy," Lavinia said. She gave me the receipt to sign. "It would be simply horrible if Maurice, or any innocent person, were convicted of murder."

"It's horrible enough just being a suspect," I said, speaking from experience. "But Maurice is holding up well. I'll tell him you were asking after him."

"Do that. Tell him I'd love it if he could drop by so we could catch up. It's been way too long." Her thin face lit up and I promised her I'd tell Maurice.

My cell phone rang when I was halfway home, and I answered it to hear my mother's voice. "I don't suppose you'd like to come for dinner and maybe a ride?" she asked with none of the "How are you doing?" preliminaries that she thinks waste so much time. As she sees it, if someone close to you wants you to know how they're doing, they'll mention it. You don't really care, Mom says, about how casual acquaintances are doing, so why ask?

I hadn't seen Mom in a couple of weeks, and an evening ride suddenly sounded like a fabulous idea. "I'd love to," I said. "Let me stop home to change and I'll come on out."

Mom's idea of proper riding attire is jodhpurs, but that's because she's into competitive dressage. I settled for a pair of jeans and low-heeled boots and drove to Mom's place in Aldie, Virginia, about a fifty-minute drive on a Sunday evening. Traffic and strip malls and overbuilding gradually gave way to housing areas with a little space between the homes, and then to tree-shaded pastures with grass so thick and green it looked like icing laid over the landscape with a trowel. Mom's house might be smack in the middle of horse country, but she didn't live on one of those multi-thousand-acre farms with miles of white fencing. Her place was small, a two-bedroom house on five acres with a fenced paddock, just enough room for her and her three horses: Carmelo, Kobe (a mare), and Bird. Mom's other passion, besides horses, is basketball. Her barn is bigger and has more amenities than her house, and I knew I'd find her there.

The barn, painted red with white trim, stood two hundred yards from the house. An old-fashioned water pump sprouted near the door, and from the shallow puddle of water underneath its spout, I deduced that Mom had recently filled a bucket to water the horses. I stepped inside, grateful for the barn's cool shade. The barn had a center aisle with three stalls on either side, only half of which were currently occupied. Bird, the twenty-two-year-old bay gelding I'd learned to ride on, whickered when I walked into the barn, and stuck his handsome bay head into the aisle. Mom emerged from the tack room on the far end, wiping her hands on a cloth. I gave her a quick hug and got a whiff of saddle soap. She endured the hug patiently—she's not much of one for physical affection—and waited while I patted Bird's neck.

"Let's have dinner first," Mom said, "so it'll be cooler for our ride." She led the way out of the barn to the house, moving with economy of motion and the slightly bowlegged gait earned from almost fifty years in a saddle. Her angular body still looked great in formfitting riding breeches. From behind, with her graying red hair covered by a riding helmet, you'd think she was thirty instead of in her mid-fifties.

Her house was simply furnished with an eclectic mix of pieces that I was pretty sure had come with the place. It suddenly struck me as interesting that both of us were living with someone else's furniture, with tables and chairs and beds that had been carefully chosen by other people. I wondered whether a happy young couple, newly married, had picked out the round oak table in Mom's kitchen that she had set for dinner with cream-colored place mats and terra-cotta-colored stoneware.

Had they eaten their first meal as a couple at this table? I shook off the fanciful imaginings and got myself a bottle of mineral water from the modern Whirlpool fridge Mom bought two years ago, when the one that came with the house gave up the ghost.

We both watch our weight carefully—Mom to be fair to her horses, and me to be fair to my dance partners—so dinner was grilled chicken breasts over a romaine-and-roasted-pepper salad. A spritz of balsamic vinegar served as dressing. We splurged on a single glass of white wine each, and Mom filled me in on the latest happenings on the professional dressage circuit. I told her about visiting Randolph Blakely at the rehab center. "It's a posh place," I said. "If I ever develop an addiction to something other than dancing, send me there, okay?"

"Do you think this Randolph had something to do with murdering his mother?" Mom asked, rising to clear our few dishes.

"I hope not," I said, "but it's a little odd that, according to his neighbor, he was apparently visited by one of Corinne's ex-husbands a few days before Corinne died. Of course, he—Hamish—didn't inherit much, and neither did Randolph."

"His son got all the money, right?"

I nodded. "Yes. Corinne's grandson, Turner. He's a piece of work. His dad thinks he did it."

Mom turned a shocked face toward me. "His own father accused him?"

"Well, not to his face, I don't think. He told Maurice and me that he figured Turner had poisoned Corinne for her money."

"That's awful. How could a father say that about his own son?"

I thought about the newspaper article I'd read earlier

in the day about a teenager killing his mother and father with a hammer, and didn't say anything. Sometimes one's children did horrifyingly awful things, and it was probably to Randolph's credit that he recognized that his son wasn't a saint. "I'm more interested in the mysterious blonde who visits him," I said.

"Why?"

Mom's blunt question made me think. "I guess," I said slowly, "it's because she's proof that there's more going on in Randolph's life than his mother or anyone knew about. They all think he's moldering away, practically a hermit, and yet this woman comes to see him. Whether she's a friend or a girlfriend or a Realtor, she's a connection with the outside world—outside Hopeful Morning, that is—that no one knew he had. I guess she makes me wonder what else he might be hiding. That's not fair." I stopped myself. "We don't know he was 'hiding' her. I guess I'm thinking that this is a case of 'still waters run deep,' or something of the sort."

"Very probably," Mom agreed. I could tell by her tone that she'd lost interest in Corinne's death and the search for her murderer. If there wasn't a horse in the story, it didn't hold Mom's attention for too long. I was used to that, so I followed her out to the stable with no hard feelings and saddled Bird, my fingers moving with the ease of long practice to slot the leather strap through the buckle, and lengthen the stirrups two notches.

We posted single file down a path that wandered through a patch of woods, and then emerged into an open pasture where we could ride side by side. Cantering on Bird, I felt myself truly relax for the first time in days, the wind sifting through my hair, the setting sun warming my face, the big, warm horse's body rocking me gently. We pulled up as we neared a stream and Mom came alongside me. "I don't suppose your sister's said anything about the trip to Georgia?"

She gave me a look out of the sides of her eyes, and I could tell that the trip was important to her, that she really wanted Danielle to come. I wanted to say she should talk to Danielle, but I knew that was unlikely to happen. Mom knew she'd burned bridges when she left us, and she wouldn't think it fair to "beg"—as she'd think of it—for attention or time from Danielle or me. "Dani's . . . worried," I said.

"What's there to worry about?"

"I think she's afraid that going to Jekyll Island again will drown out or erase all her good memories of our last trip there."

"Good memories?" Mom snorted, sounding a lot like one of her horses. "That trip ranks as one of my worst memories. Ronald was pressing me, trying to make me give up riding or, at least, competing. I think we fought from the moment we arrived at that little beach bungalow until the moment we left. He crowned the weekend by giving me his ultimatum: horses or him."

Mom's thin face looked almost gaunt as she relived the painful memories. "I didn't know," I said inadequately.

She gave a half laugh. "Why would you? Even at our worst, we tried not to fight in front of you kids. I guess I'm pleased that Danielle has good memories of the trip. I wonder what Nick remembers?" We fell quiet for a moment, trying to envision what my brother's memories of that final family vacation would be.

"That snake," I said. "I'm pretty sure he remembers the way you and I screeched when he brought that garter snake in and it got loose in the living room. Danielle thought it was cool and helped him look for it while you and I hid in the bedroom. As if a snake couldn't have slithered under the door! I wonder where Dad was?"

"Probably down on the beach with a book. I think he read every Tom Clancy novel ever written on that vacation."

We smiled at each other and started back toward the barn, the horses eager to return to their hay. Dusk had deepened, and the earliest fireflies glowed at knee level, flitting above the deep grass and at the edge of the woods. Back at the barn, I helped Mom put the horses up, gave her a hug, and left, envying, in part, her quiet country life and her relationship with the horses. I was pretty sure the Old Town Alexandria historical-preservation Nazis and/or the home owners' association would object if I turned my carport into a stable and installed an Appaloosa. Maybe I should get a gerbil. Somehow, I didn't think that would be the same.

Chapter 20

Monday, the day of the DanceSport exhibition and luncheon for the Olympics organizers and voters, dawned with overcast skies and high humidity. My morning Cheerios were limp even before I put milk on them. I spooned them up, then went upstairs, still in my nightgown—no students this morning— to do some paperwork before it was time to get ready. Zipping through my e-mails, I studied the report of our quarterly earnings and expenses that Tav had left. Tiring of the details, I skipped to the bottom line and sighed; if things didn't pick up soon, I didn't know how much longer I could continue to operate the studio. The thought of going back to working for someone else depressed me, and I brainstormed a few ideas for attracting students. Maybe if the first lesson were free?

I hadn't come up with anything brilliant by midmorning, when it was time to get ready for the exhibition. Vitaly and I were dancing the international standard dances, so I pulled my blond hair back from my face and twirled it into an elaborate chignon, anchoring it with

numerous hairpins and hair spray. Makeup came next. I
started with my false eyelashes. When I'd first applied
them as a young teen, it used to take me forty-five minutes and a lot of glue and tears to get them on right. Now
I accomplished the task in less than five minutes. Full
makeup followed, as heavy and defined as if I were doing
a stage play. If the judges and audience couldn't see a
dancer's expressions, they were missing a significant part
of the performance. I finished by curling my lashes and
layering on black mascara, then slicking a dark crimson
lipstick onto my mouth. I leaned toward the bathroom
mirror and inspected the result. *Perfecto.* Plum-colored
liner made my green eyes "pop," and the way I'd pulled
my hair back enhanced my cheekbones and showed off
the line of my neck.

Satisfied with my appearance, I checked the dress bag
that held the gown and my shoes; grabbed the dance duffel that held my bling, sewing kit for repairs on the fly,
extra makeup for midcompetition (or exhibition, in this
case) touchups, extra shoes, and miscellaneous other
things; and lugged it all out to my Volkswagen. Vitaly
and I had agreed to meet at the exhibition site, a hotel in
Crystal City, and I made the drive without holdup, happy
to hand my car over to the valet when I arrived, since the
dancers' expenses were being paid.

Changing into my exhibition dress in a public rest-
room, to the bemusement of a couple of "women who
lunch" who watched me disappear into the stall in my
jeans and T-shirt and emerge, Cinderella-like, in the pink
satin gown with its hip-high slit emphasized by a deep
ruffle, I headed for the ballroom. The reception area outside the ballroom was crowded with ticket holders drinking prelunch aperitifs and waiting for the doors to open.
I threaded my way through them and slipped through

the doors. The first person I saw upon entering the vast, echoing space was Marco Ingelido, doing a mike check at a podium near the dance floor. I'd forgotten he was to emcee the event. His eyes met mine for a moment, and he beckoned to me, but then one of the organizers claimed his attention. Other dancers milled around, some warming up on the dance floor set up in the middle of the room. Tables, set for lunch, ringed the floor, and the hotel's catering staff bustled about filling water glasses and setting out bread baskets.

"Stacy!" Vitaly sailed toward me, arms open, wide grin showing off his expensive teeth. "You are here." He wore a tux with tails over a white vest and shirt, with a bow tie and cummerbund that matched my dress. Gel slicked his stick-straight, straw-colored hair off his high forehead. "You are looking spectacularly."

I dropped him a curtsy. "Thank you, kind sir."

A photographer's flash went off and I turned, startled, to see Sarah Lewis grinning at us. "Hello again," she said in a friendly way. I introduced her to Vitaly, thinking that I couldn't go anywhere without bumping into her these days. We set a date for her to do publicity stills of me and Vitaly, and she strode off to get pictures of the other couples as a bell dinged. The doors opened and the diners and donors streamed in, making for their tables.

"Are we dancings or eatings first?" Vitaly asked.

I looked past him to where one of the coordinators was giving us urgent "get over here" gestures. "Dancing."

We gathered in a space the coordinator insisted on calling the green room and chatted with the other pros assembled to dance. Vitaly's former partner, Anya, was there in a sizzling gold lamé Latin costume that showed off her rock-hard abs, and he caught up with her while I chatted with a couple of friends I hadn't seen in a while.

This exhibition had none of the tension of a high-profile competition, and we were laughing together until someone turned up the volume on the closed-circuit TV in the corner and we heard Marco Ingelido asking the crowd for a moment of silence to honor "our recently deceased colleague and the force behind getting DanceSport accepted as an Olympic event, Corinne Blakely." In the green room, conversation dribbled to a stop as some dancers bowed their heads and others stood quietly.

When conversation resumed, I overheard someone mention Maurice's name and caught a sideways glance or two aimed at me. I flushed, certain that many of these people had heard about Maurice's arrest and were wondering whether he was guilty. Squelching my impulse to stand on a chair and declaim Maurice's innocence, I let Vitaly lead me from the room as a harried coordinator summoned us for our performance. We crossed an expanse of carpet to the dance floor as Ingelido finished reciting some of our accomplishments and led a round of applause. We began with a Viennese waltz, with Marco supplying a bit of the dance's history and describing some of the steps in an attempt to communicate to the Olympics' decision makers how complicated and technical DanceSport is.

"It's not unlike gymnastics and ice-skating," he said, "in that it requires both tremendous athletic ability and fitness, in addition to an artistic element that makes it eminently watchable." In other words, he was telling folks that TV viewership might go up if ballroom dance made it into the Olympics. It was a good spiel, I had to admit, and I wondered whether he had written the script or Corinne had.

The music transitioned to a tango, and we segued easily into the slow, slow, quick-quick-slow rhythm. The carnation pink skirt flowed around me as we promenaded. When I snapped my head frontward to give Vitaly a smoldering look, I caught sight of Greta and Conrad Monk at a ringside table. I shouldn't have been surprised, given Greta's connection with fund-raising and with dance, but I was. It didn't show on my face, however, as I hooked my leg high on Vitaly's thigh from behind and let him drag me across the floor, my face pressed to his back. Spontaneous applause broke out. We finished the set with a jaunty quickstep that left us breathless as we waved good-bye to the crowd and traded places with Anya and her new partner, who were set to demo some of the Latin dances.

The exhibition ended the better part of an hour later with all the professional dancers on the floor at the same time to take a bow. We were a glittering rainbow of greens, blues, reds, and pinks. The crowd applauded loudly, most of them getting to their feet to give us an ovation. We were each invited to join a table as dessert was served, and I was guided to a table directly in front of the podium. I knew we were supposed to talk up Dance-Sport as an Olympic event, and I'd prepared a couple of comments. They went out of my mind, though, as I smoothed my gown under my hips and sat, looking up to see Turner Blakely across the table. His nostrils flared and he looked distinctly unhappy to see me, although that didn't keep him from checking out my cleavage.

His presence was immediately explained by Marco Ingelido, still emceeing, when he thanked the corporate sponsors who contributed to the event and introduced Turner Blakely as Corinne's grandson: "Here today in memory of his grandmother, who conceived of this event and whose dearest wish was to see ballroom dancing get recognized as an Olympic event."

He invited Turner to the podium with a gesture, and the young man rose, took a swallow of his beer, and walked forward to shake Marco's hand. Pulling a piece of paper from his inside jacket pocket, Turner leaned into the mike and said, "I have here a copy of the remarks my dearest grandmother intended to make at this occasion. With your permission, I'll read them to you."

Without waiting for a response, he began to read in a clear voice. His diction and pacing were excellent, and I wondered whether he'd been studying theater before getting kicked out of college. Corinne's words were, as I'd have suspected, to the point, laced with humor, and persuasive. They were also brief. Turner finished by slowly refolding the page and saying, "Let's all honor my grandmother by making her dream a reality."

We surged to our feet, applauding Corinne rather than Turner, and I heard more than a couple of sniffles from the people beside me and behind me. My own eyes stung a bit. "That was very well done," I told Turner in all sincerity as he returned to the table. "You did Corinne proud."

"I don't need you to tell me so," he said, sinking into his chair.

"You were so good," cooed the dark-haired girl sitting beside him. She was his age, or a bit younger, and wore a hot-pink bandage dress that left little to the imagination. She planted a kiss on him that went on so long the other diners at our table, mostly couples in their sixties, rustled uncomfortably and greeted the arrival of dessert with relief.

Allowing myself one spoonful of the delicious chocolate mousse, I chatted with the folks at the table, extolling the glories of ballroom dance. Most of my mind, however, was busy trying to figure out how to ask Turner a few pointed questions. I'd about decided there was no way to do it in the current forum, with strangers seated around us and his girlfriend clinging to him like a limpet, when the other couples at the table—who seemed to know one another well—rose and said they had to be going, since they were catching a train to New York at Union Station. "Tickets to *The Book of Mormon*," one man said cheerfully.

Turner's girlfriend took their departure as the opportunity to say, "I've got to visit the little girls' room. Right back, baby." She kissed him again and I rolled my eyes.

Turner and I were alone at the table. I accepted a cup of coffee from the waiter, and Turner ordered another beer. He slumped casually, one hand dug into a pocket, a lock of black hair draped carelessly across his forehead. When the waiter had left, Turner looked at me, a calculating look in his eyes. "So."

"So." This conversation was going nowhere fast.

"You've got some moves. Hot." Lust flickered in his eyes, the same blue as his father's.

Gag me. I was about to say that I didn't need him to tell me so, when it crossed my mind that letting him think I was interested in him might yield more information than if I told him spoiled little cheaters didn't turn me on. "Thanks," I choked out.

"We could hook up sometime." He tilted his beer to his lips, his eyes never leaving my face.

"What about your girlfriend?"

"Mandy?" He shrugged. "She doesn't have to know."

So he cheated both in and out of the classroom. "I guess you have women throwing themselves at you, now that you're a millionaire."

A smug smile made me want to smack him. "The bitches are hot for me. Always have been."

I desperately wanted to prick his self-satisfaction. "I guess you were angry that Corinne didn't leave you the Warhol painting."

Turner scowled. "It should be mine. Goldberg has no right to it. They were only married for a few months, for crap's sake. I've got my lawyers on it."

"And I suppose you'll be spending big bucks on your dad, too." I sipped my coffee, noticing more people leaving. Turner would be out of here as soon as Mandy finished powdering her nose.

I thought my reminder would further anger Turner, but he laughed. "Not so much. His days in that addict resort are numbered. The will said I had to support him . . . it didn't specify where he got to live."

If Randolph had murdered Corinne with an eye toward making up with his son, or sharing the spoils with him, he was in for a rude awakening. "He could move in with you," I suggested. "There's plenty of room."

"When hell freezes over." He drained the last of his beer and thunked the bottle onto the table. "I'm putting that place on the market next week."

"If you don't like it, why did you move in there?" I asked, pleased that the conversation had come around to where I wanted it.

"Grandmother invited me. I felt sorry for her, living all alone with no one but that housekeeper woman, so I moved in."

"Aren't you the model grandson?" I drawled, unable to hold back the sarcasm. "It's terribly sad that she died so soon—mere minutes, really—after you got there. Some people might think it was a strange coincidence."

Turner's eyes narrowed. "That's all it was: coincidence. I didn't know where she kept her medicine, and

I've never bought any of that epi-whatever stuff. Where
do you get off—"

"Why did the police want to talk to you Saturday?"

Fury and a hint of fear blazed in Turner's eyes. Shov-
ing his chair back, he clipped a waiter with a loaded tray
and the man stumbled. Dirty dishes clattered to the floor
with bangs and crashes and clinks that brought all eyes
our way. White lines bracketed Turner's mouth, and he
hesitated half a second before stalking out of the dining
room.

Mandy shimmied up moments later, confusion cloud-
ing her pretty features. "Where'd Turner go?"

"Out." I pointed to the door he'd used. "He seemed
upset about something the police said Saturday."

She heaved a sigh, making her boobs rise and fall in a
way that caught the attention of the three waiters putting broken china in a plastic tub. "That is just so unfair.
I mean, there weren't any witnesses. It's a case of 'he said,
she said,' and *of course* she only said it hoping to get
money out of Turner. She's a stripper, for heaven's sake!
He's the sweetest man *ever*. It shouldn't be allowed."

"Absolutely not," I agreed, wondering whether it was
possible that some woman had accused Turner Blakely
of assaulting her. He'd gone to a bachelor party on
Wednesday night, and Detective Lissy came looking for
him at the will reading on Saturday. . . .

"I'd better go. He might need me." Mandy hurried
away.

I was debating whether to change back into my jeans
or drive home in my dress when a tap on my bare shoulder made me jump. I whirled and found myself staring
into the cold gray eyes of Conrad Monk. His suit
matched his eyes and crew-cut hair, and slimmed his

stocky figure. A fat gold wedding band inset with tiny diamonds glittered where his hand rested on my shoulder.

"A word, Miss Graysin?"

"Uh, sure." I looked around for Greta, but didn't see her. Monk led me onto the dance floor so we were out of earshot of the crew cleaning up the dropped dishes.

"I trust you've recovered from your dip in the Potomac?"

"Good as new," I said, trying to read his face. I couldn't tell whether he was taunting me or genuinely concerned.

"Good. Let me get right to the point. My wife told me you have a copy of Corinne Blakely's manuscript. I want to buy it from you."

"It's not— I don't—" How did I get myself into these things?

"Corinne Blakely, although in many ways a wonderful woman, could be a bit irresponsible. Several people, my wife among them, tried to talk her out of publishing a memoir. She wouldn't listen. Not even the knowledge that she might hurt people, innocent people, weighed with her. I hope you're more reasonable." Slightly lifted brows questioned me.

"I'm reasonable, but . . ." How to tell him I didn't really have the manuscript? And, oh, yeah, I couldn't sell it to him if I did, because it didn't belong to me.

"Good." He pulled out a checkbook. "I think ten thousand is reasonable, don't you?"

"I don't have it," I burst out.

He stared at me measuringly from beneath bushy brows. "All right. Fifteen."

"No, I really don't have it." What to do—lie some more by telling him I'd already given it to the publisher, or come clean? I decided to go, belatedly, for honesty. "I never—"

Tucking the checkbook back into his pocket, he said, "Remember, I gave you a chance to be reasonable." He didn't raise his voice, but a frigid, rigid undertone froze me. Before I could gasp another word, he turned and headed for an exit.

I was about to follow him, try to explain, when an itching between my shoulder blades gave me the eerie feeling that someone was watching me. I glanced behind me, trying to be casual, and saw Marco Ingelido mere yards away at the podium, apparently retrieving his notes. I had the sinking suspicion that he'd heard every word Monk and I exchanged. His lips curled back from white teeth in a snarl, and his glare bored a hole through me.

The phrase "if looks could kill" leaped into my mind.

Chapter 21

Dashing from the room would be undignified, so I went on the attack. Stalking over to Ingelido, my skirt billowing, I said, "You lied to me."

"*You* lied to *me*. You said there was no manuscript." He worked his jaw from side to side.

"You said you had an affair with Corinne. Her son says otherwise."

"Randolph has been so 'overmedicated' for years that Corinne and I could have gone at it beside him on the couch and he wouldn't have noticed." Scorn coated his words.

"If you didn't have an affair with Corinne, what were you afraid she'd put in the manuscript?" I asked, ignoring his last statement, although it instilled a small grain of doubt.

"Where is it?"

"As far as I know, there is no manuscript."

He snorted his disbelief. "Right."

"Greta Monk misunderstood something I said."

His face looked like it had been carved from stone, a

light olive-colored granite. "I don't know what kind of game you're playing, or why you're determined to dredge up old history—you weren't even born!—but I'm telling you now that it's a very, very dangerous game. No one can win. What happened to Corinne should tell you that."

"Is that a threat?"

He leaned into my space and I fought the urge to step back. "Take it any way you like." A change came over his face, the muscles around his eyes relaxing, and he said almost pleadingly, "Destroy the manuscript, Stacy. For everybody's sake. Burn it."

"I don't have—"

"Stacy, I am leavings." Vitaly bounded up, offered Ingelido a nod, and gave me a hug. "We will being first gold-medal winners in ballroom dance at Olympics. I am knowing this."

I smiled at him, but my eyes followed Ingelido as he walked away. I'd rarely regretted a lie more.

The rest of Monday passed uneventfully. I stopped at an ATM for cash on my way home, then spent time in the ballroom working out new choreography for a couple who had recently turned pro and were paying for my help. I chatted with my mom and Danielle by phone. Neither mentioned Jekyll Island. I took a late-afternoon ballet class, ate a light dinner, and called Tav to see when we could get together to discuss our financials. We agreed on meeting up Tuesday for lunch. More tired than usual, I turned off the lights at ten and fell asleep immediately.

I'd dreamed about the night Rafe died several times in the months since he was shot, and tonight I was in the kitchen again, moments before I heard the thud of Rafe's body landing on the ballroom floor. Usually my nightmare centered on the moment I flicked on the lights and saw Rafe lying in a pool of blood; tonight I kept hearing his body thump to the floor. *Thud. Thud.* I struggled awake and lay still a moment, trying to get oriented. It was just the dream, I told myself, breathing deeply to relax. Just a—

Click.

The sound brought me upright. My hands clutched at the sheets. *What was that?* It was a barely audible sound, not the weighty thump Rafe's body had made. Probably the wind bumping a branch against a window, or a raccoon on his nightly patrol. Nothing to worry— *Skree.* Every muscle tensed. It sounded like a door sighing open. I widened my eyes, trying to see better in the dark. Was someone in my room? No, the noise had come from farther away, maybe the living room or kitchen.

Should I cower here in my bed, hoping the intruder would steal something quickly and leave? He was welcome to the ceramic rooster Great-aunt Laurinda kept on the kitchen counter that I hadn't been able to bring myself to toss or donate to Goodwill. But he'd better stay away from my purse. I couldn't afford to lose the money I'd withdrawn from the ATM. Where was my purse? Not on my dresser where I frequently left it, I realized, not making out its shape. In the kitchen! I'd dropped it on the table when I came in because I'd been loaded down with my dress and my dance duffel. *Damn.*

I bit my lip. I could call 911. No, I wasn't even sure someone had broken in. I hadn't heard anything for the last minute or so. I was making myself all hysterical for nothing. *Shish.* A sound like fabric brushing against a screen convinced me I wasn't hallucinating. Someone was trying to break in—or might already be in! Adrenaline flooded me and I fumbled for my cell phone on the nightstand as I swung my legs out of bed. I wished I had the gun Uncle Nico had given me, but it was now permanently locked in a police evidence bin, since it was the weapon used to kill Rafe. Maybe I needed to ask Uncle Nico for a new gun, or buy one myself. Even a baseball bat would make me feel more confident. Or . . .

The poker! I eased out of my bedroom and glided toward the front parlor, where a set of sturdy andirons stood near the fireplace I hadn't used since moving in. My peach silk nightgown—I'm a sucker for slinky lingerie—rippled soundlessly around my thighs. Even though I couldn't see much, I avoided the squeaky plank near the stairs, crossed through the foyer—the front door was still locked—and reached the parlor without encountering the intruder. I paused, listening. Nothing. Was I mistaken? I fingered the phone, reluctant to summon the police for what might be no more than a curious night critter or cat prowling around outside. I was spending too much time thinking about murder, and it was making me jumpier than usual.

Figuring better safe than sorry, I crept toward the fireplace. Halfway there, my foot slipped on something that slid out from under it and I almost went down. I couldn't see what it was, so when I recovered my balance, I kept moving forward. Finally, I wrapped my fingers around the poker's iron shaft, prying it free from the stand with a slight clank. I froze. Nothing. Feeling a bit like I'd let my imagination get the better of me, I started down the hall toward the kitchen, walking more easily, the poker clutched in my right hand and the phone in my left. Two steps from the kitchen, I registered that the air was cooler just as a draft plastered my nightie against me. The back door was open!

Gooseflesh sprang up on my arms and I caught my breath, feeling a lot less brave all of a sudden. It was definitely 911 time. I brought the phone closer to my face, trying to read the numbers. A scrambling sound behind me made me whirl. I had an impression of solid blackness rushing toward me and I raised the poker like a lance, not having time to slash downward with it. Something slammed into me and the poker flew out of my hand, landing with a clatter. My fingers clutched reflexively at the phone, but my hand banged open as I struck the ground and slid. I heard heavy breathing, maybe a curse, and then my head cracked against the wall and whorls of color exploded behind my eyes.

I regained consciousness what felt like moments later, but which could have been half an hour for all I knew. My head ached. Pain in my tailbone told me I'd landed on it—hard. Not the first time. The memory of a fall from a lift—at a competition, no less—came to me, and I remembered lying on my back as people jived around me, trying to catch my breath and wincing from the pains shooting from my tailbone. There'd been an especially pretty, sparkly chandelier over the dance floor. The music had been "Wake Me Up Before You Go Go." There was no light or music now. I blinked several times, trying to blink away the pain. Panic flashed through me suddenly as I remembered the intruder crashing into me. Was he still here? I scrambled to my feet, trying to ignore the bolts of pain zinging through my head and tailbone. One hand clutched at the wall for balance. Where was my phone? I didn't see it. I tried to still my breathing. I didn't hear anything. As the thudding of my heart slowed, I realized the house *felt* empty. He'd gone.

I drew a deep breath and then forced myself to walk

toward the kitchen. With a trembling hand, I patted the wall for the switch and found it. Yellow light drenched the room. No one leaped at me. I was alone. Exhaling loudly, I felt tears burning my eyes, but blinked them away. Drawers and cabinets hung open. My purse was on the table where I'd left it, albeit tipped on its side. Hurrying to it, I groped for my wallet, not expecting to find it. My fingers closed over it and I drew it out. Untouched. Weird. I surveyed the chaos. Clearly, the burglar had searched the place. For what? Silver? I didn't know what other valuables he could expect to find in a kitchen.

The manuscript.

The thought thudded into me with all the force of the intruder and I gasped. My nightgown fluttered, reminding me that the back door was still open, and I crossed to it. Reaching toward the knob, I jumped back as the door opened wider, pulled by an unseen hand. I screamed.

Chapter 22

Backpedaling, I kept screaming. I bumped into the counter and scrabbled for a weapon. The first thing my fingers contacted was the ceramic rooster. I hefted it and raised it over my head, ready to hurl it at the intruder.

Tav stepped into the kitchen. "Stacy. I came as fast as I could. What is wrong?"

I cut myself off in midscream.

He cocked an eyebrow at me. "Were you saving that from an intruder or using it as a weapon?" He gestured to the rooster.

Sobs of relief ripped through me, and my arms went numb. The rooster crashed to the floor, shattering into a couple hundred garish pieces. *Oops.*

Sensing that I was incapable of making sense, Tav crossed the room in two strides and pulled me into a hug. "It is okay. You are okay, Stacy. Do not cry."

His arms were hard and comforting, his chest where my face pressed against it warm and reassuringly solid. His hand stroked my hair. "When I got your call and you did not say anything, I knew something was wrong. I heard you cry out and ran for my car."

I must have hit redial just before the intruder attacked me. I pulled back slightly so I could see Tav's face. His brown eyes, clouded with concern, searched my face. Using one finger, he lifted my chin. "You are all right?"

"Except for a headache." I fingered the spot on my head where it had cracked into the wall. I wasn't going to mention the pain in my derriere to Tav. "A couple aspirin will fix me right up." I smiled wanly.

"I think I should take you to the hospital to get you checked out."

"No." I didn't want to spend several hours sitting in an ER crowded with real sick people who might give me something a whole lot worse than a headache. I explained that to Tav and he half smiled.

"Okay. Well, at least sit down."

I became aware of the fact that he still held me in a loose embrace, that I was pressed against him from thigh to chest, and that his hands through the thin silk of my nightie felt way too good as they absently stroked my back. I saw awareness hit him, too. His eyes darkened and his gaze dropped to my lips. "Stacy . . ."

He pulled me closer, and the cedary scent of him made my head swim. When I didn't break away, he bent his head. His lips had barely grazed mine when a harsh voice called, "Police! Put your hands where I can see them."

Releasing me instantly and holding his hands out to his sides, Tav smile ruefully. "I called the police on my way over here. I hoped they might get here before I did." He turned to face the cop as I raised my hands to shoulder height, embarrassed at being caught in such an awkward position and almost overcome by an insane desire to giggle. My emotions had been on a roller coaster tonight.

The officer motioned Tav to one side with his gun and addressed me. "Ma'am, we got a nine-one-one call that there was an intruder at this address. Are you all right?" A sturdy-looking black man in his mid-thirties, he was all business. His gaze swept me from the top of my tousled blond head, down the length of my body in the peach nightgown, to my gold-painted toenails. His wary expression never changed. He spoke quietly into the radio hooked near his shoulder, and I glimpsed his partner as he or she checked the house's exterior.

"I'm okay now," I babbled. "There was someone.... He knocked me over. Tav is my partner. He's the one who called you. I don't know why ... he searched for ..." I gestured toward the kitchen, knowing I wasn't making sense.

"You might want to get a robe, ma'am," the cop said, lowering his gun. "Let me see some identification, sir," he said to Tav as I scurried to my bedroom. The wispy robe that went with the nightgown was not going to give much extra coverage. I yanked Great-aunt Laurinda's tatty flannel robe from the back of the closet, where it had been when I moved in, and shoved my arms into the sleeves. Tying the belt at the waist, I returned to the kitchen, comfortable but frumpy in the plaid robe that draped around my torso and puddled on the floor. Great-aunt Laurinda had been a tall woman.

Tav bit back a smile at the sight. The officer had been joined by his partner, a competent-looking woman with sandy hair in a braid tucked down the back of her shirt. They questioned us for what seemed like hours, asking me to go over the night's events several times. Showing me where the back door was splintered near the lock, they suggested the would-be thief had used a crowbar or something similar to pry it open. "Not a professional," the female cop opined.

When I led them into the front parlor, Tav following, I gasped to see that it, too, had been searched. I hadn't noticed it in the dark. A stack of dance magazines had cascaded from a pile by the couch; I must have slipped on one of them. Great-aunt Laurinda's papers from a small Oriental chest I kept meaning to sort through were strewn higgledy-piggledy around the room. "Any idea what the intruder might have been after?" the male cop asked.

I hesitated a second before saying, "No," and Tav shot me a suddenly suspicious look.

"Strange he overlooked your purse," the female officer said, her eyes narrowing as if she suspected there was more to the story than I was sharing.

I met her gaze blandly, having no intention of regaling them with my theories about Corinne Blakely's death and a mysterious manuscript no one could verify ever existed, but which the greater part of the ballroom dance community thought I had possession of.

Finally, the police officers were ready to leave. They handed me a business card, suggested I contact my insurance agent and get my door repaired, and told me to call them if I thought of anything else or found something missing. "Thank you very much," I said gratefully. As they pulled away in their squad car I noticed lights on in the windows of a couple of neighbors' houses. Great, they probably thought they'd see me on the next installment of *America's Most Wanted*.

I returned to the kitchen to find Tav pouring the coffee I'd put on for the officers but which they'd declined.

"Actually, I could use something stronger," I said, pulling a bottle of lemon vodka from the freezer.

Tav raised his brows.

"It was for a party," I explained, uncapping the bottle. "A hostess gift. I forgot to take it with me." I poured a couple fingers into a juice glass and looked a question at Tav.

He shook his head. "I am driving."

It crossed my mind that if the police hadn't arrived when they did, he might not have been driving home, and I took too large a swallow of the vodka. The lemon and cold stung my throat and I coughed. Now I knew why I didn't drink vodka. I set the half-full glass on the counter with a grimace and reached for the mug of coffee Tav held out.

"So," he said mildly after I'd had a couple of warming sips, "perhaps you will tell me what you think your intruder was after? Do you know who it was?"

"No!" I saw doubt in his eyes. "No, really. I have a guess about what he—or she—was looking for, but I don't know who it was. I would've told the cops if I did."

Tav nodded, his gaze steady on my face. "So he was looking for . . . ?"

"Corinne Blakely's manuscript?"

He raised his brows so they furrowed his forehead. "Why in the world would anyone expect to find it here?"

I winced. "Because I told Greta Monk I had it," I said in a small voice. Before he could interrupt, I hurried through my explanation.

He didn't call me a lying, deceitful, dishonest wretch, as I was afraid he might. Instead, he asked, exasperated, "Did you not realize you might be putting yourself in danger?"

"Not until Danielle mentioned it," I confessed. "And even then I didn't think I'd be in *real* danger."

"Well, you must let everyone know that you do not, in fact, have Corinne's manuscript or notes or anything else."

"I already tried. No one believed me." There was probably a fairy tale that dealt with a girl who lied and was murdered or eaten by a monster as a result, but I couldn't think of one. "I'm a moron."

"You are not a moron." Tav set his mug on the counter and crossed to me. He put his hands on my shoulders and gave me a little shake. "You are merely too impulsive, *querida*."

"Don't call me that." The words were out before I could stop them.

Tav stepped back, startled.

"Rafe used to—"

He nodded in instant understanding, but the gentle moment had passed as the specter of his dead half brother rose between us. "Of course. Let me help you secure this door and I will be on my way. We can discuss this in the morning, when we are not so tired."

I glanced at the kitchen clock, startled to see it was after four. I admitted I didn't have a toolbox and didn't know where the hammer I used to hang pictures was, so Tav and I scooted the heavy kitchen table across the floor so it blocked the back door. "That will have to do," Tav said, clearly unsatisfied with the security arrangements. "I could stay—"

"It'll be fine," I insisted, yawning. "I'll get someone to fix it first thing."

Allowing me to convince him, Tav let me show him to the front door. As I swung it open to admit the chill breath of almost-dawn, he looked down at me, the expression in his deep-set eyes sending a tingle through me. "We will continue our other ... discussion later." Without waiting for me to answer—which was a good thing, because his comment flustered me and I would only have stuttered something stupid—he stepped into the darkness. I closed the door, shot the dead bolt, and watched through the narrow windows inset on either side of the door as Tav strode to his car.

When I saw the headlights come on, I made myself turn away, hoping our one half-kiss in the aftermath of danger would not make things awkward between us in the studio. We were business partners; that was all, I reminded myself as I headed to my bedroom. Anything romantic would only complicate matters. And my life had enough complications as it was.

Chapter 23

The morning brought some clarity of mind, but no insight into who had broken in last night. My headache had diminished, but I was achy and bruised in several places, probably because the intruder had knocked into me hard. Dressed in pink shorts and a tank top for my first class, I inhaled the steam from my first cup of coffee and made a mental list of intruder candidates. Greta Monk and her hubby topped the list, since not only did they think I had the manuscript, but they clearly wanted it badly—fifteen thousand dollars badly. Good thing I didn't have it, I thought ruefully, because that sum would tempt me to sell it, even though it wasn't mine. Fifteen thousand would keep Graysin Motion solvent for a couple of months, at least.

Marco Ingelido also knew, because he'd overheard Monk. I thought about Marco. His reaction yesterday had surprised me. He was angry, yes, at discovering I had (as he thought) the manuscript. But in addition to the anger, he'd shown real fear, almost despair. And he'd been pleading with me to destroy the manuscript. I felt a pang of compassion. Whatever Corinne had planned to write about Marco, it was something much more damaging than an affair with an older woman.

Besides Marco and the Monks, who might suspect I had the manuscript? Anyone they'd told, I decided after a moment. I had no way of knowing whether any of the three of them had passed the word along; if so, almost anyone in Corinne's circle might have heard the rumor. Including, I realized, Ingelido's niece, Sarah, who was due here at one to take pictures of Vitaly and me. Forcing myself to stop thinking about the break-in, I trotted up the interior stairs to the studio, where I saw with mingled relief and disappointment that Tav wasn't there. After the drama of last night, I wasn't up for going over our financials, anyway.

Mildred Kensington greeted me with, "Any luck getting hold of that typewriter, Stacy?" and Hoover put his paws on my shoulders and gave me a lick when I walked into the ballroom. I told a disappointed Mildred that we hadn't yet come up with a way to get Turner to give up the typewriter, and introduced the elderly class members to the foxtrot. Many of them had danced it socially in the 1940s and 1950s, and memories of fraternity dances and wedding receptions lit their faces as they relearned the steps. After they left, I practiced with a student I competed with in professional-amateur divisions at ballroom competitions. Most pros make the bulk of their money off students who pay them to compete as their partners at such competitions. This man was a self-employed plumber who particularly enjoyed the Latin dances. After we worked up a sweat with the jive—me reminding him to kick sharper and faster throughout—he left and I went downstairs to shower again. Some days I showered three or four times, depending on my schedule.

The doorbell rang before I was fully dressed, and I scrambled into a tiered cotton skirt and matching knit top. I opened the door to find a strange woman on the doorstep. Sixty or so, and an inch or two under five feet tall, she had dark hair in a little Dutch-boy haircut, the kind that looks like someone put a bowl over your head and then cut around it. A blue shirtwaist dress topped with a red cardigan wrapped a wiry figure. Bright red Converse high-tops matched the sweater and made me blink. Dark eyes peered at me from behind fashionable glasses, assessing me. "Stacy, right?" Her voice was deep and gravelly, incongruous coming from her petite frame.

I nodded, automatically taking the hand she held out. "Uh, yes."

"Good. I'm Eulalia Pine, as you must have guessed." She handed me a business card that read, PINE ESTATE SALES AND APPRAISALS, EULALIA PINE, PROP. "Shall we get started?"

"Started?"

"With the furniture." She arched her brows an inch above her glasses, which made her look like she had two sets of eyebrows. In the face of my continued incomprehension, she said impatiently, "Didn't the other Miss Graysin tell you? She said you had some early to midtwentieth-century pieces you wanted appraised."

"Oh. Oh, yes." Danielle must have contacted this woman about Great-aunt Laurinda's furniture. "I didn't know today— Please come in." Mentally blasting Danielle for not giving me a heads-up, I remembered I hadn't checked my phone for messages last night or this morning.

With a sniff, Eulalia Pine stepped into the foyer, her gaze darting immediately to the grandfather clock and then into the parlor. A clipboard appeared from the tote she carried and she began taking notes.

"Would you like some coffee, Miss Pine?" I asked.

She declined with a single jerk of her head and moved into the parlor. A sharp exhalation through her nose let me know what she thought of the papers and magazines littering the room. She made to tuck her pen under the clipboard's clamp. "If this chaos is indicative of the care you give your pieces—"

"I had a break-in last night," I explained, feeling like I was failing an inspection of some sort. I straightened my spine. I didn't need to apologize to Ms. Eulalia Pine for my inadequate housekeeping. "In fact, today's not a good—"

"No need to get pissy," Eulalia Pine said, grasping the pen again. "I'm the best appraiser in northern Virginia, and I'm booked solid for the next month—I've got a major estate sale starting later this week—so it's now or never." She ran a hand over the sofa's arched back and grimaced. "Dust." She reminded me of Detective Lissy.

After that last syllable, she was all business as I trailed her through the house. She studied the matched chairs in the living room, the ones with the periwinkle blue upholstery and the arched backs I'd always thought were hideously uncomfortable. "Art moderne," she pronounced. "Textured wool frisée upholstery in excellent condition. Solid maple frames." She peered underneath them, rattled them gently, and examined a scratch on one leg. She jotted notes and took several photos before moving on to a lamp on the end table. "Hm." I could sense excitement under her noncommittal "hm" and wondered what there was about the ceramic lamp with its green and white jagged stripes to interest her. It was ugly with a capital U.

"Hedwig Bollhagen," she said in an awed voice after carefully lifting the lamp to examine the base. "With an original paper shade. Pity about the watermarks, but still." More notes and photos. She seemed less interested in the three-tiered mahogany table the lamp sat on, and muttered something about "Michigan Furniture Company" and "post-1950." We moved into the dining room, a room I'd barely set foot in, and she was dismissive about the table, but said she could have a buyer in minutes for the "art deco oak sideboard" with its low backsplash and brass hinges. "It's French." I couldn't tell whether she thought that enhanced its appeal or cut its price by half. I ran a hand over the silky wood as Ms. Pine marched back into the hall, wondering whether Great-aunt Laurinda had acquired the piece in France, and whether she'd bought it on a whim or saved for months to afford it. I suddenly wondered whether I wanted to sell this furniture steeped in memories and history.

"Miss Graysin!" The appraiser's impatient call cut through my thoughts, and I joined her by the staircase. She seemed disappointed when I told her nothing upstairs needed appraising. "It's my ballroom dance studio," I said.

"Ballroom dancing? Really?" Her mobile brows flew up again. "How bizarre. The estate sale I mentioned is for the heirs of a woman who used to be a ballroom dancer. Maybe you knew her? Colleen Blakely."

"Corinne," I corrected her, a little shiver running through me. "Her grandson told me he was selling the house. I didn't realize he was getting rid of all her stuff."

"A feckless young man," Eulalia Pine said, apparently having no qualms about dissing her employer. "When Mr. Goudge hired me—I've worked many an estate sale for his firm—he warned me about him."

Ah, so she was working for the lawyer, not Turner Blakely. A brilliant idea lit up my mind. "Are they selling everything?"

"As I understand it."

"I happen to know that Corinne owned a Smith Corona electric typewriter. I'm most interested in acquiring it for a friend."

"Collects typewriters, does he?" She nodded as if she ran across typewriter collectors every day. Maybe she did.

Conscious of the consequences of my last lie, I hedged. "He wants this particular typewriter pretty badly. If you are conducting the sale, would it be possible to put that aside for me?"

She eyed me shrewdly. "Perhaps. The sale starts Wednesday at eight. The dealers'll line up early and get a number for entry, but I'll let you in. Stop by early and I'll have it for you."

"Sooner would be better," I hinted.

She shrugged. "You could approach Mr. Turner Blakely about it."

Been there, done that. I gave in gracefully and thanked her.

Eulalia Pine pushed her glasses up her nose. "I'll see what I can do. And I'll have an appraisal report for you later this week. Say Thursday or Friday?"

"That's fine," I said, anxious to tell Maurice about the imminent arrival of the typewriter with, hopefully, the cartridge that would reveal some, at least, of the manuscript's secrets.

After Eulalia Pine left, I called Danielle to thank her for setting up the appointment, and then Maurice to tell him about the typewriter.

"Excellent work, Anastasia," he said.

"I think you were right about the manuscript being the key to Corinne's murder," I said, and told him about the break-in.

After a few questions about my well-being, he hung up, saying he had an appointment with Detective Lissy. "Don't worry," he forestalled my next comment. "Mr. Drake is going with me."

Chapter 24

I didn't have time to worry about what Lissy might want with Maurice, or to straighten up the mess left by the intruder, because Vitaly would be arriving any moment for the photo shoot with Sarah Lewis. I applied makeup in record time, then brushed my long blond hair and secured a fake hibiscus above my left ear. Slipping into the lime green samba costume with the halter top and the fringed pants, I made it upstairs moments before Vitaly arrived in a matching outfit, with a green shirt open to his navel and black slacks. I filled him in on the night's excitement while he slicked his hair back with gel, all the while grinning at his reflection in the mirror.

"You are stayings with Vitaly and John," he announced when I finished.

I was touched by his concern, but said, "I can't come to Baltimore, Vitaly. I've got too much to do here. Besides, I can't imagine the intruder will come back."

"He is not searching your bedroom yet, *da*?" Vitaly leveled an unusually serious look at me.

The thought made the hairs on my forearms prickle; no, the intruder hadn't gotten to my bedroom.

A knock at the outer door signaled Sarah Lewis's arrival, and I went to let her in. She wore jeans again, and a photographer's vest whose pockets bulged. She carried a bag with lots of zipped compartments, and her braid swung forward as she bent to set it down. "Hi, Stacy. You look great. That green is a wonderful choice. Where do you want to do this?"

I led the way into the ballroom, and she looked around curiously, greeting Vitaly with a smile. "Good light." She peered out each of the windows, stripping the drapes as far to the side as she could to let in more light. "We'll do a few shots in here, and then I think it might be fun to get some down there." She pointed out the rear window to the tiny courtyard. "That tree would look marvelous in the background. And it would be a bit different from the standard ballroom backgrounds."

"You is being the expert," Vitaly said agreeably.

At her command, we posed and danced and smiled while she moved around us, finding different angles. My smile started to feel stiff by the time she said, "Okay, let's go out back. Did you want to use a different costume?"

We nodded, and Vitaly ducked into the bathroom to change while I whisked down the interior stairs. I donned the red dress with plunging neckline and the black ruffle that detached to become a cape. My hair had to change, too, to match the character of the paso doble, and I quickly twisted it into an updo, sticking an elaborate enameled comb into it. Most of my makeup was okay as it was, but I slicked a dark red lipstick onto my lips before hurrying out of my bedroom.

I stopped so quickly I stumbled. Sarah Lewis stood at the threshold to the parlor, camera raised to take photos of the mess within. She must have followed me down from the studio. "What are you doing?" I asked, my brows snapping together.

She whirled at the sharp note in my voice. "Taking photos. For your insurance company. Vitaly told me about your break-in. That must have been scary."

I eyed her, uncertain whether to believe her or not. Her expression was guileless. She couldn't be interested in the manuscript, I reminded myself; she was far too young to feature in any of Corinne Blakely's memories. "Thanks," I said. "It was scary." I moved toward the kitchen and she followed me. "Oops." I'd forgotten the table blocked my back door. Together, Sarah and I heaved it out of the way and exited through the back to find Vitaly waiting in the courtyard, his matador costume a dramatic splash of black and red against the green grass and blue sky of the late-spring day.

"I love photographing trees," Sarah said as she positioned Vitaly and me under the draping limbs of the old magnolia. "I like to think about all the history they've seen. Who knows what this old guy might have observed in his day?" She patted the tree's rough trunk. "Slaves washing sheets on laundry day in this very courtyard, British soldiers occupying the town during the War of 1812, a midwife slipping through the night to help a scared sixteen-year-old wife give birth."

I stared at her. "You sound like a historian," I said.

"Smile. I was a history major at William and Mary before I got bitten by the photography bug. My mom—she's a history professor at Georgetown—got me a job as a tour guide at Christ Church one summer. George Washington used to go to services there, you know."

I was pretty sure everyone in Old Town Alexandria knew that bit of trivia, but I said only, "A history professor, huh? Not a dancer like her brother?" I dropped into a deep lunge, looking up into Vitaly's face with simulated passion. He steadied me when my foot slid off an exposed root.

Sarah lowered the camera and stared at me. "My mom doesn't have any brothers."

I was confused. "But your uncle Marco—"

Understanding dawned and she laughed. "No, no, he's my uncle by marriage. He's married to Mom's sister, my aunt Marian."

"But you look—" My eyes widened and I gasped. Vitaly, thinking I'd hurt myself, hauled me upright. I leaned into him for a moment to hide my face.

"Is it hurting, your head?" he asked.

"No, I'm fine," I said, plastering a fake smile on my face. "Just dizzy for a moment." I resumed the pose.

It seemed like Sarah hadn't heard my last half-comment, because she didn't react. My mind raced, and I knew none of the photos she took in the last five minutes of our session would be usable, because my head wasn't in the paso doble. I was mentally back in the early 1980s, when Ronald Reagan was president, disco was king, and Sarah Lewis and I were infants. We wrapped things up minutes later, and Sarah packed up her equipment, promising to have proofs for us to review the next day. Vitaly dashed off to meet John, and Sarah followed me back upstairs to the studio so I could write her a check for the sitting fee. I was saying good-bye to her, trying to catalog her features without seeming to stare, when Maurice pushed through the door. He and Sarah exchanged greetings, and he held the door for her as she slipped out, descending the stairs bolted to the house's exterior.

I grabbed Maurice by his blazer lapels and dragged

him into my office. "Maurice! Could Sarah Lewis be Marco Ingelido's *daughter*, rather than his niece? I always thought she looked like him, but I thought that was because his sister was her mother. But her mom's not his sister; her mom's his wife's sister."

Surprisingly, Maurice didn't look surprised. I took him through it again. "But you can see she's related to him by blood," I finished. "She's got his coloring, his facial structure."

"I tried to tell you about their relationship," he said, "that day Mildred and I went to get the typewriter from Turner."

I stared at him in astonishment. "I thought you meant they—Ingelido and Sarah—were having an affair. So it's common knowledge that she's his daughter?" So much for Marco's being desperate to stop the memoir's publication to keep his secret.

"By no means," Maurice said. "I happen to know because Ingelido was dating Corinne at the time. I found her sobbing her heart out one evening. She told me she had to break up with him because he had gotten another woman pregnant. He'd been acting strangely, and she suspected he was cheating on her. She wasn't proud of it, but she'd hired a private detective and managed to piece it together."

"Why didn't he marry Sarah's mother?"

"She was already married," Maurice said.

Oh, the tangled webs we weave . . . "Would Corinne publish something like that?" I asked. "Making a scandal like that public would hurt a lot of people—Sarah, her mother, and Ingelido's wife, just to name a few."

Maurice gave it some thought, shrugging out of his blazer as if it were suddenly too warm. "I just don't know," he said, clearly troubled. "I would hope not, but . . ."

I flashed on Sarah Lewis taking photos of my front parlor. "Do you suppose Sarah knows? What about the man who's married to her mom?" I couldn't call him Sarah's "father," since it seemed clear he wasn't.

Maurice rubbed a finger along his lower lip. "I don't know him well; I've met him at a few functions when he and his wife — Phyllis, I think her name is — came to watch Ingelido dance. He's a university professor. Physics. Marian, on the other hand, I know pretty well. I attended their wedding about six months before I signed on with my first cruise line. She comes from money. If I'm not mistaken, her money bankrolled Take the Lead with Ingelido."

We exchanged significant looks. "So if she found out her husband fathered a child with her sister . . ."

"She might pull the rug out from under Ingelido's business," Maurice finished.

"That certainly gives Marco a strong motive for not wanting Corinne's book to get published," I said.

"I don't like Ingelido much," Maurice said, "but I can't see him sneaking poison into Corinne's pills. How would he have gotten access to them, for one thing?"

"Good question." Crossing to the window, I looked down onto the street, twiddling with the blinds' cord. "I think you should at least mention him to Phineas Drake, though. One of his investigators might turn up something more."

At the mention of Drake's name, Maurice's face sagged, and I remembered he'd had another session with Detective Lissy and his merry band of interrogators.

"What? Did the police . . ." I didn't finish the question.

"They didn't spring any new evidence on us, if that's what you're asking," Maurice said, sinking onto the love seat. I sat beside him and put my hand on his. "We covered the same old ground, several times. It's clear they think I'm their man, that I killed Corinne. The worst part is that since they've arrested me, they're not even looking at anyone else."

"But I'm sure Phineas Drake is," I said, remembering the way the lawyer dug up other suspects when the police thought I had killed Rafe.

"He's got investigators on it," Maurice said with a shrug that said he thought it was hopeless.

"Then they'll turn something up that will exonerate you," I said with hearty cheerfulness. I stood and tugged at his hand. "Come on."

He looked a question at me but got obediently to his feet.

"I'm taking you down to the river and buying you an ice cream." I knew ice cream couldn't fix Maurice's situation, but my dad took me for ice cream when I didn't do well at a competition or a teen boyfriend dumped me, and it always made me feel a bit better, at least temporarily. And temporarily was better than nothing, I thought, following Maurice down the stairs.

Chapter 25

After our expedition to the river (where I had a lemon sorbet to keep my calorie intake within the strict levels I stuck with to maintain my weight, while drooling over Maurice's double scoop of coffee fudge ripple), I left Maurice at Graysin Motion, practicing with one of his competitive students, and headed for the flagship studio of Take the Lead with Ingelido. I had debated calling Marco Ingelido and setting up an appointment, but I decided that surprise might work better. I was going to confront the dancer-turned-entrepreneur with the news of my break-in and see how he reacted. I couldn't stand to see Maurice so sad and worn-down; I needed to do something to jolt Corinne's murderer into betraying himself or herself.

Take the Lead with Ingelido was in the Tysons Corner area, and I fought rush-hour traffic around the beltway to get there. Late-afternoon sun streamed through the Beetle's window, and my air-conditioning didn't seem to be as cool as usual, so I arrived flushed and sweaty. The dance studio occupied a former skating rink, and the familiar top-hat logo signaled potential dancers from atop a neon sign that towered over the private parking lot. I eyed the lot with envy. In crowded Old Town Alexandria, where my studio was located, students either had to park on the street—a chancy thing—or use the parking garage two blocks down. I knew a fair number of female students didn't feel comfortable attending our evening events because they didn't like the parking situation.

A sprinkling of cars populated the lot, and I figured Marco had a class going on. Entering the building, I looked around curiously; I'd never been in here before. The color scheme was all black and gold, like the logo, with flocked wallpaper and gilt mirrors in the entryway. An unmanned reception counter where some pimply kid used to pass out roller skates now held class schedules, brochures, and a selection of dance shoes. A door, half-open, sat just past the counter, waltz music pouring out, and I poked my head in.

The dance floor was huge, the former rink covered with wood flooring, I guessed, noting the waist-high wall that encircled it with gaps for dancers to enter or leave the floor. Approximately fifteen couples circled the floor, and I bit back the envy that surged in me; we were lucky to have six or eight couples at any given class. Clearly, people liked Ingelido's concept. Marco himself was moving among the dancers, correcting a gentleman's frame, demonstrating a turn with a flustered woman student. I had watched for three minutes or so, not willing to interrupt the class to speak with Marco, when a familiar voice spoke from behind me.

"Were you interested in lessons, ma'am?"

I spun to see Solange Dubonnet standing behind me. Her expression faded from helpful to sneering when she recognized me. "Come to see how a successful studio operates, Stacy?" she asked with false sweetness.

"I didn't know you worked here," I said. Solange was the reason Rafe Acosta became my ex-fiancé four months before his death. I caught them in bed together. Waves of red hair rippled to Solange's shoulders, bared by a halter-top dress, and her green eyes gleamed with malice. She'd tried to buy Rafe's half of the studio after his death, but her plan had fallen apart.

"I've been teaching here since just after the Emerald Ball," she said, referring to a ballroom dance competition in L.A. "Working with Marco is fabulous—he's got such a head for business, and the students love him. What are you doing here?" She eyed me with suspicion, as if I were here to kidnap Marco's students and drag them down to Graysin Motion.

"I just wanted a word with Marco," I said, determined not to get into it with her.

After studying my face for a moment, she sashayed onto the dance floor and spoke in Marco's ear. He glanced toward me, handed the class off to Solange, and headed my way. I had to admit he moved well as he approached me with the gliding motion that had made him famous back in the day.

"Stacy." He greeted me with lifted brows. "Have you come to find out about our franchise opportunities?" The glint in his eye told me he knew better.

"Actually, I came to tell you someone broke into my house last night."

His face went expressionless for a moment before he said. "Really? And why would I be interested?"

"Because whoever it was was looking for Corinne's manuscript."

Taking my elbow, he guided me toward a small office

I hadn't noticed earlier. I noted dark wood, an excellent sound system, dance trophies, and a sleek laptop before he closed the door and turned to face me. "Did they get it?" His dark eyes searched my face.

"You should know."

"Are you accusing me?" He seemed caught between astonishment and scorn, and any hope I cherished of getting him to confess dwindled. He snorted and passed behind me to get a cigarette from a box on his desk. "Filthy habit, I know," he said, lighting up. "I feel it in my wind more and more each year. Yet . . ." He shrugged.

I tried a different tack. "Sarah Lewis seemed very interested in the scene of the crime. I caught her taking photos of my parlor."

"Sarah?" Marco took a step toward me. "What was she doing there?"

"Vitaly and I hired her to do our publicity stills," I said. The tension in Marco's face unsettled me and I stepped back.

"Leave Sarah out of this," Marco warned. "It's got nothing to do with her."

"Oh, I think it does," I said. "Your determination to keep Corinne from publishing her memoir—I think it's got everything to do with Sarah."

Marco reared back as if I'd slapped him. The cigarette burned down, unnoticed, between his fingers. After a moment, he lifted it to his lips and drew deeply. It seemed to calm him and he turned his head to exhale smoke over his shoulder. "Whatever you think you know, I had nothing to do with Corinne's death. And that's all I'm going to say on the subject. I don't need to prove anything to you or anyone else: The police already have their man."

I sensed a deep weariness in the dancer that almost

made me feel sorry for him. "Maurice didn't do it," I said. "He had no possible motive."

"Really?" Marco squinted and his voice turned nasty. "Perhaps you should ask him about a certain ruby necklace that 'disappeared' during one of his cruises. Come to think of it, that's a story that might interest the police, if they haven't already dug it up. And I'm sure it's a story Corinne was including in her damned memoir, since she was instrumental in resolving the situation."

The certainty in his tone took me aback. "What are you talking about?"

His gaze mocked me. "Ask Maurice. I'm not one to tell tales out of school on another man. I've got a class to teach." On that note, he stubbed out his cigarette in an ashtray and ushered me out of the office, leaving me in the entryway as he returned to the dance floor. I knew Solange, eyes bright with curiosity, watched me as I exited.

I pointed my Beetle toward home, troubled by Marco's insinuations about Maurice. I hoped to be able to talk to him about them when I got back to Graysin Motion, but an accident on the beltway had traffic backed up for miles, and by the time I reached Old Town ninety minutes later, he was gone for the day. I phoned his house, but got no answer. Reluctantly concluding I would get no answers that evening, I called Danielle and talked her into meeting me at the gym for a workout.

"Isn't that Eulalia Pine something else?" Danielle whispered as we did vicious ab exercises in a Pilates class—Danielle's choice, not mine.

"She seems to know her stuff," I said, crunching my body into a vee with my arms extended over my head and my legs almost perpendicular to the floor. "She's in charge of an estate sale at Corinne Blakely's house that starts tomorrow. I'm going to show up early to buy Corinne's old typewriter."

"Why?"

The women on either side of us shushed us, and Danielle and I exchanged guilty looks and then giggled. The instructor frowned at us, which only made us giggle more.

"I'm not going to be able to walk upright for a week," I complained to Dani as we straggled out of the class at nine p.m. I rubbed my abused abs.

"You're the professional athlete," she said. "Suck it up."

"Hmph."

As we showered in the locker room, Danielle came back to the estate sale, and I told her about the typewriter and Maurice's theory that the cartridge would reveal Corinne's outline and provide more suspects for her murder.

"An estate sale sounds like fun," Dani said, squirting shampoo into her hand and massaging it through her thick curls. "I'll come with you."

"I have to be there by eight tomorrow morning."

"Shoot. I've got to work."

I faced the shower spray, closing my eyes and lifting my face to the drumming water. "I'll call you as soon as I get finished and let you know how it goes. Any luck finding a couch yet? I could keep an eye out for one at the estate sale."

"I've been to a couple more stores, but I haven't settled on a couch yet. I'm making progress, though: I know I don't want leather. Sure, let me know if you see something at the sale."

We toweled off, dressed, and left the gym as the last glimmers of sun faded from the sky. Before we separated outside the gym, I asked Dani whether she wanted to go swimsuit shopping with me on Saturday. "I need a new suit for Jekyll Island," I said casually.

She eyed me with affectionate scorn. "Is that your subtle way of trying to nudge me into a decision?"

I don't know why my subtlety was so obvious to everyone. "Maybe."

She laughed, punched my shoulder, and strode off with a toss of her red curls.

"Is that a 'yes'?" I called after her.

I arrived at the estate sale the next morning moments after it began, Tav, surprisingly, in tow. He'd shown up at Graysin Motion before heading to his business downtown, hoping to have the talk about our financial situation which we'd postponed from yesterday. He'd caught me shooing out the sweaty ballroom cardio students, anxious to get to Corinne's house before someone snapped up the typewriter, and had decided to ride along when I told him where I was going.

He let out a low whistle when he caught sight of the mansion. "Ballroom dancing pays better than I thought," he said.

"Marrying well pays better than ballroom dancing," I said dryly, maneuvering the car down a side street where arrows indicated we should park.

"Maybe I should try it," he said with a sidelong look at me.

"Great work if you can get it," I said, refusing to take the bait.

He laughed and freed himself from the seat belt. "Which way is the house now? I got lost two turns back—I have no sense of direction."

I put my hands on his shoulders and pointed him in

the right direction. The number of cars parked on both sides of the street between here and Corinne's filled me with dismay, and I found my pace quickening as we approached the house. "I hope it's not gone," I muttered, as we came within sight of the house, the lawn crawling with dozens of people pawing through goods set up on card tables outside, while a steady stream of buyers disappeared through the front doors or into the open garage.

A fortyish woman and a man sat behind a six-foot-long folding table with a cash box in front of them and a professionally lettered sign proclaiming PINE ESTATE SALES propped to the side. The woman wasn't Eulalia Pine, but I approached her anyway. She looked up from making change for a dealer apparently buying several pieces of furniture and gave me a harassed look over the tops of her reading glasses. When I introduced myself and told her I wanted to speak to Eulalia Pine, she shook her head of frizzy brown hair. "Mom tore a ligament in her ankle out appraising some antique farm equipment last evening," she said with an exasperated sigh.

"She was going to put a typewriter aside for me," I said anxiously, scanning the boxes and items stacked behind and under the table.

The woman threw open her hands in a "nothing I can do" gesture. "She didn't say anything to me. Your best bet is to find it in the house. All I can say is we haven't sold any typewriters today." She turned her attention to a customer behind me.

I grabbed Tav's hand. "Come on. Thanks," I threw over my shoulder to the woman, who was now haggling with a portly man about the price for a life-size ceramic tiger he towed on a child's sled.

Tav and I threaded our way through the throngs of shoppers; it felt as crowded as Christmas Eve at the mall.

"Who knew a garage sale would draw so many people?" I said.

"Estate sale," corrected a thin woman holding a laundry basket full of what looked like antique linens. "Very different. I don't do garage sales."

"You say tomahto, I say tomayto," I whispered to Tav as we made our way into the high-ceilinged foyer. I thought of all Great-aunt Laurinda's stuff I wanted to get rid of and wondered whether either an estate sale or a garage sale would net me enough to buy a few new pieces of furniture. Maybe if I combed garage sales for bargains, I thought. I hadn't been to a garage sale in years; last time I'd purchased an *Aladdin* VCR tape with a quarter from my allowance. I started for the stairs.

Midway up, a young couple, each toting one end of a rolled-up carpet, bumped into me. Tav's arm clamped around me as I teetered on the stair. He drew me tight to his side.

"This is more dangerous than playing football"—I knew he meant soccer—"on the highway."

"The possibility of bargains can drive even usually sane, calm people to hitherto unknown acts of violence," I said, trying not to show how his closeness affected me. His warmth and the woodsy scent of his shampoo or deodorant made me lose focus for a moment.

"Do you suppose that woman woke up this morning saying, 'I must have a bronze planter engraved with scenes from an African village, because my life is incomplete without it'?" Tav asked in my ear as an elderly woman tottered past us with just such an item clutched to her chest.

I stifled a laugh and continued up the stairs. On the landing, practically within sight of my goal, I bumped into Turner Blakely. A knowing smile oiled across his face when he recognized me, and I could tell he thought I'd come looking for him. He threw an arm across my shoulders. "Too many people around right now, Stacy," he said. "But I'm free tonight."

I wiggled out from under his arm and drew Tav forward. "Tav, this is Turner Blakely, Corinne's grandson. Turner, Tav Acosta, my partner." I deliberately didn't specify what kind of partner.

The men eyed each other with instant, mutual dislike and shook hands briefly. "I am sorry about your grandmother's death," Tav said.

"What are you doing here, then?" Turner asked me, suspicion darkening his eyes now that he knew I hadn't come chasing after his hot bod.

"The same as everyone else," I said as casually as possible. "Looking for a bargain."

"They're not charging enough for Grandmother's treasures," Turner said. His face wore an expression of discontent. "I tried to tell the woman in charge that she was pricing things too low, but she wouldn't listen to me. Told me she knew her business and to butt out."

I grinned inwardly and wished I'd been present for the confrontation between Eulalia Pine and Turner Blakely.

"I know Grandmother paid twenty times more for some of her things than that Pine woman is asking for them."

"Things always go cheap at a garage sale," I said.

"Estate sale." Turner glared at me.

I suddenly thought of Maurice's painting. I knew he didn't have possession of it yet. "Where are the items that Corinne willed to people?" I asked.

"In storage," Turner said. "Goudge's staff collected the bequeathed items. They also removed all the good art, Grandmother's jewelry, and pieces of furniture; it'll be auctioned off later." He looked a bit happier at the prospect of making more money.

"Look, Verena, this chest of drawers is only one hundred dollars," exclaimed a woman's voice behind us.

"That can't be right!" Turner brushed past Tav and me and went to confront the women attempting to lift the chest.

As soon as his back was turned, I grabbed Tav's hand and pulled him down the hall to Corinne's office. Only a couple of shoppers browsed in the small room. One was standing on tiptoe to take down a clock mounted on the wall. The desk had a "sold" sticker on it. Gaps in the bookshelves showed where buyers had removed books. The desk chair was gone.

So was the typewriter.

Chapter 26

I must have gasped, because Tav turned to look at me. "Stacy?"

"It's gone," I wailed. "But the woman said they hadn't sold it yet." I rushed to the desk, looking under it and around it, in case someone had moved the typewriter so they could examine the desk better. "It's not here."

"Stacy." Tav hauled me to my feet. "Someone must have just walked out with it. If we hurry, maybe we can catch up with them at the cashier and make them an offer for it."

"Good thinking." I dashed out the door in front of him, saw the stairs clogged with people to my right, and headed left, hoping to find a lesser-used flight of stairs. Many of these old houses had servants' stairs, I knew. This end of the hallway was quieter, empty bedrooms opening off to either side. I flung open a door at the end of the hall to find a narrow flight of stairs leading downward. With a triumphant smile at Tav, I took the stairs two at a time, erupting into what appeared to be a butler's pantry near the kitchen.

"Excuse me," I said, squeezing between two couples squabbling over an ugly china tureen ornate enough to have graced the table of Queen Victoria or some such.

Hoping Tav was still behind me, I threaded my way through the kitchen, its counters laden with stacks of china and serving dishes in three or four patterns, bins of silverware and stainless, glassware, small appliances, and all the other detritus that ends up in kitchen cabinets: linens, baskets, holiday-themed dishes, candlesticks, garlic presses and mandolins, and a George Foreman grill. A brief vision of the impeccable Corinne bent over a little grill on her patio flashed through my mind as I opened the back door to said patio and stepped outside with a sigh of relief. Fresh air! I hadn't realized how confining the house felt with so many people panting for bargains.

"Over there." Tav grasped my arm and pointed toward a young man disappearing around the side of the house, our typewriter tucked under one arm while he struggled with a standard poodle on a leash. We took off after him. My kitten heels sank into the soft turf with every step. I finally paused to slip them off and sprinted barefoot to catch up with Tav as he rounded the corner of the house. The grass was crisp and cool, and I would've enjoyed the opportunity to stand and scrunch my toes in it, but our typewriter was getting away.

"Sir, sir!" I called to the man, who had, luckily, stopped to examine a copper birdbath.

The poodle barked and the man looked up, light brown hair the color of the poodle's curly hair falling into his eyes. He was in his mid-twenties, with a soft look about him like he didn't exercise much and spent most of his time indoors. "Quiet, Tammy," he told the dog, resting a hand on her head.

She curled her lip at us, but quieted. "Yes?" He looked from me to Tav inquiringly.

"My name's Stacy Graysin," I said with a winning smile, "and I came here today specifically to buy that typewriter for a friend of mine."

The man's arm tightened around the machine. "I'm buying this for my mother. She wants to write a book. A romance."

"Wouldn't she rather have a computer?" I asked. "Much easier for editing and such."

"She doesn't trust them."

Oh, boy. Tammy the poodle growled at me, and I wished Hoover were here to teach her a few manners.

"How much are they asking for the typewriter?" Tav asked.

The young man righted the typewriter and checked a sticker. "Twenty-five dollars."

"I'll give you forty," Tav said. Tammy nosed at his hand until he stroked her head.

"Done." The man handed me the Smith Corona while Tav pulled two twenties out of his wallet.

"Thanks." I tossed the word to Tav and the young man as I beelined for the cashier's desk before anything else could happen. The way the morning had been going, I expected Turner to pop up and rip the typewriter out of my hands, telling me it wasn't for sale, or for a sinkhole to open up and swallow the machine.

"I see you found it." The woman we'd talked to earlier smiled when I reached the front of the line.

"You know," I said, clunking the typewriter and my shoes down on the folding table, "I really only need the cartridge, and I think that man"—I pointed to the man with his poodle, still talking to Tav—"would like to buy the typewriter." Popping the cartridge out, I wished I'd thought of it before we'd paid Poodle Guy the forty dollars.

"Two bucks."

Handing her a fiver, I turned to look for Tav, waving the cartridge triumphantly.

Tav and the poodle guy were inspecting a display of framed movie posters, some of which looked like they were from the 1940s and 1950s, and I started toward them, tucking the cartridge and my shoes into my purse. Before I had taken two steps, though, I caught sight of a tall, skeletally thin man clad in a trench coat skulking at the edge of the property, half-hidden by a spiky-leafed hedge. Hamish MacLeod! What was he doing here? On impulse, I headed toward him, pretending to glance at the tables of knickknacks and pieces of furniture on the way. When I got to within hailing distance, I looked up— artistically, I thought—and pretended to spot him for the first time.

"Why, aren't you Hamish MacLeod?" I said, heading toward him with a big smile. "I saw you at the will reading. You were husband number four, right? I work with Maurice, who was husband two." I beamed at him.

He shrank back, practically wedging himself into the hedge, and his eyes darted from side to side. I got the distinct impression he wasn't happy to see me. Too bad. "It's sad, isn't it," I babbled on, gesturing to the crowds of people trampling the grass and making off with Corinne's treasures. "Sad to see it all go."

"It's sacrilegious," he muttered, his Scottish accent blurring the words. If I'd closed my eyes, I could have been listening to Scotty from *Star Trek*. "It's like desecrating a saint's resting place."

I didn't quite see the parallels: Corinne was no saint, and this wasn't her resting place.

"These ghouls don't appreciate who Corinne was," he said, a bit louder. He inched out of the hedge with a rattle of branches and glared down his beaky nose at me. He must have been sweltering in the trench coat, because sweat beaded his forehead and slid down his temple.

"Were you here to get a memento?" I asked.

"Why would you ask that?" he shot at me, one hand sliding into his coat pocket. Only then did I notice the way the pockets bulged.

Hm. Perhaps the Reverend MacLeod was helping himself to mementos without paying for them. I said soothingly, "I'm sure it must be hard to see the things that were special to you and Corinne sold off like ... like ..." I couldn't think of a comparison.

"They have no right! That vase there." He pointed to a huge cut-crystal vase a heavyset woman was carrying in both hands. "That held the first offering of tulips I ever made to my gorgeous Corinne. It was the night after we met. She had told me tulips were her favorite flower, and I rounded up every one I could find in the city and gave them to her in that vase." He turned away, as if the sight of the vase being sold was too much for him.

"Very romantic." Clearly, the man had been gaga over Corinne. Completely unbalanced about the woman, in my humble opinion. If he had felt slighted by her, if she'd told him she was going to write something that dissed their relationship, how would he have reacted? Of course, I reminded myself, she'd divorced him and married twice more, and slights didn't get much more "in your face" than that. The divorce hadn't prompted him to harm her, so why would he poison her now? He hadn't had the opportunity, either, as far as I knew.

"When did you last see Corinne?" I asked.

"I went to every competition and exhibition she participated in." He straightened and threw his shoulders back, clearly waiting for me to applaud his devotion.

Uh-oh. Stalker city. "Don't you have a job?" I asked.

He frowned at me. "I'm retired from the ministry. My time is my own." I imagined he used that exact voice in the pulpit when he wished to emphasize a scriptural point. The effect was diminished somewhat when a small, faceted perfume bottle tumbled from beneath his coat and landed in the grass. We both ignored it.

"I guess you spend time with Randolph, too."

He froze momentarily, then leaned toward me. Hunched over like that, with his long, skinny neck and beaky nose, he reminded me way too much of a vulture. "Why would you say that?"

"I was chatting with Randolph this weekend and someone mentioned you'd stopped by," I said, forcing myself not to back away. What could he do to me on this grassy lawn with hundreds of bargain hunters nearby?

Some emotion flitted across his eyes; it looked like fear. "What I do and where I go is no business of yours, young lady."

"I'm just trying to keep Maurice from being convicted of Corinne's murder."

"Whoever killed my beloved Corinne should be burned at the stake. It was an evil thing to do. Evil!"

He said it with an intensity that made me wonder whether he had all his marbles. "I think you have an ulterior motive for being here today," I said, stooping to retrieve the perfume bottle. I held it on the flat of my palm, the way you feed a horse so you don't get bitten, and he snatched it.

"As do you, young lady!"

His accusation startled me, and I gripped my purse

tighter. Could he know about the typewriter cartridge? Was he here for more than the odd memento? Was he looking to retrieve the manuscript, too?

His next words dispelled that fear. "You're here, like they are"—he gestured to the crowd—"out of vulgar curiosity. You're here to feed on the beauty, the gentleness, the incandescent light that was Corinne. Scavengers, all of you! Ghouls!" He threw one arm up dramatically, and a foot-tall bronze figure of a dancer *en pointe clink-clank*ed to the turf. Without another word, he bent, picked it up, thrust it into an interior pocket of his coat, and left. He strode rapidly across the lawn, trench coat flapping about his legs. I stared after him for a moment, not sure I'd accomplished anything by confronting him, then trotted toward where Tav and Poodle Guy were chatting by a pile of coffee-table art books.

Tav broke away from his conversation, joining me with a grin. I grabbed his arm and pointed to Hamish MacLeod as he disappeared down the driveway. "That's Hamish MacLeod," I said, "Corinne's fourth husband." I relayed our conversation and my conviction that the man was stealing easily portable items.

Tav looked after Hamish with interest. "Corinne certainly had eclectic taste in husbands," he said.

I hadn't expected him to go tearing after MacLeod and accuse him of theft, but his comment seemed anticlimactic. "Why do you suppose he was visiting Randolph at Hopeful Morning?"

Shrugging, he looked down at me quizzically. "Probably not for any nefarious reason. Perhaps you are so caught up in keeping Maurice out of prison that you are seeing suspicious behavior in very ordinary activities?"

His words stung a bit. "Well, I don't call thieving 'ordinary' activity," I said huffily.

We had reached the driveway by this time, and I stopped to put my shoes back on, using a hand on Tav's shoulder to balance myself. I tried to slip him forty dollars, but he shook his head. "I want credit for doing my part in keeping Maurice out of jail. I only hope this cartridge contains something useful after all the hassle we went through to get it."

The sun highlighted yellow flecks in his brown eyes as I smiled up at him. "You and me both."

Since Tav was late for a meeting, I dropped him off at the Metro station before returning to the studio. Vitaly and I taught an international standard class at Wednesday lunchtime, and I had to hustle to get back for it. We introduced the Viennese waltz—harder than the regular waltz—to applause and groans.

"I don't know how you manage to look like you're floating, Stacy," one woman said. "I feel like I'm wearing cement shoes."

"Practice," I said with a smile. "It's all about practice. You can float, too; I promise."

The class wrapped up at twelve thirty, and Vitaly stayed in the ballroom to coach an amateur-amateur pair who were excited about entering their first competition. I descended to my kitchen and called Maurice, leaving a message to let him know we'd finally acquired the typewriter cartridge. My hand was still on the phone when it rang, startling me.

"Stacy, I've got the CD with your proofs on it," Sarah Lewis said when I answered. "I'm going to be at Tate Slade's Fine Arts this afternoon, taking photos for a brochure for their new exhibition, and I can drop it by afterward, if you like."

"How 'bout I meet you at the art gallery," I said, feeling restless. "It's on Royal, right, near the Episcopal church?"

I mopped the kitchen floor and then changed into white cotton slacks with a thin red stripe and a red peasant blouse before scooting upstairs to tell Vitaly I was leaving and to ask him to lock up when he finished. Walking the few blocks to the art gallery, I felt myself relaxing, sinking into the moment. I deliberately put aside thoughts of Corinne's murder and the studio's precarious financial position to enjoy the beautiful day. A calico cat looked down on me from his perch in a bay window, bricks herringboned the sidewalk in a hypnotic pattern, and the drone of an airplane high overhead made me glance up briefly. Reaching the gallery before I was ready to, I strolled past it to linger in front of St. Paul's Episcopal Church, letting the sand-colored stones of its Gothic revival facade warm me, and admiring the swooping arches that fronted the church. Reluctantly, I retraced my steps to the art gallery and went in.

Dimness cloaked me, and I blinked while my eyes adjusted. The space was largely open, with bleached wooden planks on the floor, white panels for walls, and lighting provided by stainless-steel fixtures directed toward the paintings. A thin man on a stepladder and a minion struggled to hang a wall-sized painting that seemed to consist of little more than a canvas painted off-white with a wavy blue line bisecting it.

"We're closed to set up for the exhibition. The opening's Friday night," the man on the stepladder called.

"I'm looking for Sarah Lewis," I said, wandering closer to see whether the painting offered anything more up close. Nope. I peered at the discreet price tag on the wall and almost gasped: twenty thousand dollars. *Eep*.

"Back there." The man jerked his balding head toward the rear of the gallery. As he spoke, a flash of light told me where I'd find Sarah.

"Thanks." I wended my way around the panels and past more paintings as monochromatic and inscrutable as the first one. I like my art to have recognizable objects in it—people, dogs, flowers—or at least to feature bright colors. As far as I was concerned, these paintings took minimalism, or monochromatism or whatever the style was called, to heights of boringness seldom scaled by an artist. I left off critiquing the paintings as I rounded a corner to find Sarah Lewis adjusting a light on an aluminum pole.

"Do you think you could hold this just so?" she asked, spotting me. "It keeps slipping."

I obligingly wrapped my fingers around the cool metal, and watched as she checked a light meter and then took a few photos of the canvas in front of us.

"Thanks." Letting the camera hang from a strap around her neck, she reached into a multipocketed duffel and withdrew a CD case. "Let me know which ones you want. Eighty dollars each."

I took the case from her, noting that she seemed a bit stiffer than when we'd last met. She broke eye contact almost immediately to shift the strap around her neck.

"Vitaly and I will look at them and let you know," I said. I hesitated, wanting to ask her about Marco, but feeling awkward about it.

"Look," she said as I was on the verge of leaving. Her head snapped up and her eyes met mine squarely for the first time. "Marco told me about your visit yesterday."

"Um."

"He said you know."

"I didn't know you knew."

"Since I was eighteen." She tossed her head so her

dark braid slipped over her shoulder. "He and Mom took me aside to tell me that I wasn't my father's daughter, that I was Marco's daughter. They thought I should know the truth for medical reasons and what have you. Great birthday present, huh?"

"It must have been hard to hear."

She met my gaze, unsmiling. "The hardest. Not only did I have to come to terms with the fact that I wasn't who I thought I was, but my mom wasn't the person I thought she was either. All her blather about integrity and living authentically was just so many words. Great for spouting in the classroom but without any applicability to real life. We didn't talk for a couple of years."

"I'm sorry," I said, feeling intensely uncomfortable in the face of her anger and grief.

"Yeah, well, a lot of therapy has gotten me—us—through the worst of it. But then Corinne Blakely told Marco she was publishing her memoir, and that she was including the story of their romance and why she broke it off." Sarah popped the lens off the camera and stowed it roughly in the duffel. She was silent for a moment, searching for a new lens and fitting it to the camera body. She mumbled something I didn't catch.

"What?"

"I said I didn't want Dad to find out that way. He loves my mother; he still thinks I'm his biological daughter. It would break his heart." She looked up, her chin tilted a bit, defiantly. "That's why when Marco told me you had the manuscript, I broke into your house to find it."

My jaw dropped. "Say what? It was you?"

She nodded. "It wasn't hard. I bought a crowbar at a hardware store and waited till I thought you'd be asleep. The waiting was the hardest part. I pried the door open and started searching, but then you woke up." She loosed a long sigh. "I'm sorry I knocked you down. I hope you weren't hurt?"

"I'll live." This conversation felt surreal. This woman had broken into my house with burglary on her mind, and now she was looking at me with concern. I tried to muster some anger, but the fact that it was my own lie that led her to break in kept me from working up any righteous indignation.

"Were you telling the truth when you told Marco you don't really have it?"

I nodded.

"Then what am I to do?" Tears filmed her eyes.

"I think it's totally possible there isn't really a manuscript," I said, relating what Mrs. Laughlin, Corinne's housekeeper, had told me.

"Really?" Sarah stood a little straighter. After a beat, she added, "So someone killed Corinne for nothing?"

"Why would you assume Corinne was killed over the memoir?" I asked.

"Because the thought crossed my mind. And if it occurred to me, chances are someone else thought of it, too."

I stared at the woman in front of me, so like me in many ways: She was close to my age; she worked for herself in an arts-related field; she was single (I thought) and childless. Had she just confessed to planning a murder?

"I didn't do it, of course," she said, perhaps reading my face. "I couldn't. I couldn't kill someone, not even to save Dad pain and keep my parents from divorcing. But I can't really blame whoever did it—Corinne was asking for it."

The tight expression on her face dared me to contradict her. Tap-tapping and a muffled "Damn!" floated over the nearest panel, and I started at the reminder that we weren't alone.

"Do you suppose it crossed Marco's mind?" I asked.

There was a barely perceptible hesitation before she burst out, "He wouldn't! Marco's a good man."

Evidence of a daughter fathered on his wife's sister to the contrary. I raised my brows.

"Sex is different from murder!"

No argument there.

"Just because he and my mom had an affair thirty years ago doesn't mean he killed Corinne to keep it secret. Or that my mother did, either," she added.

Hm, now there was a suspect I hadn't thought of. Would Sarah's mother kill to protect her marriage . . . or her job? It might be worth learning more about Phyllis Lewis. Except how would she have put epinephrine in Corinne's pills? I decided Phyllis didn't get a priority rating on my suspect list, although I might mention her to Phineas Drake.

"Are you going to tell the police?" Sarah asked in a low voice.

My thoughts were jumbled; I didn't know what was best. "My concern is Maurice Goldberg. He's my friend, and I'm not going to sit by and watch him go to prison for a crime he didn't commit."

I hadn't really answered her question, but she nodded. "Fair enough. Look, I know it's costing you time and maybe money to get your door fixed and all. Just pick the photos you want and I'll get you another disk that's not copyright protected—you don't owe me anything."

I regarded her somewhat cynically, recognizing a bribe when I heard one. "I'll let you know." I wasn't sure what I'd let her know, but it sounded good.

We eyed each other awkwardly for a moment, not

sure how to part, but then she half nodded and turned away to fiddle with the light stand again, and I slipped silently around the nearest panel. Out of sight of Sarah, I took a deep breath, blew it out, and hurried for the door, raising a hand in acknowledgment when the gallery owner called, "Don't forget! Friday evening. There'll be wine and cheese, and you can meet the artist in person."

Whoop-de-do.

Chapter 27

Seven o'clock that night found me at the Fox and Muskrat watching Maurice compete in a darts tournament. Anxious to get the typewriter cartridge to him, and to find out what Marco Ingelido had been referring to when he talked about a necklace disappearing on one of Maurice's cruises, I'd finally gotten hold of Maurice and asked him to meet me for dinner. He'd countered with an invitation to the darts tournament. "I've been signed up for weeks, Anastasia," he said. "I can't back out now."

Accordingly, clad in slim-fitting jeans and the red shirt I'd worn earlier, only with an extra button undone, I cheered for Maurice while he tossed darts at the target. Clumps of people gathered around the competitors aiming at two well-lit targets set on age-darkened beams. The rowdy participants included men and women and people of all ages, from a girl in a GWU sweatshirt who was maybe twenty, to a man who looked like he could have swabbed decks on the *Titanic*. Pretty much everyone was wearing jeans and sucking on a beer. Even Maurice had dressed down for the occasion, leaving his blazer at home to compete in a blue-and-yellow-striped rugby shirt and pressed jeans with loafers.

I'd been tickled to see that he had a little case containing his own darts. "You take this seriously," I observed.

"There's a lot riding on it." By his tone, he might have been talking about the first space launch or the D-day invasion or a heart transplant. But then he winked at me and I laughed.

The "lot riding on it" turned out to be a free six-pack of English ale for the winner, and a free beer for Maurice, who came in second. I'd had no idea he was doing so well, since the scoring system totally mystified me. I clapped my hands as he rejoined me at a high-top table near the dartboards after collecting his winnings. Setting his beer on the table, he pulled out my chair. "Come on, Anastasia. It's time you learned how to throw darts."

Most of the crowd had dispersed, many of them leaving the pub, and no one was watching the twosome still tossing darts toward one of the targets. No danger of public embarrassment. "How hard can it be?" I asked, grabbing a hasty sip of my own beer before Maurice pulled me to a line on the wooden floor and handed me a dart. Showing me how to position my fingers on the ridged metal, he drew his arm back and pushed it forward to demonstrate the throwing motion several times. "Push the dart at the board. Don't fling it. There's no break in the wrist."

I lobbed the feathered missile toward the board; it nicked the corner and clattered to the floor. Okay, so the game was more difficult than it looked. Maurice handed me another dart. "Not so hard. Relax into it."

I tried relaxing and the dart nose-dived into the floor a foot in front of the target. I pouted.

"Not quite so relaxed," Maurice said, hiding a smile.

I could see he was enjoying himself, maybe for the first time since his arrest, and I didn't want to spoil his mood, but after another fifteen minutes of the darts lesson, during which I managed to sink most of my darts into the pockmarked beam supporting the target and a couple of them into the target itself (to extravagant praise from Maurice), I dragged him back to the table.

Squirming onto the bar stool, I said, "I've got some good news and a question."

"Good news first," Maurice said, signaling for another beer. He was drinking something dark and foamy that looked like it would hold a fork upright; I prefer a beer that light can penetrate, an India pale ale or the like.

Pulling the cartridge from my purse, I waved it aloft. "Ta-da."

His brows climbed as he reached for it. "Anastasia! How did you acquire it?"

I told him about going to the estate sale with Tav and the stratagems we'd had to employ to secure the cartridge. "The Quest for the Cartridge ended in triumph," I declaimed, "due to the perseverance and resourcefulness of the knight and his fair lady." *Whew*. I'd had too much beer.

Maurice wiped away a foamy mustache and smiled. "Well done. Mildred and I will get started on deciphering it first thing tomorrow. I just hope that what it contains is worth all the money and effort you put into finding it."

"If not" — I shrugged — "we're no worse off than we were before."

"You said you had a question?"

Someone plugged quarters into an old jukebox that had been turned off during the tourney, and a Kenny

Rogers song drifted our way. It was incongruous in the British-feeling pub. "I talked to Marco Ingelido yesterday," I said. "And to Sarah today." Uncomfortable confronting Maurice with Marco's story, I gladly wasted some time telling him about my conversation with Sarah.

"I can't believe she broke into your house," he exclaimed. "Good heavens!"

Fortifying myself with a swallow of beer and trying to block out the irritating chorus of "Wake Me Up before You Go-Go" that was now bouncing from the jukebox, I said, "Marco claims Corinne knew something about you that you wouldn't want to see published."

"Corinne knew many things about me I wouldn't want to see in print, starting with my waist size," Maurice said humorously, but I could see the uneasiness in his eyes.

"He mentioned a necklace." I let the comment hang there.

"Ah." Maurice stared into his beer.

The silence lengthened, broken only by the dulcet tones of Wham!, and I pleated a bar napkin.

"I was young," Maurice started, still gazing into his beer as if it were Dumbledore's Pensieve. I wondered what memories it contained. "But that's no excuse."

I stiffened. Was Maurice going to confess to theft? I didn't really want to hear it.

"It was my second cruise. The ship was called *Starlight Maiden*. I only ever sailed on her the one time. Anyway, our second night out, I asked a woman to dance. That was my job, you know—to 'entertain' unaccompanied ladies of a certain age on the dance floor, or even accompanied ones, if it looked like their escorts would be relieved if someone else danced with them. This woman's name was Julia. She was maybe sixty to my thirty. Attractive, self-assured, from Oklahoma. Oil money.

"You may have heard jokes about dance hosts being little better than gigolos?" He didn't wait for me to answer, but hurried on. "In this case . . . we 'hooked up,' as the kids say today. For the remaining seven nights of the cruise. It was fun. I was attentive; she was generous."

I squirmed in my seat, intensely uncomfortable, appalled that I had forced Maurice into reliving this. "You don't have to—"

"Midway through the cruise, she bestowed a necklace on me, a ruby pendant, a smallish one, set in gold. She said she was tired of it, that I should give it to my mother or my sister. I tucked it away, planning to do just that, and didn't think any more about it until after the passengers debarked back in Florida and it transpired that Julia had told the purser her necklace was stolen. Before I could come forward, the crew's quarters were searched and the necklace was found in my suitcase."

"Bitch."

Maurice pursed his lips. "A very troubled woman, at the least. The cruise line fired me immediately, and I was in danger of going to jail. Corinne saved me."

"How?" I envisioned the dancer going toe-to-toe with the mysterious Julia, pulling out her fingernails one by one until she agreed not to prosecute.

"She hired a private investigator. He discovered that Julia had pulled the same trick three times on separate cruise lines. Gotten three dance hosts fired. One went to prison. Corinne presented this information to the appropriate authorities and the charge was withdrawn; in fact, Julia was prosecuted. I was still fired, though, for 'fraternizing' with a passenger."

"My God, Maurice."

"Not an incident I look back on with pride. You'd better believe all my future dealings with passengers were strictly on the dance floor." He gave me a strained smile.

Leaning across the table, I hugged him awkwardly. "I'm sorry I brought it up."

"No, it needed to come out. I suppose I should tell Drake, let him advise me as to whether or not I should give the information to the police. It wouldn't do to have them stumble across the old arrest somehow. Or to get a copy of Corinne's manuscript or outline and find the tale in there." He tapped the cartridge on the table.

It was well past nine o'clock by now and the crowd had thinned out. A waiter came by and we both shook our heads at him. He collected our glasses and swiped at the table, leaving a damp swirl on the polyurethaned wood. Tucking the cartridge under his arm, Maurice slid off his stool. I followed suit. We headed for the door and Maurice collected a few "congrats" and "good nights" from the remaining drinkers. "See you in the morning," I said, trying to sound natural and spritely.

"*À demain*," Maurice said, walking me to my car and declining a ride home. I watched from behind the steering wheel as he started down the sidewalk toward his house, shoulders slumped just a little, stride a bit less sure than usual. Striped by a car's headlights, he crossed a street and I lost sight of him.

Vitaly stomped into the studio the next morning for our practice, tossed his designer sunglasses on top of the stereo cabinet, and announced, "John is being a total fanny."

I had to think about that one for a moment. "Ass?"

"*Da!*" He nodded, adding a phrase in Russian that probably translated to something ruder than "ass."

He marched in place to warm up, each foot pounding down in a way that suggested he was envisioning his partner's head under his heels. I'd never seen him so worked up. His thin cheeks were flushed, and his straw-like hair flopped as he marched. He had moved from Russia to live with John in Baltimore three or four months back, and I'd met John several times since Vitaly and I had become partners. He was a bit older than Vitaly—in his forties, I'd say—and seemed like a steady, kind man. I carefully didn't ask what John had done to merit being called an ass, since getting involved in Vitaly's love life—even peripherally—seemed like a bad idea.

"You is wanting to know how John is being an ass, yes?" Vitaly said, launching himself across the room in a series of deep lunges. "Well, I am telling you. He is insist we must kennel Lulu when we is vacation in France next month."

My brain worked to dredge up Lulu. Their boxer puppy. "Um," I murmured, going through my own warm-up routine. Frankly, it didn't seem too ass-ish to me. A not-yet-house-trained puppy in a hotel on the Côte d'Azur sounded like a big pain in the ass to me.

"Lulu is being lonely without I and John. She is not like living in a box."

"Maybe Lulu's afraid of flying," I said. Damn, I hadn't meant to get involved.

"You think?" Vitaly looked struck.

"There are lots of very good pet sitters who stay in your house and take care of your pets. Walk them, feed them, keep them company." In for a penny, in for a pound. "I'm sure if you asked around, some of your dog-owning friends could recommend someone."

"John should have thinked of this," Vitaly announced. "I will telling. Now, we dancing."

He pulled me toward him and spun me away and we

sprang into the jive, spending a sweaty hour practicing our side-by-side figures and our lifts. Our timing still wasn't quite right on some of our lifts—we'd been working together only a couple months, after all—and if I didn't want to end up on my nose when he swung me up so my heels kicked toward the ceiling, I had to hit his hands just right with my pelvic bones, my hands and locked-elbow arms bracing against his shoulders. Our foreheads clunked together at one point, but we kept going until our trembling arms forced a break.

I was collapsed on the floor sipping a bottled water, and Vitaly was downing his usual grapefruit juice, when I heard the outside door squeak open. *WD-40*, I reminded myself as Hoover bounded in. His toenails clicked on the ballroom's wood floor and he skidded to a stop in front of me, licking my face and then sniffing at the bottle I held.

"Hi, Hoover." I patted his head, edging away from the strand of drool about to decorate my tank top. The Great Dane trotted over to see whether Vitaly's bottle held anything more tempting than water, and Mildred entered the room, a beatific smile on her face.

"Hello, everyone," she said as if Vitaly and I were a crowd of dozens. "We have news!"

"We" turned out to be her and Maurice, who entered moments after her, looking more his usual self than when we parted last night. I smiled at him. "The cartridge?" I asked.

"Yes, Anastasia, the cartridge." Maurice held up the black plastic case, which now had a loop of ribbon hanging from its pointy end.

"We have decoded it," Mildred announced importantly, waving a thin sheaf of paper. Her white hair bounced happily around her plump cheeks. "We have

divined the mysteries of Corinne's manuscript." She
flourished one hand into the air like a fortune-teller an-
nouncing messages from the great beyond. "All is revealed."

Vitaly looked confused. "What is this cartridge?"

Taking turns and talking over each other, Maurice,
Mildred, and I explained what the cartridge was and how
we had gotten it. "Now," I finished, "they're going to tell
us what they learned."

Vitaly and I turned expectant gazes on the older pair.

"It's not quite what we were hoping," Maurice
hedged. "It turns out this must have been a new cartridge, because there were only a couple pages' worth of
material on it. That's why we were able to copy it off
pretty quickly."

"So tedious," Mildred put in. "Letter by letter. I don't
understand why dear Corinne"—I didn't think she'd
ever met Corinne Blakely, but Mildred was the kind of
person who made friends immediately, even with a dead
woman—"didn't use a computer. I can't imagine life
without a computer."

That was rich, coming from a woman who'd lived
more than half her life before the invention of the silicon
chip.

"Why, it's so much easier to keep up with my sorority
sisters and friends with Facebook. I remember when one
had to write letters by hand and hunt for one's address
book to address them, and then wait for the postal service to deliver them, and the friend to find time to write
back—phah! Twitter's the way to go. I have seventy-four
followers, you know." She beamed at us.

"The manuscript?" Maurice nudged her gently.

Hoover settled beside me, his heavy head on my lap,
as Mildred began to read. "It starts in midsentence. '. . .

lucky to have lived most of my adult life in the world of dance, surrounded by friends and family who venerate the art form. Although it might seem, from some of the reminiscences I've shared with you, that the world of ballroom dance is rife with scandal and backbiting and skullduggery, I suggest that this passion finds its way into the dance and makes it the art form that it is. In every walk of life, there are husbands who cheat, children who disappoint, friends who betray. In dance, at least, there is also beauty and movement, expiation and forgiveness in the sweat and rigor and partnership. In dance, it really *does* take two to tango, so relationships become paramount.

"'As I pen these words, the International Olympic Committee is deciding whether or not DanceSport should become an Olympic event. If you've stuck with me through the last two hundred some-odd pages, you know how I hope the vote comes out! But even if Dance-Sport does not receive the IOC's blessing, it has still blessed my life in innumerable, immeasurable ways. And I am thankful for it.'"

Mildred glanced up from the page and wiped a tear from her eye. "So beautiful."

I locked eyes with Maurice. "But ... two hundred pages! This isn't an outline—it's a final chapter."

"Just so, Anastasia," he agreed.

"Then ... then there is a completed manuscript."

"Unless she is starting at the end?" Vitaly suggested.

I considered it briefly before shaking my head. "No, the page count makes it sound like she's already written the whole thing." I jumped up, dislodging Hoover. "Mrs. Laughlin lied!"

Chapter 28

Maurice tapped a finger against his lips. "Now, Anastasia, maybe there's some other explanation. Maybe Corinne didn't share the manuscript with Mrs. Laughlin."

I looked at him from under my brows. "Friends for half a century? Lived in the same house?"

"It seems unlikely that Mrs. Laughlin wouldn't know," he admitted.

"Who is being this Mrs. Laughlin person?" Vitaly asked.

"Corinne's housekeeper," I said.

"Where can we find her, dear?" Mildred asked.

"England," I said gloomily, at the same time Maurice said, "The King's Arms."

"What?" "Where's that?" "How do you know?" Hoover added to the bedlam by scrambling to his feet and barking. Mildred shushed him with a hand around his muzzle.

Maurice answered my question first. "I spoke with her briefly at the will reading and she mentioned she would be putting up there—it's a bed-and-breakfast place in Arlington—until after the funeral."

Mention of the funeral quieted us all. It was being held the next day. Turner Blakely had delayed it, he'd said, so Corinne's "many, many friends from the international ballroom dancing community" could arrange to attend. He'd hired a funeral coordinator and was doing it up like a Hollywood wedding. I knew all this because there'd been a black-boxed announcement about it in the program handed out at the exhibition for the Olympics folks. (The announcement hadn't actually said the bit about a Hollywood wedding, but it was clear the solemnities would be pompous and glitzy and overdone.) Vitaly and Maurice and I were attending together.

"I'm going to the King's Arms," I said. I pushed to my feet, my muscles stiff after sitting cross-legged for so long on the hard floor. I was getting old.

"I'll go with you," Maurice said.

Shaking my head, I started for the door. "Uh-uh. She lied to *me*. I'm going to have it out with her. I'll give you a call when I get back. Can you cover the ballroom aerobics class for me if I'm not back in time?"

When Maurice looked like he would have followed me anyway, Vitaly put a hand on his arm. "No one is doing anythings with Stacy when she is making up her minds. Much smarter to keep away and take cover." He mimed ducking and covered his head with his arms.

Everyone laughed, defusing the tension. Hoover barked, and I hurried out, not bothering to debate Vitaly's assessment of me. I might be *impulsive* now and then, but I didn't create chaos, for heaven's sake.

Pausing only to toss a lemon-colored T-shirt over my

sweaty workout top, I grabbed my keys and slammed the back door on my way out.

The King's Arms, when I finally found it—I should have taken time to MapQuest it before driving off—was a two-story, Tudor-style home on a quiet cul-de-sac in nearby Arlington. It was all whitewashed walls, dark beams, and mullioned windows; it looked old and out of place next to the brick, 1960s-era ranch house beside it. Flowers frothed in the classic English garden that fronted the home, roses spilling open so bumblebees could get drunk on pollen. I recognized lavender and daisies and petunias, but I couldn't name most of the blooms. A carved wooden sign announced, THE KING'S ARMS, EST. 1805, BED AND BREAKFAST. Crunching up the oyster-shell path to the front door, I paused. Did one ring the bell or just walk into a B and B? Playing it safe, I knocked. When no one answered, I pushed the door open and peeked in.

"Hello?"

A small reception desk with old-fashioned cubbies for keys was four paces in front of me, but no one staffed it. A rag rug covered the floor, and an iron chandelier hung low, providing dim light from curly CFL bulbs that didn't have near the ambience that candles would have. A broad staircase ascended to my right, and I could see a door with the number one affixed to it just off the landing. I had one foot on the stairs, determined to knock on every door if I had to, to locate Mrs. Laughlin, when a thin teenager came around the corner, steadying a pile of pink towels with her chin. She looked startled to see me, but then smiled. "Hi." The towels muffled the word by not giving her enough space to open her mouth properly.

"I'm looking for Mrs. Laughlin," I said.

"Number four," she said.

"Thanks." I trotted up the stairs, not pausing to inspect any of the botanical prints arranged on the wall.

Number four was the last door on the right. I rapped with one knuckle.

"Come in, Shelly," a voice called.

I turned the black metal doorknob that might have been original to the house, and pushed the door open. Mrs. Laughlin, still looking as sweet and gentle as a Hallmark-card grandma, had a suitcase open on the bed and was placing folded clothes into it. "Just leave the towels on the dresser," she said without looking up.

"You lied to me," I said, stepping in and closing the door.

Mrs. Laughlin didn't exclaim or scream, but the pile of utilitarian undies she was tucking into the suitcase tumbled out of her hands, spilling on the bed and the floor, when she jerked her head toward me. "Oh, my goodness, you gave me a start," she said, right hand pressed to her chest. She peered over the red-framed bifocals. "Stella, right?"

"Stacy."

She bent to retrieve a pair of undies from the floor. "I wasn't expecting . . . Why are you—"

"I think you know." I'd been scanning the room, and I'd spotted a stack of paper on the antique oak washstand by the window. Crossing the room, I studied the top page, which proclaimed *Step by Step: A Memoir*. Corinne's name appeared next, followed by a list of some of the ballroom dancing titles she'd won.

Mrs. Laughlin watched me riffle through the pages, doing nothing to stop me.

"This is Corinne's memoir. Why did you lie to me and tell me it wasn't finished?"

She sighed and stretched for a pair of undies that had

drifted half under the bed. Her girth got in the way, and I bent to pull them out for her. "Thank you." She folded them precisely and laid them gently atop the others in her old-fashioned, hard-sided suitcase. It looked battered enough and antique enough to have been the one she packed her clothes in when she came from England half a century earlier.

"Well, I really didn't think it was any of your business," she said at last, turning to face me. A look of resolution stiffened her seamed face. "I lived all this with Corinne," she said, gesturing toward the manuscript pages, "and I helped her write and organize the book. When she died, it seemed only right for me to continue where she'd left off and see the book through to publication."

"It's part of the estate," I pointed out. "It must belong to Turner."

"Pish."

She turned back to her packing and I watched for a minute. "Corinne's agent said they were working with someone to finish the book—that was you?"

She nodded. "I got in touch with them immediately after learning Corinne was dead. I've added a chapter about her death—the editor says it's quite moving—and I mailed off the completed manuscript Monday. That's a copy." She indicated the pages on the dresser.

"The police should have this," I said, laying a hand on the manuscript.

"There's nothing in there that will help them," she said, "but by all means, take it to them if you want."

"What do you mean, there's nothing that will help them? So many people were worried about what Corinne was saying and were angry at her for revealing their secrets."

"Maybe so, dear," Mrs. Laughlin said with a world-weary air, "but do you really think Marco Ingelido would kill to keep his illegitimate daughter a secret?"

I did, actually.

"Or that Greta Monk would do murder to keep Corinne from spilling the beans about a spot of embezzlement twenty years ago?"

Possibly. Or her husband might.

"Or that one of her ex-husbands might do away with her in order to keep sexual inadequacies a secret—Lyle; or keep the world from hearing how he beat his son from his first marriage—the Reverend Hamish; or conceal his past as a gigolo accused of theft—your friend Maurice." Her gaze gently mocked me. Giving me her back, she hauled on the suitcase, pulling the top half up and over so she could latch it. A gap of about eight inches made closing it unlikely. "Could you just press down on this, dear?" she asked.

Obligingly, I moved to the bed and leaned all my weight onto the suitcase while she fumbled with the latches. They snapped shut after a moment's struggle. Breathing heavily, Mrs. Laughlin sank onto the coverletted bed, and I swung the suitcase to the floor, nearly dislocating my shoulder. What was she taking back to England with her—her bowling ball collection?

"People don't kill out of embarrassment," she said after catching her breath.

Hm, wasn't there more to it than shame? I wasn't so sure that the prospect of humiliation, divorce, loss of income or prestige, or a prison sentence didn't make good motives, but I let her continue.

"People kill out of greed or for revenge," she said with the air of a teacher instructing a student.

Where had she gotten her degree in the psychology of

murder? "If greed's a motive, you stand to make a lot of money off of this," I said.

My near-accusation didn't faze her; in fact, amusement bloomed on her face. "I didn't kill Corinne."

"It would have been easy for you to tamper with her medication."

"Maybe so, but I didn't do it. However, that doesn't mean I was going to look a gift horse in the mouth. The manuscript," she said when I looked confused. "Corinne left me enough to live on in her will, but do you have any idea what taxes are like in England? And the VAT?" She shook her head in disbelief. "Besides which, I don't want to spend the rest of my days trapped in that cottage with Abigail. We didn't get along so well as teenagers, and I doubt that old age has increased our tolerance for each other. I want to be able to get away, to travel. The advance for the book—I negotiated a new one when I explained to the publisher that they'd never get the manuscript if they didn't deal with me—will pay for a little holiday in Majorca. And when the royalties start coming in, I expect I'll be able to manage the safari in Botswana I've always dreamed of, and maybe a tour of Cambodia." She gave me a serene smile.

"Turner will sue you," I predicted.

"Let him try." Steel threaded her tone. "I'll claim the manuscript was one of the mementos I chose in accordance with dear Corinne's will."

Whew. If she hadn't been so thoroughly English, I'd've thought she had an ancestor named Machiavelli.

Getting to her feet, she said, "Now, dear, I'm afraid I have to shoo you out. I need a nap before my dinner date this evening."

Date? This octogenarian on the verge of moving back

to England had a date when I hadn't had a date in over half a year, not since Rafe and I broke up?

She primmed her mouth. "Mr. Jonathan Goudge has invited me to dine with him," she said coyly.

Corinne's lawyer. I couldn't help it: I laughed. "Well, have a nice evening," I said, scooping up the typewritten pages. They weighed more than I anticipated.

"You, too. I expect I'll see you at the funeral tomorrow."

I arrived back at the studio midway through the ballroom aerobics class and immediately took over for Vitaly, who was leading the class with verve. The students seemed to be enjoying him, even though he had them doing spins until they staggered around the room like drunks, since they didn't know how to spot properly. I waved good-bye to Vitaly as I got the women started on some quickstep footwork sequences guaranteed to raise their pulses.

As soon as class ended, I went downstairs to shower and change. Refreshed, and dressed in a minidress with a mod floral print straight out of the sixties, I tucked the manuscript in a tote and lugged it to a copy place. Once I'd made myself a copy, I drove to the police station and asked for Detective Lissy. A young admin type escorted me back to his office, and I looked around with curiosity while Lissy finished a phone conversation. My prior experience of the police station included only a grim interview room; it was interesting to scope out Lissy's private space.

As I would have expected, the place was scarily neat, with case folders stacked precisely, papers in his in-box aligned so their edges touched the top and right-hand sides of the box, white mug centered on a ceramic coaster. What caught my attention, though, were the photos. All in identical black frames, and all lined up with the front edge of the credenza behind his desk, they featured kids ranging in age from infanthood to adolescence, smiles on most of their faces. Somehow, I had never pictured the neat-freak Detective Lissy with children. Unless he had them trained to military standards, they must drive him insane with clothes dropped on the bedroom floor, makeup left on bathroom countertops, and mud tracked into the house.

When Lissy hung up and gave me a long-suffering look, I asked, "Are they yours?"

"You think I keep photos of someone else's grandkids in my office?"

"Grandkids?" *Wow*. My mind was busy processing this hitherto unknown side of the persnickety detective and I missed his next remark.

"What do you have to show me, Miss Graysin?" he asked impatiently. "The desk sergeant said you had new information related to the Blakely murder."

"Oh, this." I hefted the tote onto my lap and dug out the manuscript. Proudly, I deposited it on his desk. It looked out of place there with its dog-eared pages ever so slightly offset.

Lissy poked at it with a stiff finger. "'This' would be . . . ?"

"The manuscript," I said. "I discovered that Corinne had completed it after all, and I managed to retrieve it." I waited for his words of praise.

"Oh, that," he said dismissively. "We've already got a copy. One of my officers is reading it, but I don't expect any revelations."

"You've already got a copy?" My face fell.

Sensing my disappointment, perhaps, he smiled maliciously. "Why, yes. Angela Rush, the agent, faxed it to us yesterday."

I bit back the words that sprang to mind. *Damn. Double damn.* I'd thought I could curry favor with Lissy by bringing him the manuscript, but it was old news to him.

"I've been doing this job for twenty-seven years, Miss Graysin," he said. "I'm better at it than you think." He used the backs of his fingers to edge the manuscript closer to me.

I wanted to point out that if he were really good at it, he wouldn't have arrested the wrong man. However, I just stood, tucked the pages back into the tote (instead of strewing them around his psychotically neat office, as I was tempted to), and said with as much dignity as I could muster, "Thanks for your time. I've got to hurry if I'm going to drop this at Phineas Drake's office before they close for the day." I gave him a sweet smile.

The mention of Drake's name gave Lissy a dyspeptic look, as if he had tummy troubles, but he didn't say anything besides, "I've told you before: Stick—"

"Yeah, yeah, I know. Stick to dancing."

I dropped a copy of the manuscript off with Phineas Drake, getting a few minutes with the lawyer himself, even though I told his receptionist I didn't need to see him. His smile was partly hidden by his beard as he came forward to greet me. When I told him what I had, he gave me all the praise Lissy had denied me, extolling my initiative and my cunning. He laughed, a sound like rolling timpani, when I told him about Mrs. Laughlin and Mr. Goudge.

"That's one way to create conflict of interest and ensure Goudge won't be able to represent the estate if the grandson sues her for theft of the manuscript," he said admiringly. "Sounds like my kind of gal."

I raised my brows, wondering whether Mrs. Laughlin's liaison with the lawyer was as deliberate as Drake was suggesting, and decided it probably was.

Drake riffled the manuscript's pages and plunked it onto his massive desk. "I'll get one of my associates on this right away. I have high hopes that it'll provide me fodder for creating reasonable doubt, my two favorite words in the English language." Still chuckling, he escorted me back to the elevators and I rode down, anxious to get home and read the book myself. I called Maurice on the way, telling him what Mrs. Laughlin had said and about giving the manuscript to Drake.

"Good thinking, Anastasia," he said. "I'll keep my fingers crossed that you find something useful in the book."

"I can make another copy, if you want one," I offered.

"Thank you, but no. I'm sure I'll read Corinne's book one day, but I don't think I can deal with the memories right now."

"I understand." The melancholy in his voice subdued me. "I might have some questions for you, though, as I read."

"By all means."

I hung up, thinking about what a weird thing a memoir was. Was it possible, I wondered, for Corinne, or anyone, to write a wholly truthful memoir? Not, I decided, thinking about how Danielle's and my memories of our last trip to Jekyll Island differed. Nothing told from one person's perspective could be more than one facet of truth, if that. I amused myself the rest of the way home imagining how my life story would differ if written by me or Danielle or an "objective" author like a reporter.

Chapter 29

I couldn't dive into the manuscript right when I got home, since I had back-to-back private sessions with two of my competitive students. As I said good-bye to the second one, Danielle breezed in, still in her work "uniform" of gray suit, pale blue blouse, and low-heeled black pumps. Dullsville. Only her red curls saved her from a blandness that would make Muzak look innovative. "I thought we'd get dinner somewhere first," she said, wrinkling her nose at the sight of my sweaty, grubby self.

"First?"

"Aren't you the one who invited me to go swimsuit shopping?"

"You didn't take me up on it," I said, releasing my ponytail from its elastic.

"Well, I must have, since I'm here." She grinned unrepentantly.

"Fine. Let me shower," I said, resigned. I didn't want to go swimsuit shopping now; I wanted to read the manuscript. However, if there was a chance of getting Danielle to agree to vacation with me and Mom, I had to take it. Sisters.

An hour and a half later, me showered and both of us fed, we descended on the swimsuit department at T.J.Maxx. They had a large selection of suits and were relatively uncrowded in the early evening. Danielle and I each selected eight or ten suits and headed to the fitting room to try them on. We emerged from our dressing rooms simultaneously to inspect our first efforts in the three-way mirror. I wore a tomato red bikini with ruffles, and Danielle had on a black one-piece.

Danielle glared at me balefully. "No woman in her right mind goes swimsuit shopping with a professional dancer."

I grinned and pirouetted, letting my hair fly. "Oh, come on. You're in good shape, too; you're just hiding your great bod under the world's most hideous suit."

Looking down at her tank-style suit, Danielle said, "You don't like it? It fits well."

I made a raspberry. "Let me pick one out for you." Ducking into her dressing room, I sorted through the suits she'd selected. "Black tank, black tank with a zipper, navy tank—ooh, going out on a fashion limb there—another black tank, black tank with shirring," I said, tossing them aside. "Boring, boring, boring! Stay here." I marched out of the fitting area and back to the racks, forgetting I was still wearing the red bikini until I noticed people staring, especially a middle-aged man buying golf shirts who got tangled up in the spinning clothes rack. Ignoring the attention, I pulled three suits off the rack and took them to Danielle.

"Here."

She took the suits reluctantly. "They're so . . . unblack."

"They're bright, colorful, happy. Try them on."

When Danielle came out in the first suit, a one-shoulder number in dark green with pink and coral flowers splashed across it, I gave her a wolf whistle. With her red hair tumbling over her shoulders, she looked like a tropical siren. Turning to and fro in front of the mirror, she gave a tentative smile. "You don't think it's too noticeable?"

"There's no such thing," I said with all the positivity of almost twenty years of dancing in skintight outfits spattered with sequins or rhinestones, or slit up to *here* and down to *there*, or with sheer illusion panels that skirted the FCC's decency guidelines, or all of the above. "You look hot. Buy it."

"Okay." She giggled and tried on the other suits, and we walked out of the discount house an hour later, the happy owners of two new suits each. Deep dusk had settled over the parking lot, but plenty of traffic still zipped by on Highway 50. Late rush hour—the commuters who worked late to avoid the worst crush of traffic. With the possible exception of midnight until three a.m., every hour of the day in the greater D.C. area was rush hour of some kind.

"Does this mean you're coming to Jekyll Island?" I asked.

She gave me a "don't push me" look. "It means I'm planning for all eventualities, keeping my options open."

"Spoken like a true union negotiator."

Tucked up in bed an hour later, I started in on the first page of the manuscript, even though my eyelids were drooping. The first chapter consisted mainly of introductory-type comments—why Corinne was writing the memoir and a bit of ballroom dance history. The second and third chapters concerned her childhood and I skimmed those, even though her accounts of her father's harshness (verging on abuse, it seemed to me) and her younger brother's death from pneumonia at age four were riveting. The following chapters dealt with the way she fell in love with ballroom dance by watching all the old musicals in the local theater on Saturday afternoons, and her earliest dance lessons, paid for by the money her mother made sewing for neighbors in the evenings after her day's work was done.

Corinne had just moved to New York City when I must have drifted off, because I awoke the next morning, one manuscript page crumpled under my cheek, the rest of them scattered on the floor where they'd fallen during the night. *Great.* A glance at the clock told me I didn't have time to sort them out; Maurice would be here in half an hour to pick me up for the funeral. Hastily scooting the pages together, I stuck them in my bedside table and dashed for my closet. I didn't have a single outfit anyone would call "solemn," so I had to settle for a zebra-striped sheath dress that went almost to my knees, with black hose and strappy black sandals. I twisted my hair into a simple chignon and, thinking it was kind of Corinne-ish, added a small black hat with a wisp of veil that I'd worn when Rafe and I performed a foxtrot on the *Ballroom with the B-Listers* results show a couple years back. A slick of light makeup and I was waiting in the front hall when Maurice pulled up.

When we arrived at the Presbyterian church, Maurice deserted me with an apology to join the other ex-husbands in a front pew, across the aisle from Randolph and Turner Blakely. "Corinne drew up the seating charts," Maurice explained in a low voice before he headed toward the altar, "and selected the music and the scripture passages for reading, and the flowers. It looks like Turner's done a nice job of fulfilling her wishes."

I gave Turner a silent apology for assuming he'd been the one determined to turn Corinne's funeral into a spectacle; rather, it was Corinne orchestrating the drama from beyond the grave. I shivered and slotted myself into a pew near the back, where the scent of lilies and carnations wasn't too overwhelming. I could just glimpse the oiled mahogany of the casket. I didn't think I'd feel compelled to draw up a script for my funeral when the time came.

We were a few minutes early, and I watched as other mourners trickled in. Mrs. Laughlin entered on the arm of Jonathan Goudge, and they were ushered to the pew behind the ex-husbands. Marco Ingelido and his wife arrived and followed an usher to a pew only two in front of where I sat. I guessed they hadn't made Corinne's A-list. Lavinia Fremont arrived soon after in a beautifully cut black linen suit and a wide-brimmed hat with enough veil to hide Jimmy Hoffa. I recognized her by her limp, and by the fact that she was shown to the pew Mrs. Laughlin occupied.

I recognized many, many of the other mourners, dancers I'd competed against, or ballroom dance legends I'd revered—Corinne's contemporaries. My pew was filling up, and I looked up in semiannoyance when a newcomer squeezed in beside me. My annoyance turned to pleasure when I recognized Tav.

"I didn't think you were going to make it," I whispered. I'd mentioned the funeral to him a couple days earlier, but he'd been unsure about getting away from his business long enough to attend.

He scanned the church with slightly lifted brows. "Judging from the crowd, I wouldn't have been missed."

"I'd have missed you." *Oops*. I hadn't meant to say that.

He gave me a warm smile that elicited all sorts of feelings not appropriate for a funeral. I resolutely faced forward as the service began, but I was conscious of his muscled thigh pressed against mine and his every movement as he flipped a page in the program or stood for a hymn. A photographer—not Sarah Lewis—took pictures discreetly, and if people had been wearing brighter colors and the music had been a bit more up-tempo, I'd have thought I'd stumbled into a wedding rather than a funeral.

We were spared any eulogies, and the service itself was mercifully brief and tasteful. The interment was in the cemetery attached to the church, and we all filed outside while the organist played a dirge-y piece I didn't recognize. I was grateful for my sleeveless dress as we emerged into the swampy heat. Tav stayed beside me as we angled toward the grave site, his arm lightly draped over my shoulders. Something black moved under the awning set up to shade the mourners, and I took a closer look as Tav asked, "Is that—"

"Black swans," I said, suppressing a giggle. Six of the large birds were corralled in a roped-off area to the left of the grave opening. A scrawny man in black jeans and a black T-shirt with SWAN WRANGLER stenciled across the back cast seed for them and headed off an aggressive bird that pecked at the patent-leather shoes of a woman who walked too close.

"Now I have seen everything," Tav said in a wondering voice. "I have seen doves at weddings a couple of times, but this is my first experience of swans at a funeral."

"Something to keep in mind for when your own time comes," I said with an impish smile.

"Absolutely not."

He said it forcefully, and a couple in front of us turned to glare. I buried my head in his shoulder to stifle my giggles and felt him shaking with laughter, too. "This is a solemn occasion," I managed to squeak after a moment, straightening up. The minister was saying something, but we were too far back, and a breeze was blowing her words away, so I couldn't hear. What we did hear was a sharp *yap-yap*. I looked around, thinking a stray dog might have wandered into the graveyard, but didn't see one until Tav poked me gently and directed my attention to a furry mop of a dog sticking his head out of a woman's purse to tell the swans what he thought of water fowl at a funeral.

The dog's owner tried to silence her pet with a hand around his muzzle, but the dog continued to *mrrf* and growl. People nearby began to smile or frown, and a wave of muffled laughter and comments spread through the crowd. The lowering of the casket caught the dog owner's attention, and the pooch seized the opportunity to leap to the ground. Threading his way through people's legs, he beelined for the swans. Despite the fact that they were three or four times his size, he dashed under the rope and stood barking at them. The minister spoke louder to compensate. A couple of the swans waddled away uneasily, more disturbed by the shrill yapping, I was convinced, than by any threat the tiny dog represented, but another swan moved toward the pup, hissing.

Before the swan wrangler could shoo the dog out of the enclosure, the aggressive swan fanned his wings wide and snaked his head toward the dog. With startled yips, the mop dog turned tail and ran, the swan chasing him. People backed away as the angry swan sailed over the rope and the wrangler cried, "Not yet, Ebony, dang it!"

The other swans, apparently taking Ebony's departure as their cue, beat their wings heavily and took to the sky, a dark phalanx rising over the cemetery. It was stirring in its way, I had to admit, but slightly undermined by the first swan still chasing the hapless pup. I had to think this wasn't quite what Corinne had in mind when she requested swans at her funeral. The dog's owner had entered the chase as well, wailing, "Gumdrop!" as she trailed the pair, staggering on her high heels. The dog had reached the lip of the grave, and I was afraid that the farce was going to turn really ugly, but Corinne's son, Randolph Blakely, leaned forward and scooped up Gumdrop before he could barrel into the gaping hole. With a smile, he restored the dog to her grateful owner. A blond woman about Randolph's age laid her hand on his arm and smiled. My investigative antennae pricked up, and I wondered whether she was the "girlfriend" Randolph's neighbor had told us about. She carried a few extra pounds and had a long face, but she was attractive in a comfortable, middle-aged sort of way.

Randolph looked more alert today, and his expression was lighter, in marked contrast to his son, who scowled at Gumdrop as if wanting to drop-kick him into the next county. "That was well done of Randolph," I whispered to Tav.

Ebony, deprived of his prey, flapped his great wings and followed his buddies into the sky.

"I wonder how the swan wrangler catches them again," Tav said, his gaze following the elegant bird.

With a determined look on her face, the minister began a rousing chorus of "Nearer My God to Thee" and we all chimed in.

As the service ended and people began wandering off, I excused myself to Tav and angled toward where Randolph was accepting condolences, the blond woman still by his side. I made it to the front of the line and offered my hand to Randolph, saying sincerely, "Your mother meant a lot to all of us in the ballroom dancing world. I'm so sorry for your loss."

He nodded his acceptance of my condolences and turned to the older gentleman behind me. I stuck out my hand to the blond woman. "I'm Stacy Graysin. I don't think we've met."

"Alanna Vincent," she said with the gratitude that spouses and girlfriends frequently betray when someone pays attention to them at their husbands' or boyfriends' events.

"How did you know Corinne?" I asked.

"I didn't, really," she admitted with a small smile that crinkled the skin at the corners of her eyes. "Randolph and I met at Hopeful Morning. I'm an alcoholic, and we overlapped there for several months." She said it with no trace of self-consciousness. "When I left this past February, we stayed in touch. Things are progressing." She gave me a sweetly mischievous smile and squeezed Randolph's arm. Still conversing with the elderly gentleman, who seemed to have an inexhaustible flow of reminiscences about Corinne, Randolph patted her hand where it lay on his arm.

"That's lovely," I said. "I hope things work out for both of you. It was very nice meeting you."

"You, too, Stacy." Alanna smiled.

A bit bemused by this evidence of Randolph's romantic life, I went in search of Maurice to see how he was holding up. He stood near the grave with the other ex-husbands. Lyle was apparently demonstrating a golf swing, and the Reverend Hamish was bawling, while the fifth husband, the African-American whose name I couldn't remember, patted his back. I assumed the short, dumpy man I hadn't seen before was Baron von Whatever, and I studied him curiously. I was somewhat disappointed to see that he was ordinary in every respect, except for a gray mustache waxed and twirled into points that looped up against his pudgy cheeks.

Spotting me, Maurice said something to the baron and edged toward me, only to be intercepted by Turner Blakely. The young man looked svelte and sophisticated in a black suit with a black-and-gray-striped tie. His dark hair was brushed straight back from his forehead, revealing a pale, narrow brow.

"Goldberg." He planted himself in front of Maurice and pulled an envelope from an inner jacket pocket.

Maurice cocked his head slightly, waiting for Turner to explain himself.

"I'm contesting the will," Turner said, thrusting the envelope at Maurice, "and in particular the painting that you tricked Grandmother into leaving you."

"There was no trickery involved, Turner, as you well know," Maurice said calmly. "However, it's your prerogative under America's right-to-sue-and-be-sued legal system to contest the will, so contest away."

The tips of Turner's ears reddened at the light contempt in Maurice's tone. "Murderers can't benefit from their crimes," he spit. "When you're convicted, the painting will revert to the estate anyway."

"Then if you're so sure of my guilt, save your money and wait for the justice system to grind its wheels. It shouldn't take more than eight or ten years, what with appeals and everything." Maurice gave Turner a pseudo-sympathetic smile. "Who knows? Maybe by then the painting will have appreciated in value. Or maybe I will have sold it to pay my legal bills." With a nod, he left Turner fuming and walked to me, saying under his breath, "Get me out of here, Anastasia, before I really *am* guilty of murder."

I could tell by his ragged breathing that maintaining a facade of calm while talking to Turner had cost him, and I took his arm to lead him back toward the car, distracting him by telling him about having discovered the identity of the mysterious blonde who had visited Randolph. Tav joined us and, summing up Maurice's state of mind in one comprehensive glance, offered a quiet comment on the funeral and what a lovely tribute the crowd was to Corinne. Maurice responded in kind, and his breathing had slowed by the time we neared the car.

The car parked in front of mine was a black limousine, and a chauffeur opened the door for Randolph Blakely, Alanna Vincent, and—to my surprise—Hamish Mac-Leod as we approached. The reverend was still sobbing into his hands, and Alanna was murmuring soothingly to him. The chauffeur stood stiff as a fence post, perhaps used to ferrying blubbering passengers around the city.

"It'll be okay, Hamish," Randolph said bracingly. "You made a good decision to admit yourself to Hopeful Morning. They'll help you. Look what they did for Alanna and me."

The chauffeur clunked the door shut behind them, and I couldn't hear any more. My gaze flew involuntarily to Tav, and he gave me a smug "I told you so" look that I couldn't even get mad about. Apparently Hamish's presence at Randolph's cottage *was* completely innocent, as Tav had suggested. He'd been considering admitting himself to the rehab center. I smiled sheepishly and walked around to my door.

Maurice slid into the passenger seat and shut the door, and I looked at Tav gratefully over the hood of the Beetle. "Thanks. So, how does the swan wrangler get them back?" I guessed he'd gone to talk to the man when I went to find Maurice.

He grinned, confirming my guess. "They fly home," Tav said, "like homing pigeons. And in case one gets the idea of escaping, they have got GPS devices on their collars."

"The wonders of technology," I said.

His expression grew more serious, a bit uncertain. The wind riffled his dark hair. "Stacy, will you have dinner with me one evening? Not this weekend—I must fly to New York on business—but next weekend?"

My breath caught in my throat. "Are you asking me for a date at a funeral?"

A wry smile slanted his mouth. "Is that bad?"

"It's a first for me."

"Me, too."

I fell silent, biting my lip. I'd been attracted to Tav all along, but I was afraid to get involved again, especially with a business partner. If we dated and then broke up, it would be messy, awkward, like it had been after I caught Rafe cheating and ended our engagement. But we weren't talking about "getting involved," my free-spirit self argued. We were talking about a single date. *Ha!* my sensible side said.

"I'm not sure I'm ready," I told Tav, brushing a wisp of hair off my face.

"I know. I promised myself I would wait six months before asking you, but my willpower is not up to the task of waiting." The rueful awareness in his eyes, the crooked smile, the memory of that almost-kiss Monday night made my chest feel tight.

Maurice rolled down the window and said, "Are you coming, Anastasia?"

"Yes," I answered both men.

Chapter 30

Friday afternoon I locked up Graysin Motion, shut off my cell phone, and took Corinne's manuscript into my kitchen. Making a big pot of coffee, I sorted the pages back into order and sat down to read. The tale of Corinne's life, her excitement as she fell in love and married, only to find herself restless and unsatisfied soon after; her love for baby Randolph, and her anguish as the son she loved turned into someone else under the influence of drugs; her dislike of the daughter-in-law Randolph brought her, a girl ten years his junior who was more interested in partying than in mothering the child who came along six months after they married; her ballroom dance successes and her drive to win more titles and recognition; and the stories about people she met along the way kept me glued to the manuscript as the level of coffee in the pot steadily declined.

Greta Monk's story was here, along with Corinne's confrontation with her about the embezzlement. Conrad Monk, Corinne said, had repaid the money his wife embezzled and spread hush money around liberally to keep her from being indicted. Corinne had gone along only to keep scandal from tainting the dance scholarship foundation and its good work. Marco Ingelido's sordid story was here, a cautionary tale of lust run amok. She'd loved Marco, Corinne admitted, and had hoped to marry him before he got Phyllis, Sarah's mom, pregnant. When he'd become engaged to Marian, Phyllis's sister, Corinne had warned Marian, told her that Sarah was, in fact, Marco's child. My eyes opened wide at that. So, Marco's wife had known all along and never let on. I wondered whether the knowledge that her husband had slept with her sister, had fathered a child with her, had eaten at her over the years.

I made notes as I read, planning to pass my ideas along to Detective Lissy (whether he appreciated it or not) and Phineas Drake. Corinne gave Maurice's story of cruise ship romance gone bad a humorous spin, and I wondered how he'd react to that. It didn't seem to me, even forty-some years after the fact, that he found anything funny about the incident. I knew Detective Lissy would have latched onto the story already, so I didn't include it in my notes. There were a couple of stories I hadn't heard before, one featuring a ballroom dance judge who was a closet homosexual in the early 1970s who had been blackmailed by a former partner. Since he had died of AIDS in the late 1980s, I didn't put him in my notes either. The other tale I was unfamiliar with involved Turner and cheating. He'd done more than cheat himself, according to his loving grandmother; he'd run a cheating racket that involved buying copies of tests, hacking professors' computers, and selling the tests themselves and/or answers to a startling number of students. I wondered whether he could be prosecuted for the hacking; even if not, having the tale publicized was likely to ensure he never got admitted to another university. Not that failing to get a degree would matter much to his future, now that he had inherited Corinne's millions.

Lavinia Fremont's story came late in the manuscript, with great descriptions about their trip to England and the excitement of competing. Corinne described the attack outside the nightclub in horrific detail, and included a confession that rocked me back in my chair. I turned the last page over with relief and regret. I imagined the book would sell well. Draining the last bit of coffee from my mug, and feeling a caffeine-overdose headache coming on, I tapped my pen on the table and stared into space. My thoughts tumbled semiaimlessly. If I wrote a memoir in my seventies, would I have the same wealth of stories to tell that Corinne did? Would the people whose secrets Corinne laid bare in the book recover from the revelations? I thought about Mrs. Laughlin and her statement about greed and revenge being the only credible motives for murder. I'd thought all along that greed had twisted someone into a murderer. Maybe Turner or Randolph in order to inherit early, maybe Marco or Greta, who were greedy for acclaim and success and whose quests for those might be curtailed by Corinne's brutal openness. Maybe even Mrs. Laughlin, greedy for autonomy and new adventures.

The more I thought about it, though, the more I became convinced that I was wrong. Greed hadn't prompted Corinne's murder.

Revenge had.

Chapter 31

I thought about calling Maurice and talking it over with him, or even Tav or Danielle, just to run my suspicions past them. In the end, I called Detective Lissy. He was the one who would have to make the arrest, after all.

I caught him as he was leaving the office for the weekend, and he seemed strangely unwilling to make time for me, even when I told him I knew who had killed Corinne Blakely.

"So do I," he said wearily. "Maurice Goldberg. We arrested him, remember?"

"It wasn't Maurice. Look, I read the manuscript—"

"So did one of my officers. We talked to a couple of the folks mentioned in the book, including the Monks and Mr. Ingelido, and we're satisfied they didn't have anything to do with the murder."

"They didn't," I agreed. "If you'd just hear me out—"

"Ms. Graysin, my grandson is pitching the first game in the Little League championships in forty-five minutes. The only thing I'm listening to this evening is the crack of the ball against the bat and the insults of parents abusing the ump."

"Where?"

A hint of disbelief in his voice, Lissy told me.

An hour later, I joined him on the metal bleachers set up around a baseball diamond out near Vienna, Virginia, a D.C. suburb off of I-66. The sun beat down hotly, and I was grateful for the Baltimore Orioles cap I wore with my ponytail threaded through the back. The metal bleachers had absorbed enough heat to be uncomfortably warm against the backs of my thighs as I settled in beside Lissy. He looked casual and much more grandpa-ish in multipocketed khaki shorts and a faded blue golf shirt. Despite that, the shoelaces on his athletic shoes looked like they'd been ironed, and not a smudge of dirt sullied their whiteness. He slid me an exasperated look when I sat down and didn't introduce me to the woman on his other side, whom I assumed was his daughter.

"You know Virginia has stalking laws, right?" he greeted me.

"I'm not stalking you!"

"Hmph." He turned away to applaud as a team of adolescent boys in red-striped shirts took the field. "My grandson," he said proudly, pointing to a burly lad throwing balls from the pitcher's mound. He sounded more human than I'd ever heard him.

"Looks like he's got an arm," I said, parroting something I'd heard my dad say once about an Orioles pitching prospect.

I'd hoped that praising his grandson would soften Lissy up, but he merely said, "Give it to me." He kept his eyes on the field while I talked, turning his head to face me only when I'd finished.

"You want me to arrest Lavinia Fremont?" he said

incredulously. "The woman who benefited most from Corinne Blakely's generosity, whose business was financed by Blakely?" He sounded as if he'd have had the ump throw me out of the game if it were possible.

"It was blood money," I said. "In her memoir, Corinne confessed to being the one who orchestrated the attack that cost Lavinia her leg. Listen." I'd brought the page with me, and I dug it out of my pocket and unfolded it. "It's from the next-to-last chapter."

I began to read. " 'This memoir would be neither complete nor honest without an accounting of what happened in London in 1964 when my best friend, Lavinia, was attacked outside a nightclub and subsequently lost part of her leg and the ability to dance.' " I looked up to gauge Lissy's reaction, but his face was expressionless. "She goes on to explain about the dance competition and who all was there in London, and then says, 'To my everlasting shame, I paid a man, a thug, to injure Corinne so she wouldn't be able to compete. I told him where we'd be and even made sure we lingered at the nightclub until most of the patrons had left. I have regretted it from the moment he jumped out from behind that car. If I could have stopped it, I would have, but it was too late. I watched as he attacked Lavinia, watched as she crumpled to the sidewalk, and listened to her cries of pain. I could try to excuse what I did by talking about my passion for ballroom dance, and how badly I wanted to win the competition, but that would only make me more contemptible. I was so sick with grief and remorse that I could barely dance; indeed, I gave up dancing for several months after that. Everyone thought it was so I could be with Lavinia and help her, but it was because every turn, every chassé, reminded me of what I'd caused to be done. I swear, if I could have traded places with Lavinia on that operating table when the doctors removed her leg, I would have.'"

I lowered the page, affected as I had been on first reading it by the honesty—belated—and the pain that quivered in the words. "Even though Corinne meant only to put Lavinia out of commission for a week or so, she's the reason her friend had to have her leg amputated. She felt so guilty about it that she helped Lavinia financially—"

"Helped her get on her feet," Lissy said with mordant humor.

I winced and continued. "She put up the money to start Lavinia's design studio and did what she could to funnel business Lavinia's way. All because she felt genuinely awful about what she'd done."

"Perhaps you'll explain why Fremont waited until now to get her revenge?" Lissy asked, politely skeptical.

"Because she didn't know Corinne was behind it!"

Cheers erupted around us, and the boys on the field headed for the dugout while a green-shirted team took up positions around the bases and in the outfield. The scent of hot dogs drifted our way, and I realized I was hungry, but not hungry enough to eat a hot dog.

"And since the book isn't published, she found out about the scheme how?" His tone was not-so-politely skeptical now.

"Because Corinne told her."

He looked at me from under his brows. "Ms. Graysin—"

"No, really. Corinne told each of the people mentioned in the book—well, maybe not all of them, but the major players—what she was writing about. Greta Monk knew. Marco Ingelido knew. Maurice knew. I'm sure her son and grandson knew something about what she was writing about them. She talked to everyone. She must have talked to Lavinia Fremont, but Lavinia didn't mention that when we talked, which proves she had something to hide." I finished triumphantly and leaned back, bumping into someone's knees. "Sorry," I muttered to the man behind me.

"In each of those cases, Ms. Graysin, Blakely was revealing something negative about another individual; maybe you're right and she felt some obligation to warn them. With the Fremont tale, however, she was confessing to something herself, not outing someone else's secret, so I don't see that she'd have the same motivation to discuss it in advance."

I'd been through it fifty times in my mind and I knew I was right. Frustrated with what I saw as Lissy's deliberate obtuseness, I started, "Detective—"

"Ssh!" His grandson had come up to bat. I resigned myself and watched as the kid whiffed the first pitch, fouled the second one, and then connected with the third one to send the ball skittering between first and second bases. When he arrived, panting, at first base, he turned to grin at his grandpa, and Lissy gave him a thumbs-up. If I'd thought his pleasure in his grandson's accomplishment would soften him up, I was in for a disappointment.

"Go away, Ms. Graysin," Lissy said. "I appreciate what you're trying to do for your friend, but you have no evidence. Nada. Nothing but a story made up of speculation and wishful thinking."

"But—" I stopped. "What if I had proof?"

"If you had evidence, we could talk." His tone made it plain he didn't think we'd be conversing anytime soon.

Without giving a lot of thought to what I was going to do next, I pointed my Beetle toward Washington, D.C. At this hour on a Friday evening, most of the traffic was crawling out of the city, so I didn't hit any major traffic jams. As a result, I slid into a curbside parking space a block from Lavinia Fremont's shop at half past seven. The sun was low on the horizon, still providing plenty of light, but stretching shadows halfway across the street. A Middle Eastern restaurant offered sidewalk tables, and the scent of falafel mingled strangely with exhaust. Diners laughed, and a belly dancer emerged as I made my way toward Lavinia Fremont's studio.

The door was locked, and a "closed" sign hung in the window. I bit my lip. I'd rushed over here without a real plan, in my usual impulsive way, and now I didn't know what to do. I stepped back on the sidewalk and craned my neck. A light shone from the windows above the shop; I thought Lavinia lived up there. A taupe-painted door to the left of the shop had a sign above its doorbell that read, PRIVATE RESIDENCE. NO SOLICITATION. I wasn't a salesperson. I rang the bell.

Nothing happened for several minutes. I was about to give up and go home to formulate a better plan—heck, any plan—when I heard footsteps descending the stairs. "Yes?" Lavinia called from inside the safely closed door.

"It's Stacy Graysin, Lavinia. May I talk to you for a moment?"

The door eased open a crack, stopped by a chain, and half of Lavinia's face appeared. She was makeupless, and her severely red hair made a stark contrast with her pale, tissue-frail skin. "Stacy!" She sounded astonished to see that it was really me. "What on earth—"

"I know it's late, and I shouldn't bother you at home, but it's about Corinne. May I come in?"

She hesitated long enough for me to know she considered my appearance on her doorstep an imposition, and then pulled the door wider after removing the chain. "I suppose so." Her voice was querulous; she sounded a lot like my Nana Graysin did once she decided she was old and decrepit, not like the vibrant Lavinia I was used to.

She wore a gray chenille robe, and I followed her up the stairs, conscious of her one bony, blue-veined ankle bare above a black, moccasin-style slipper, and the hard, too-uniform flesh color of the prosthetic. Her apartment door stood open, light spilling onto the landing, and she gestured for me to precede her inside. I looked around curiously, noting a sofa and love seat covered in pale green velvet, with striped pillows and a patterned rug providing contrast. Framed photos were the only art on the walls. I moved closer to study them, smiling at the 1960s hairdos and fashions of the ballroom dancers. An auburn-haired dancer in an ice blue gown caught my eye. I half turned to Lavinia, who stood watching me. "You?"

She nodded. "Me and Ricky." I realized with a start that there were no dance photos in her design studio, no photos of her at all. Glancing at the collection on her walls, I also realized that all the displayed pictures pre-dated the attack in London. Suddenly uncomfortable, I backed away. A dining nook beyond the seating area held a round table and four chairs in a warm wood of some kind, and a single bowl of soup and glass of wine sat on the shiny tabletop.

"I interrupted your dinner," I said, feeling worse and worse about my invasion. "I'm sorry."

Lavinia shrugged as if to say, *You're here now*, and offered me some soup. "Chicken barley," she said. "A family recipe."

"It smells delicious," I said, accepting.

Limping into the galley-style kitchen, she ladled soup

into an eggplant-colored bowl and handed it to me. "Wine?"

"I'm driving."

Without asking, she poured me a glass of water, carried it to the table, and seated herself. "I assume you're not here to talk about dresses?" she said with a hint of asperity. She sounded more like the usual Lavinia, and I relaxed a tad.

"No. I wanted to talk about Corinne."

Lavinia nodded. "There's something about a funeral that brings out the need to tell stories, isn't there?"

That wasn't exactly it, but I nodded. "You were best friends."

Lavinia spooned up soup and didn't reply.

"It's amazing what she did for you after your accident."

"I wouldn't call it an 'accident.'"

"The attack." I let the words sit, trying to prod her into saying something. No joy. We ate for a moment in silence, and I glugged some water, beginning to wish I'd accepted the wine. Finally, I said, "I read Corinne's manuscript."

That brought Lavinia's head up. She observed me through narrowed eyes. "I heard she never finished it."

"Oh, she did," I said. "Her housekeeper—Mrs. Laughlin—took it over after Corinne's death."

"Stole it?" Lavinia wasn't one to pussyfoot around with euphemisms.

"I guess so. She finished it up, added a bit, and sent it off to the publisher. I guess the book'll come out in time for the holidays."

"Merry Christmas," Lavinia said in an unjolly voice.

"She's got a whole chapter about the trip to London," I prodded.

Lavinia downed the rest of her wine and rose to fetch the bottle, her limp more pronounced than earlier. "What does she have to say about it?"

"I think you know." There. I said it. I kept my eyes fastened on Lavinia; her gaze flitted to my face and then refocused on the wine bottle as she poured the last of the straw-colored liquid into her glass.

"I suppose I do know," she said, and I felt a brief flare of triumph before she continued. "I was there, after all." Did her steady gaze hold a hint of mockery?

I expressed my frustration by dropping my spoon into my bowl with a clatter. "She admits to paying some thug to attack you."

Lavinia drew her breath in sharply and said, "Oh, my."

"'Oh, my'? You learn your best friend was responsible for an attack that cost you your foot, your ability to dance, and you say, 'Oh, my'?" Scraping my chair back, I got to my feet. "I think you knew. I think she told you."

Lavinia faced me calmly, only her whitened knuckles around the wine bottle's neck betraying tension. "I'm just surprised that she confessed to it in writing," she said. "I've known for years."

"I don't believe you." I knew I sounded like an eight-year-old on the playground, but I couldn't help it. She was skillfully, deftly, cutting the ground from under my feet. By saying she'd known for years, she was building a defense based on Lissy's logic: Why would she seek revenge all these years after the fact? "I think she told you not long ago, like she told everyone else about what she was writing. I think you felt angry, stunned, betrayed. I think you went off the deep end, that you . . ." I found I couldn't utter the accusation out loud.

"That I killed her?"

I nodded, taken aback by the grief in her voice.

"We buried my best friend today, and you show up here accusing me of causing her death. I didn't think you were so callous, Stacy." Before I could respond, she asked, "Have you ever experienced betrayal?"

An image of Rafe in bed with Solange, of her red hair splayed across my pillows, of pale skin, gasps, and the scent of sex, overpowered my mind. I nodded.

As if reading my thoughts, she said, "Oh, men. Men don't count." Finally putting down the wine bottle, she walked to the table and gathered up our bowls and spoons, transporting them to the sink. The sound of rushing water played over her next words. "I mean betrayed by a friend. By someone you trusted, someone you shared secrets and dreams with, someone you thought believed in you, supported you, loved you."

I thought of Danielle, my mom, my good friends from high school and beyond. There'd been the usual sniping and making up, the waxing and wanings of friendship, but no scar-making betrayals. Unless you counted my mom deciding she would rather hang out with her horses than with us. "No."

She nodded, as if I'd confirmed something. "No. So you can't possibly hope to understand how I felt when Corinne told . . . When I discovered that she paid someone to hurt me."

"No, I can't."

"No one could understand who hasn't been through it," she half whispered, and I wondered whether she was thinking of juries.

Part of me wanted to comfort her, and part of me wanted to snap, *Get over it already. We all have to deal with betrayals of one kind or another, with disappointment, with tragedy.* So I stood there like a dolt, not knowing what to do or say.

"Corinne helped me come to terms with the loss of my foot. She set me up in business. She held me while I cried, got me to AA when I took to drinking to deal with the disappointment of never dancing again." She saw me glance at the wine bottle, and half laughed. "I don't think I was really an alcoholic—just headed that way. I've drunk socially for decades now with no problem. So it was like finding out that my whole life was built on quicksand when she told me. I knew how old-time explorers must have felt upon learning the world was round; their whole worldview was called into question, everything they believed turned overnight into a lie, a falsehood."

She slid a cutting board and knife into the soapy water, and her hair swung forward as she scrubbed them, hiding her face. "I think I could have forgiven the attack," she said, her voice little more than the rasp of an autumn leaf against a window. "It was the lying. The years and years of lying. The friendship I believed in, counted on, was a big pile of lies, no more substantial than clouds seen from an airplane window, seemingly so thick and soft they look like they'd cushion you when you jump into them. But when you make the leap, you fall straight through them. To the ground. To death."

The intensity in her voice creeped me out a bit. "So you ground up some cold tablets and put them in her heart medicine. You were her friend—you knew what kinds of meds she was on. I'm sure it wasn't hard to find an opportunity to slip the bottle out of her purse and doctor a few pills. Or maybe you did it on a visit to her house, sneaking the bottle out of the medicine cabinet."

"There was no guarantee it would kill her."

That sounded perilously close to an admission of guilt. My brief flash of elation was cut short when she turned to face me, a large chopping knife in her hand. My gaze froze to it and I stumbled back a step. Lavinia looked confused for a moment, then startled. "I'm not a murderer! I wouldn't hurt you." She laid the knife on the counter and I breathed again, conscious of my heart still going *thumpity-thump* against my ribs.

I needed to get out of here. I'd pushed as much as I could push, and Lavinia hadn't cracked. I was completely convinced she'd killed Corinne, but I didn't have any more solid evidence to offer Lissy than I'd had when I walked in here. "Maurice shouldn't have to pay for what you did, Lavinia. He's going to trial, and there's a good chance he'll be convicted."

"The evidence is only circumstantial," she said, a hint of uncertainty in her voice.

"It's the painting," I improvised, playing on that uncertainty. "It's motive. He was with her when she died, he could have substituted the poisoned pills for her heart medicine anytime over the weekend, and she left him a painting worth millions. Means, opportunity, and motive, as the cops say. He's screwed."

I waited a beat, hoping . . . for what? That she'd leap in a taxi and drive straight to the nearest police station to confess? After a moment, it became clear she wasn't going to say anything more. Feeling tears start to my eyes, I hurried to the door, glancing back when I reached it. Lavinia stood by the sink, tugging her robe around herself as if she were cold, and tucking her hands into her armpits.

I left.

Chapter 32

A rude pounding on my door woke me early Saturday morning. I glanced at the digital clock on my bedside. Six twenty-eight. Who in the world was at my door at this ungodly hour? My mind leaped to my mom, my dad, Danielle. Something had happened to one of them. Swinging my legs out of bed, I grabbed my robe and shrugged into it as I made for the door. A peek out the slit of a window beside the door showed me Detective Lissy. *Oh, no.* A homicide cop on my doorstep at this hour wouldn't be good news.

Fumbling with the lock, I jerked the door wide, anxiety making my heart pound in my chest. "Is it my sister? My mom or dad? What's happened?"

Lissy showed me an irate face, not one pulled down by having to impart tragic news. He was immaculately turned out, even at this hour, in a dark suit, crisp shirt, and patterned tie. "Your sister? What? Oh. No, your family is fine."

I pulled the door wider, silently inviting him in, still coming to terms with the fact that nothing had happened to my family. Breathing easier, I faced him in the hallway. "What happened?"

"I need you to come with me. Throw some clothes on and let's go." His face, impassive, told me nothing.

I was half-startled, half-curious. "Where? What? Are you arresting me?" Suddenly conscious of the sheerness of my nightgown and robe, I crossed my arms over my chest. Lissy seemed totally unmoved by my state of partial undress, his eyes staying on my face seemingly without effort.

"Have you done something I should arrest you for?"

"Of course not!"

"Just get dressed, Ms. Graysin. We're wasting time."

Confused, sleepy, but relieved that my family was okay and that he wasn't arresting me, I closed my bedroom door and scrambled into a summer skirt, peasant blouse, and sandals. Brushing my teeth and running a brush through my hair, I rejoined Lissy in less than five minutes.

"Impressive," was all he said as he gestured me to the door.

I climbed into the front seat of his brown Crown Victoria and buckled up. "Can we get coffee?" I asked.

For answer, he pulled into the nearest fast-food drive-through, and we both ordered extra-large coffees, black. I shot him a glance; it felt weird to have something in common with Lissy, even something as minor as how we liked our coffee.

"Where are we going?" I asked as we headed out Route 1 toward D.C. There was virtually no traffic this early on Saturday, and we sped along above the speed limit.

"In due time, Ms. Graysin, in due time."

I relaxed back into the seat, sipping my coffee, but

after a few moments the silence got to me. "Did your grandson win his game?"

Lissy slid his eyes my way and said, "You're not really interested."

He had me there. I relapsed into semisulky silence, irritated at having my sleep interrupted and irritated with his high-handed, secretive behavior. What in the world could possibly have come up that would make a homicide detective kidnap me at the crack of dawn? Maurice! I sat up straighter and was about to ask Lissy whether our field trip had anything to do with Maurice when we crossed the Arlington Memorial Bridge and I realized we weren't headed toward Maurice's house.

I had just raised my cup to my lips for a sip of coffee when Lissy jolted into a pothole. Coffee splashed out of the cup and onto my blouse and I yelped.

"Don't get it on the seat," Lissy said, reaching over to liberate napkins from the glove box.

"I'm fine, thanks," I said. "Second-degree burns— nothing to worry about." Blotting coffee off my yellow blouse, I didn't notice we'd arrived until Lissy parked at the curb. An ambulance, doors wide, and a couple of police cars were parked askew in the narrow street fronting Lavinia Fremont's studio and apartment. *Oh, no.* "What happened?" I whispered.

"Why don't you tell me?" Lissy said. When I didn't say anything, he opened his door and got out. I followed suit, scrambling onto the sidewalk and staring as EMTs carried a stretcher down the stairs from Lavinia's apartment. The sheet-shrouded figure lay still except for movements induced by the jostling descent. The sheet covered her face, but I knew it was Lavinia.

A young cop looked at me curiously, and I realized I was holding the coffee cup so loosely that coffee was dribbling to the sidewalk. I chucked the cup into a nearby trash can and moved to join Lissy at the door. "Don't just stand there," he said, starting up the stairs. "And don't touch anything—put your hands in your pockets."

I did as he said. When we entered Lavinia's apartment, I glanced around, expecting to see signs of mayhem. But everything appeared as it had last night: orderly, warm, cozy. It didn't look like a homicidal maniac had gone rampaging through the place. I looked a question at Lissy, whose gaze hadn't left my face since we came in. Finally, it seemed, he was ready to tell me why he'd dragged me down here.

"You will have gathered that Ms. Fremont is dead," he said. He paused a moment, as if waiting for me to argue with him. When I didn't say anything, he went on. "It looks like a heart attack, not an unusual occurrence for a seventy-three-year-old. A neighbor found her—"

"At six in the morning?"

"They walk together every day at five thirty, apparently," Lissy said. "As I say, her death would normally not have occasioned much remark, except . . ." He paused for emphasis. "Except that last night you were on me like paparazzi on Angelina Jolie, trying to convince me that the now-dead Ms. Fremont murdered Corinne Blakely. To top that off"—he raised a hand to stop me as I opened my mouth—"your fingerprints are all over the apartment, and the video camera at the jewelry store down the block shows you passing by at seven thirty-eight last evening. "So I ask you again, Ms. Graysin: What happened here?"

Damn. No good deed goes unpunished, as they say. I came down here to help Maurice by prodding Lavinia into a confession, and I ended up as a murder suspect. "Should I call Phineas Drake?" I asked.

"Hell, no," Lissy said, wincing. "You're not a suspect."

"I'm not?" Then what was with the gestapo routine, the visit to Lavinia's?

"The same camera that showed you arriving caught you leaving forty-five minutes later. Shortly after that, Ms. Fremont called her doctor's office to cancel an appointment for today. The camera and the doctor's answering machine have accurate time stamps. It's pretty clear that it was suicide. She took a few handfuls of the same medicine that triggered Corinne Blakely's heart failure—the packets are in her bathroom, and only her fingerprints are on them. Judging by the prescription meds in her medicine cabinet, she had much the same heart condition as Blakely, so the result was identical: myocardial infarction and death. At least, that's what it looks like pending autopsy. Plus, there's a note. I just want you to tell me how it came about."

"A note?"

Lissy beckoned to a white-overalled woman who obligingly produced a note in a plastic bag. It was handwritten on cream-colored stationery with a stylized LF at the top. "Life without friends isn't worth living. The friendship I believed in all these years was a lie. No one should be blamed for Corinne's death except Corinne herself. And no one should be blamed for mine except me." There was no signature.

I looked up from the grim words to find Lissy still staring at me. "I came here last night," I said, "hoping to goad Lavinia into confessing to murdering Corinne. I wasn't expecting . . . this." The weight of responsibility crashed down; I felt like someone had dropped a grand piano on me. I had pushed Lavinia Fremont over the edge, nudged her into committing suicide. I struggled to be objective. Of course, Lavinia had a murder weighing on her conscience, too. Even though her note made it clear she thought Corinne deserved to die, I knew guilt must have been eating at her.

"It's not your fault," Lissy said dispassionately. "She was depressed over her best friend's death, perhaps overwhelmed by what she'd done. Did she admit to killing Blakely?"

"Pretty nearly." I related as much of the conversation as I could remember. "When she first learned Maurice had been arrested, I remember that she seemed upset about it, so I implied that his case was desperate, that he was likely to get convicted. I thought her conscience might get the better of her if she thought an innocent person was going to go to jail for what she'd done." And it had, but not in the way I'd imagined. "Can I go home now?" I whispered.

"Yeah. I'll have a uniform take you back. Thanks for your assistance."

"Maurice?"

He puffed out his cheeks. "I'm sure the DA will want to review the charges in light of recent events."

That was good news, at least. I tried to focus on that as I descended the stairs, trailing one hand against the wall to steady myself. I felt dizzy, off balance. It was going to take me a while to process all this. A good long while.

Chapter 33

Friday evening, almost a week later, the DA had dismissed all charges against Maurice, and he, Vitaly, Danielle, and I were gathered in the ballroom, celebrating. Only Tav was missing, still on his business trip. He'd be back tomorrow, and I was looking forward to our date with equal parts anticipation and anxiety. I looked around the now-empty ballroom, weary but content. We'd hosted our monthly social dance, where students and others paid a fee of seven dollars and came here to dance for fun and practice their steps, and the last straggler had just left. We'd had a good turnout tonight—nineteen people—and I was tired, but not so drained that I turned down the glass of champagne Maurice offered me. He'd brought along a couple of bottles to celebrate the good news from the DA.

"To Maurice," we toasted, raising our glasses to drink.

"I still can't believe it was Lavinia," Maurice said for about the twelfth time. "Lavinia!"

"She felt betrayed," I said.

"Revenge is powerful motivationer," Vitaly said, downing his champagne in two glugs and holding out his glass for more. "I had an uncle once who wanted revenging on the man who is having affair with his wife, my aunt Magda. Uncle Sergei is spending ten years in the planning, but he is destroying man's business—canning the fishes—and strangling the man outside where he gets his hairs barbered. The police is not catching him, but in the family, we know. We Russians is knowing how to hold the grunge."

"Grudge," the rest of us chorused.

"I'm just glad you don't have to go through a trial," I told Maurice.

"Me, too," he added fervently.

Danielle slipped off her shoes and scrunched her toes open and closed against the cool hardwood floor. "So, if this dress designer person killed Corinne, who pushed you off the paddleboat, Stacy?"

"My guess is Conrad Monk. I think he meant it as a warning, or to soften me up for his attempt at buying me off when he thought I had the manuscript."

"Are they still going to publish it?" Danielle asked.

"I don't know. You probably saw the news story: Turner is suing Mrs. Laughlin and the publisher over it, but Randolph is contesting Corinne's will and trying to wrest control of the estate away from his son, so who knows how it will turn out."

"Turner should have known better than to try to move Randolph out of Hopeful Morning," Maurice said with a head shake. "If he'd left things as they were, Randolph would probably have been happy to spend the rest of his life there, bothering no one."

"At least now Turner's so busy with Randolph's lawsuit and fighting the sexual-assault allegation that he doesn't have the time or money to fight for your painting," I said. "Did you see in the paper that he was arrested but released on bond? Someone told me there was a video on YouTube of him going after the stripper at the bachelor party, but I haven't seen it. Phineas Drake says he'll buy his way out of it—pay off the woman who's accusing him—but still. What will you do with the painting?"

"Hang it in my house for a while," Maurice said, smoothing his hair back, "then probably donate it to the Smithsonian. It belongs in a museum, where thousands of people can admire Corinne every day. To Corinne." He raised his glass, tiny bubbles spiraling upward, and we toasted again.

"To ballroom dancing," Vitaly offered.

"To ballroom dancing," we chorused.

"To Anastasia," Maurice said, "whose tenacity—"

"Pigheadedness," Dani chimed in.

"—and insight spared me an ugly trial, at the very least." He mouthed *Thank you* at me as the others swallowed more champagne.

Danielle pulled me aside as the men popped open the second champagne bottle. "Did you ever hear back from Eulalia Pine about the furniture? Did she give you an estimate?"

"She did better than that," I said, raising my champagne glass. "She bought most of it. She's sending a truck on Wednesday."

Danielle stared at me. "Really? And it doesn't bother you to let it all go?"

Shaking my head, I said, "No. I thought about it. I mean, there're a lot of memories in that furniture, but

you know what? They're Great-aunt Laurinda's memories, not mine. I want to start fresh, with a clean slate and
all that, and decorate this place in a way that means
something to *me*. I'm keeping a couple of pieces, the
grandfather clock and Great-aunt Laurinda's portrait,
for instance, but most of it is out the door." I made brushing movements with my hands.

"Did she pay you enough to buy all new furniture?"

"I wish. I can buy a few pieces—maybe we can go
couch shopping again!—but it'll be pretty bare in here
for a while."

Danielle looked down into her almost empty champagne flute and mumbled something.

"What?"

"I said I bought my ticket today." She met my gaze
almost defiantly.

"Ticket?"

"For Jekyll Island."

I gave a whoop and hugged her hard. "I'm so glad
you're coming! You didn't have to buy a ticket, though;
Mom said it was her treat."

"I'll pay my own way, thank you," Danielle said. "That
way, if I feel like canceling, I can, or if I want to come
home early because it's just too awkward or the memories are hard to take, I can."

I smiled and released her. That was my sis, always
planning for all eventualities.

Music suddenly blared from the speakers—Carrie
Underwood's "Cowboy Casanova"—at decibel levels
guaranteed to net complaints from my neighbors. Danielle and I whirled to see that a tipsy Vitaly had plugged
his iPod into the stereo system and was now free-dancing
to the strong beat. With a laugh, Danielle joined him,
doing the same dorky box step she'd been doing since

her first middle school dance. Maurice set down the champagne bottle and glided toward me. With a smile, he offered his hand.

"Anastasia?"

"Let's dance," I agreed.

If Nigel told me one more time to manufacture a wardrobe malfunction for the show's first night of live competition, I was going to slap him.

"Stacy-luv," he said, Cockney origins evident in his accent, "we can make this strap a breakaway so sometime during the dance it will separate and—pop!" He ran a stubby forefinger with manicured nail down the purple spaghetti strap of my costume, stopping with his finger indenting my left breast through the satin. "Pop goes your boob and pop go the ratings!" He beamed.

I slapped him.

Three weeks ago, when Nigel Whiteman, coproducer of the hit series *Ballroom with the B-Listers,* phoned to announce the show was going to film its next season in the Washington, D.C., area, and said he wanted Graysin Motion to be one of the featured studios, I leaped at the opportunity. The chance to teach a Hollywood has-been or never-quite-was to dance on national TV was not one I was likely to pass up. I immediately said yes, not stopping to consider that my new business partner, Tav Acosta, might object.

Tav frowned in concentration when I told him about the opportunity and explained how the show worked. "It's not like that other ballroom dancing show, where it all happens in Hollywood," I said. Sitting on the edge of my desk, facing Tav where he sat on the loveseat under the window that looked out on the busy Old Town Alexandria street, I swung one leg with excitement. "*Ballroom with the B-Listers* goes to a different city each time and pits local ballroom dance studios against each other by giving them each two celebrities, a man and a woman, to train. The broadcasts are done from different local venues, so it's sort of a dance show, reality show, and travel show in one." I kicked so hard my flip-flop flew off, landing in Tav's lap. "Sorry."

He gave a half-smile and handed me the orange rubber shoe. Then his handsome face got serious. "But, Stacy, how does a studio have time to work with the celebrities and do everything the show requires, and still run classes and train its private students?" His faint Argentinean accent gave the words a sexy edge.

He could recite a grocery list and make it sound sexy, I thought, before consciously squelching the idea. Tav Acosta was my business partner. I'd learned the hard way that mixing business with romance was a bad idea when I caught my former fiancé and business partner, Tav's half-brother Rafe, in bed with a Latin dance specialist. Rafe's murder—no, I hadn't shot him, although I'd certainly thought about it—had brought Tav to Virginia. In his late thirties, he looked far too much like Rafe—lean face, long legs, dark hair and eyes—for my peace of mind. He'd inherited Rafe's share of my beginning-to-be-successful ballroom studio and had decided to open a branch of his import-export business in the area and stay for a while to help run the studio. He was a whiz with money, payroll accounts, and expenses—all the things that made me want to drive a skewer into my temple. I handled the teaching and our instructors and the competing. Our partnership was working well. Until now.

"We'll have to cut back on some of our classes," I admitted. "But I'm sure our private students will be okay with a little rearranging of their lessons, too. They'll be as excited about the show as we are."

Tav looked decidedly unexcited, so I added hastily, "Think of the amazing free advertising we'll get when twelve million people watch the show every Thursday night!"

"There is that," Tav admitted. "Still, Stacy, we cannot afford to discourage any of our regular students. Long after this *Ballroom with the*— What did you call them?"

"B-listers. It means sort of second-tier celebrities." Or third or fourth tier, I added to myself, recalling previous seasons' competitors.

"Thank you. Long after the show is over, Graysin Motion will be depending on the competitive students to pay our bills and keep us in business." A shock of black hair fell onto his forehead and he brushed it aside impatiently.

"They'll still be here," I said. "The show only runs six weeks, after all. Don't forget we'll have tons of new students brought in by BWTB, too." Pushing myself off the desk, I approached Tav and bent so our faces were on the same level. My blond ponytail dangled over my shoulder. "Don't you want to be on TV?"

"Por Díos, no!" He looked so horrified at the thought that I laughed.

"Well, I do." I'd been on television before, of course, as a participant in international-level ballroom competitions, but this was different. This time the show would be about me, about my dancing and teaching. It would be fun.

"You will be breathtaking," Tav said. "You will be so popular with the viewers that they will whisk you away to Los Angeles to start a new career."

Was there a teeny hint of insecurity in his voice? I studied his face but saw nothing there other than his usual calm confidence. Still . . . "I wouldn't go," I said. "My life is here. I don't want to be a celebrity forever, just long enough to double our student numbers."

Tav threw up a hand. "Okay, Stacy. You win. Tell them Graysin Motion will be happy to compete."

Since I'd already committed the studio, I was relieved I'd gotten Tav to agree. "It'll be fun," I said. "You'll see."

"Oh, my graciousness, this will being fun!" Vitaly Voloshin exclaimed, clapping his hands together. Originally from Russia, Vitaly now lived in Baltimore with his significant other. We'd become ballroom partners after Rafe's death.

We were warming up in the ballroom, the long room that ran the length of the historic Federal-era town house I'd inherited from my great-aunt Laurinda, which housed Graysin Motion on the top floor and my living quarters on the ground floor. Harsh July sunlight poured through the front windows, making my eyes water, and I moved to draw the drapes.

"'My gracious'?" The phrase didn't sound like Vitaly. I *shush*ed the drapes closed.

"John's mother, she is visiting," he explained, "and this she is saying all the times." He smiled at himself in the mirrors that lined our ballroom studio, admiring his teeth, I knew. John had paid for extensive cosmetic dentistry not long ago and Vitaly was still fascinated with the toothpaste ad smile that had replaced his formerly crooked and tannish teeth.

"Where's she from?"

"The Alabamas. She is being very nice, but I am not liking the grist for breakfast."

"Grits."

"*Da*." Lunging the length of the ballroom, his thigh muscles visible through the thin warm-up pants, Vitaly asked, "When does the show coming here?"

"Three weeks." I joined him in the lunges, adding a high kick every time I straightened. "We've got a lot to do to get ready. We'll have to let all our students know, see what changes we need to make in the class schedule . . . Maybe Maurice can pick up some of the classes I teach and work with your private students, since he won't be competing." Maurice Goldberg was our other instructor, a former cruise ship dance host who admitted to being "sixtyish" but whom I suspected was more like seventy. He was a big hit with our more mature, well-off female clients, the bread and butter of any ballroom studio. I hoped he would be okay with the fact that he wouldn't be featured on the show. BWTB assigned only two celebrities to each studio and they'd specifically said they wanted me and Vitaly to partner this season's competitors.

"You told them Vitaly is not dancing with fat womens, yes?"

"Absolutely," I lied, crossing my fingers. I'd only seen a handful of heavy-set celebrities on BWTB in all its seasons, so I was hoping they didn't pair Vitaly with a hefty partner since he had refused from day one to dance with our overweight students. I didn't know the source of his prejudice, but he was adamant, so I hadn't pushed the issue. "I'm sure they'll pair you with someone skinny and sexy and beautiful." Ninety-five percent of BWTB's female celebrities fit that description, so I figured I was on safe ground.

One week later, once again in our ballroom, Vitaly stared at his BWTB partner in disbelief. "You is taller than Vitaly."

"You are a runt." Phoebe Jackson looked down her nose at him. Perhaps half an inch taller than his six feet, with medium dark skin and a half-inch-long Afro that hugged her skull, she exuded strength in a tank top that showed defined biceps and triceps. Strong, slightly arched brows drew in toward a broad nose as she extended a hand for Vitaly to shake.

Vitaly appraised her, running his gaze from her shoulders to the muscled thighs and calves displayed by a short denim skirt. "You is seem reasonably athletic," he said approvingly. "Why is you being famous?"

"You've never heard of me?" Her tone hovered between affront and amusement. "I'm a kick-butt action star, baby. I whupped up on Jackie Chan in *Shanghai Serenade* and beat the crap out of Sly Stallone in *Rambo Meets Bimbo*. He was even shorter than you," she added. "But, baby, was he in good shape, even though he's got to be in his sixties. Mm-mm." She smacked her full lips appreciatively.

I guessed Phoebe was in her early forties, but she looked damn fit for her age. "Nice to meet you, Ms. Jackson," I said. "I'm Stacy Graysin." We shook hands and eyed each other. The microphone pack was uncomfortable at the small of my back and I wiggled.

"Call me Phoebe. Miz Jackson is my granny." She smiled. "You'll get used to the mike pack."

"Okay, okay," Nigel Whiteman broke in from where he stood, arms crossed, behind the cameraman. In his mid-fifties, he had a compact body, a spray tan, and eyebrows that winged up from the bridge of his nose like Nike swooshes. His light brown hair was receding at the corners of his forehead, creating a widow's peak effect I didn't think he'd had in his twenties. He wore blue jeans and a gray T-shirt, which would have made him look like just one of the guys if he weren't also wearing a platinum Rolex and Italian loafers. I'd learned in the three days since I'd met him that his smile rarely made it to his eyes, and even when he laughed at people's jokes, it was more to avoid looking too cranky than because he found anything funny.

"Stace, Phoeb. Let's not make nice, hm? Viewers like conflict and tension, not nicey-nicey. Try it again. Think two lionesses meeting up on the savanna, fighting over a mate." He gestured at Vitaly.

Vitaly looked offended, and I pressed my lips together to keep a giggle in. We were getting a quick lesson in how much was real about reality shows. "Sure, Nige," I said.

"Grrrrr." I growled at Phoebe.

She burst into laughter, showing enough white teeth and gums to intimidate a real lioness, then high-fived me while Nigel frowned. "I like your style, girl."

Vitaly and Phoebe and I filmed our "first meeting" three more times until Nigel was satisfied that we'd snarled enough.

"Where's my partner?" I asked. I'd been on pins and needles for days, wondering who I'd be paired with.

"He couldn't make it today," Nigel said. "You'll meet him tomorrow."

"But you can tell me who it is now, right?"

"Uh-uh." Nigel smiled, closed-mouthed. "We want to

record the real surprise when you two meet for the first time. Makes for better television."

I stifled my frustration and my urge to point out that we'd just filmed Vitaly's and Phoebe's "real" reactions to each other four times. "I can't wait," I said brightly, conscious that the camera was running and that I'd signed a contract saying the show could use whatever footage they obtained. I didn't want to come across as surly or uncooperative; that would scare away potential clients. But at that moment I began to get an inkling that being part of BWTB for two months might not be all fun and dancing.